Spiral Bound Brother

Spiral Bound Brother

Ryan Elliot Wilson

Winchester, UK
Washington, USA

First published by Perfect Edge Books, 2013
Perfect Edge Books is an imprint of John Hunt Publishing Ltd., Laurel House, Station Approach,
Alresford, Hants, SO24 9JH, UK
office1@jhpbooks.net
www.johnhuntpublishing.com
www.perfectedgebooks.com

For distributor details and how to order please visit the 'Ordering' section on our website.

ISBN: 978 1 78279 141 6

A CIP catalogue record for this book is available from the British Library.

Design: Stuart Davies

Printed in the USA by Edwards Brothers Malloy

CONTENTS

Part I Craft 1
Part II Burgundy Five Star 83
Part III The Kingdom 149
Part IV Whirlybird 223

For Larry and James, the teachers

Part I
Craft

1

I hadn't been to a doctor in six years. I'd hit an age where I preferred a series of arcana, to let it be a surprise, whatever foul thing was growing inside me. Sitting in Earhart High School's charmingly round library, reading *Prufrock* as if listening to a song that began anew immediately after fading out, I mashed my hair down with my hand. Finding it moist, of course, and stuck to my scalp like I'd applied rubber cement, I found reason to read the poem for the fortieth consecutive time.

"I'm not insane."

My delusion must have been audible, because Mike Dunham, a senior now (I taught him as a freshman), stopped me with a gentle hand on my shoulder. All-star second baseman, great glove man, Mike Dunham, B+ on every paper, every test, for participation, every quiz, B+. It was astounding consistency. I once gave him a D+ on a paper, which was actually very solid if not exactly powerful, just to see what he'd do. I wrote the same kind of notes I always write in the margins of his essays:

- *Good start identifying Poe's theme of Unity, but go further here. You're cowering from the fire-breathing dragon!*
- *Keen Observation! Bravo! You're almost faculty!*
- *Missing a quote! Looks like someone was watching ESPN while they wrote this part of the essay.*
- *This quote reveals much more about the narrator than you're illuminating! Illuminate, Mike! Poe wants you to shine a light.*
- *Mike, A very solid and convincing argument concerning the narrator's unavoidable path to meet all aspects of himself in death. Everything you point out is on target throughout. But try to identify more of the jaw-dropping choices Poe makes in his description, in mood—in other words, make an incision and look inside! Go past the skin!*

  Then: D+

He approached me after class with the essay between his thumb and index finger, just cocked his head ever so slightly and walked away. I'd meant it as raillery, no harm to his semester grade, but then again I was consciously ignoring what I knew about Mike Dunham. He always seemed poised to explode. He was friable despite his steady glove-work up the middle, the reliably straightforward analyses in class. He made every play he was supposed to, and the hard shots, too, the tough hops, made something like two errors his entire senior season, and at least one of those was due to the Earhart High scorekeeper guarding his own son's earned-run average. But he rarely seemed to come up with the incredible catch, and never did I see him celebrate with the lowest octane of high-fives after turning the double play, still somewhat rare in high school, or at least for Earhart teams. He just didn't dance with it.

I called Mike in during his period in *Flyer*, our school newspaper. Chuck Loder taught journalism, a lovely guy and one of my two friends on campus. Bitter as Job and unafraid to make the administration squirm. They would have fired him years ago, but those Famous Barr Clearance Suits that made up the Earhart administration didn't have one body part heaving with life, not a one between them.

"Mike, I'm very sorry about that D+. I meant to write B+."

"I know what you did, Mr. Craft."

"Oh?"

"You wanted to see if you could rattle me. Like I'm some kind of robot. I get it. But let me tell you, okay, I have some very serious crap going on at home right now, and I don't think it's funny at all."

"Mike, you have me all wrong. I was only trying to light a fire."

Mike's cheek muscles dropped, and his eyes welled up, not with tears, but pity, for me, the liar.

"I thought you were the kind of teacher who would own up

to it, Mr. Craft."

I wanted to pull him to my chest and hold him there a moment, but you can't do that sort of thing anymore.

"I'm not familiar to myself, Mike, and I don't get much pleasure from life. Do you understand?"

"Yeah."

"I used to be different—that's not true, exactly. I used to honor the idea that the future was important. That's it."

"Yeah. My sister loved you."

"Really? She hardly said a word in class."

"She's like, a real good listener. So, anyway, I gotta go."

"Okay, Mike. I'm sorry. If you need someone to talk to—"

"No, thanks."

Three years after our little talk that day, there he was again. I was set to implode at the library study table, with the delusional and masochistic notion that I could tangle with this death-panic episode, whatever it was, armed only with T.S. Eliot. The man had a soft spot for dictators (my former colleague, John Marauder, who actually now lives in a shack in Hawaii, wrote a brilliant, if a bit overreaching, paper on Eliot's Nazi imagery in *Burnt Norton*). And Mike, emitting the same nervous calm for which I'd known him, a senior now, an impressively full beard, his hand resting there on my shoulder, watched me read Prufrock for the forty-first time:

Like a patient etherised on a table …
I have gone at dusk through narrow streets
And watched the smoke that rises from the pipes
Of lonely men in shirt-sleeves, leaning out of windows …
And in short, I was afraid.

I looked peripherally at Mike, and I thought of my mother, how she'd always envisioned me to be a bold child, and how I'd disappointed her, slowly, until we only feigned closeness and true care, warmth. Thinking of how she toiled the beauty right out of herself, and hunched herself over, dazed from life's invisible blows to the head.

Would the same blows overtake me? My sanity hung there, under attack, in the occupation of *saints and idiots*, as my department chair and old friend called our line of work. Via the cover of ninth-grade English, I managed to avoid anything that truly matters, presupposing that anything truly matters. I'd become, or more likely, I discovered I'd always been a tragic, grotesque creature, filled with beautiful memories that only made things sickeningly more difficult.

I closed my eyes and *Prufrock* echoed in my head, narrated by my mother's voice, morphing into Eliot's, then mine, then mine as a child, at which point I must have begun vocalizing, some kind of guttural sound usually associated with anguish.

"*Ahhkahh*," I said.

"Mr. Craft… Mr. Craft… Mr. Craft… Mr. Craft."

"Mike. Hello. *Ahhkahh*!"

The slippages were beyond my control, a kind of possession.

"Mr. Craft, you haven't turned the page since I've been here. And I've been here for a while. Like an hour and a half."

"I'm reading, Mike. *Ahhkahh*!"

"Are you okay? What's that sound you're making—like, where's it coming from?"

"I'm thinking of teaching this poem—*Ahhkahh*—class next year. I was just going over it."

"You're not taking any notes or anything."

"Mike, you know, you're observant to a point—*Ahhkahh*—and honest, but there's a reason you got B+s, and not As in my class. *Ahhkahh*!"

"You shouldn't equate life with grades, Mr. Craft. That's so like, teacher, like, stupid."

"Mmm. But you should realize that with literature, it's up to the reader to decide!"

"That's doesn't make sense," he said.

"That's what makes it powerful. *Ahhkahh*! When you've spent an hour with one page, pouring over the tiny explosions of language, really seeing—A*hhkahh*—the...the maelstrom of the human mind, talk to me!"

"Okay."

"*Ahhkahh*! Things of beauty shouldn't be given up so easily!"

I sent my face plunging onto the table, unconscious. Some of the faculty, when alerted to the situation, thought of driving me to the ER, but they were all far behind schedule in their grading. Essays really do take forever, if you do it right. Chuck Loder told me I was comatose for about an hour and a half, but they were diligent about putting a pocket mirror under my nose every fifteen minutes or so, presumably the time it takes to grade one essay and drink a small Styrofoam cup of Folgers Crystals. The next day I figured I ought to at least check in with my old, senile medicine man, Dr. Paul Trisk.

"There's no good reason," he said, "for you to have your pants down right now. Pull them up."

"The nurse told—"

"Damn the nurse."

Trisk, an authentic asshole of the first order, wearing the inscrutable beard of a debilitating hand condition, was my first doctor out of college, so I stayed with him, to limit my already gargantuan dose of paperwork in my life. It would have come as no surprise to me if he told me I had a few months to live. Instead he just scowled.

"Breathe. No. Breathe," he said.

He touched me on the abdomen, roughly. I cringed.

"You're fine. Stop smoking or nobody will care when you die. That's how it works. I've seen it."

"What if I pass out like that again, out of nowhere?"

"It's harmless probably. Anxiety. You seeing any women?"

"No."

"Why not?"

"None will see me. No, that's not true. I stopped trying. "

"Start getting intercourse regularly again and I won't see you for another six years. You're going to live to be a hundred if you quit cigarettes. Longevity curse. And better yours than mine, believe me, Craft."

2

I stood up there every day, submerged in a windowless hole in the southwest suburbs of St. Louis, my place of origin, performing maniacally (they say) in front of the eager achieving, ruddy faces (a few brown ones mixed in), for twenty-five years. T-w-e-n-t-y-F-i-v-e. I taught a section of the slower kids, of course. All the honors teachers had to take our share, "What can you do?!" we used to chortle, all the young teachers, in the spirit of post(post)Woodstockian revival camaraderie, "The fucking war!" You actually have to love some aspect of being in a trench with no way out, or the children eat your spleen. Can anyone outside of the classroom appreciate, truly, how teaching high school whittles portions of a person away, regardless of gender, genetic make-up, experience, patience, accomplishment—irrelevant—it squelches, if not your electricity, then at least the ability to feel your own broken glass heart. And, all right, it replenishes, but only the moment before you dissolve.

My favorite book to teach though, by far, was the first book of the year—*Call of the Wild*. It lights an animal fire in the children's minds, as if the class is on ice skates, gliding, falling down, racing, and suddenly their whole little pond is ablaze. It brought me great joy for years, watching their faces, listening to their sobs as Buck gallops into Alaska's infinite expanse. You could feel the wind. The children with loving mothers and fathers, and more so the ones who courageously managed, somehow, to make it through alone, thought the ending affirming of that essential, unnamable sensation in their intestines that felt like untamed joy. London gave them answers to their questions about freedom and nature—what are they, really, freedom, nature—in a time that dragged those words behind the donkey to the point that they'd become scavenged corpses.

And there were children who drowned in it, the grinding truth of it, and so denied themselves. London's husky transcends the story of Christ in terms of answering *the summons*. This, the children who read it understood. They added something of value to themselves, something substantial to pull from in the face of a world of decay, hollow hearts, and prostitution. It never got easy to stomach the shallow end's whining, though, the pleading with me—*give a goddamn test and be done, can't you see, Craft, we're finished with you and your affected voice, the death, Craft, your perverted leers, your creepy side-part-comb-over, swooped like that, and the boys, you like boys, Craft, we know, don't think you're putting anything past us, we see you, Craft. We're done with this sled-dog shit, we can't hear it, can't see it, don't want to, and we're more than done with your rat face.*

Thesis-Contrary idea-Lead in-Quote-Lead out-Intensification-Provide evidence-Discovery of irony-The absurd-The transcendent-Devices-Thesis expanded-Conclusion. The kids loved it some and hated me, maybe loved me some and hated it. Then one day it was simply over.

The events that seem to be few dominoes that knocked over the rest, thus handing me this life, are intricately connected to a student I'd taught seven years before. Lila Bell. She was captain of the Earhart Hockey Cheerleaders, a notoriously bawdy group, but Lila was an earnest girl, plugged into a socket, always conscious of her words, an advanced writer at fourteen. Subtle-subtle-subtle then pow! Well, one evening not long ago, my home phone rang, a true rarity. She'd returned home from Prestige Small New England Liberal Arts College, just before winter break of her senior year. There were a few wealthy families at Earhart (we prided ourselves on being better than the private schools), but not one had money like the Bells. Her great-great-great-great grandfather started the first law firm in St. Louis, which evolved into one of the largest and most respected law firms in certainly the Midwest, if not the entire country, Bell, Higley, & Williams.

Lila had aged to twenty-one when I heard her say my name

again, *Hiya Craft*. I was forty-seven years old, divorced, clearly, and had just, days before, lost consciousness in the library, on the verge, I suspected, of unraveling once and for all, despite what old Dr. Trisk said. Lila suggested we meet for coffee down the street from my apartment.

An English major, *because of me*, she said, *the way I didn't fuck with the stories,* she said, *but gave them some overdue fucking glory,* she said (somehow she managed another *fuck* with no context I could discern). I'll never forget an early discussion in class on "Stopping by Woods on a Snowy Evening." Her voice—not her voice, exactly—her method of utterance caused me to flip a few ounces of coffee onto my nipple and my already barely usable copy of Frost's collected work.

"Joan of Arc!" I shouted into my scalded chest. And the children laughed, of course.

"Shut up!" she scolded them. "Are you all right, Craft?" Lila asked. When she participated, it was always as if she and I were alone.

"Go on, go on, you were saying something marvelous about the horse, about loving that the man considers his horse's feelings. That's called pathos by the way."

"Yeah, but then the woods become death suddenly! And it's like he likes it, looking at death, and he just goes home because he made some stupid promise. And now it's too late because you like him, so you care. And death is what he really wants. This is not a 'nice pretty, like really nice poem' or whatever the hell *Julie* said. I stop listening when she starts speaking. No offense, Julie," she said, raising a hand in Julie's direction.

"Is it possible he views death as something good?" I said.

"Only if he hates being alive, I guess. The guy is ill. He's going to do it, probably with a shotgun, you know, out in the woods."

I scanned the class and found furrowed brows from corner to corner. They always became contemptuous when someone had *something to say*. But this was an assault. I went through the stop sign anyway.

"Lila, do you think it's possible that a person could reach a point in life where those woods might say something reassuring about *eternity*, for lack of a better term?"

"I don't know anyone like that."

"No, I don't either," I said, realizing how conspicuous my present state of mind had become.

"Except like hardcore Christians, I guess, but they'll believe just about anything they're told to," Lila added.

If I didn't take a hard turn, the class was going to fold in on itself, and, because I didn't care, I pressed on.

"So are you concluding that the speaker, and that Frost by extension, is offering us a load of manure. To feel tempted by the woods is just fantasizing about death and to think that way is a capitulation to real life."

"What does that mean?"

"To give up," I said.

"Yeah, pretty much. This is the saddest thing I've ever read, 'cause it's all in his head."

"Yes, that's precisely where it is," I said, noting that most of the class had placed their heads upon their desks or created hand pillows.

Thankfully, the bell rang, resetting them for biology, geometry, gym, the day's class forgotten, except by Lila.

At the café all these years later, as I spoke about my threadbare life and my fainting spell, she looked at me and laughed, an extended warm laugh that ended with her forehead in her hand, a little snorting at the end. I could see in the mirror on the wall behind her head that I didn't have anything smeared on my face, so I knew it was, at least in part, my utter ridiculousness, and her familiarity with me, the man, the fool.

"I've missed you so much, Craft."

The corkscrew curl of hair on her forehead was long enough to submerge itself in her coffee. That she never noticed, and dunked it again and again, well, that finished me off.

"It feels good to be here. It's not weird at all, you know?" she said, holding my eyes in hers.

"Thanks for the coffee. It's delicious," I said.

"You suggested this place," she said, "so you shouldn't be surprised."

"Mmm. Yes."

"Craft."

"Yes, Lila."

"Okay, listen. I've made some stupid choices with boys at school. Nothing horrible, I wasn't raped, thank God, a friend of mine was, right outside a Bank of America."

"That's awful."

"She's strong. But, that's not what I want to talk about right now, okay?"

"Fine by me."

"I'm just going to say this."

"Please do."

I heard the chink of porcelain breaking apart, and crying behind us. A little girl, four or five, spilled her hot soy milk.

"I can't get off unless I'm by myself. Do you know what I'm talking about?"

"Yes," I said.

"You know what I'm saying?"

"Precisely, yes."

"I'm not offending you? Making you uncomfortable?"

"I'm not offended. No, I can imagine it's hard to find a boy with any real feeling in his hands."

"Exactly! Exactly, Craft! It's their hands, they're either these clumpy claws or totally spastic. Like they're playing a video game called *Fingerfuck!* where the object is like, make the girl uncomfortable and frustrated without causing actual pleasure."

"Are you sure there is no such game already?"

"Oh, my God! That's the future isn't it!"

"I imagine so. Maybe we should have a glass of wine instead. It's nearly a quarter after five."

And so in a sort of hyper-rationalized stab at free love via pedagogy, we strolled in blissful silence on the chilly old sidewalks of Soulard until we reached my brownstone, where I knew it was my duty to give Lila a friendly orgasm on my kitchen counter. We'd finished off the first cheap Cabernet bought from Walgreens on the walk home. I was uncorking the second bottle when she approached me from behind and placed my hand exactly where I'd never allowed my ever-wandering mind to imagine too vividly. Now, our faces next to each other, we gently huffed and sighed, slow enough to let it remove the rest of the world, allowing just she and I, animals, to move together. It was flattering, to be selected for that moment, so I concentrated on the import of the work.

We relaxed on my rug afterward—I think I might have even put on early Leonard Cohen. She hadn't heard him. A *fucking revelation,* she said. I was as hard as a mountain, even if I was proportionally the image of a more modest Renaissance sculpture. But neither of us did anything about my side of it, just didn't seem like the spirit of the thing. No matter.

"Craft, remember *'Ex-basketball Player'?"* She provided a lit joint, which I declined.

"Of course, I've taught the poem for twenty-five years."

"When you read it in class, I knew I'd get naked with you someday. And I got really freaked out. It was a terrifying thought. Disgusting even."

"Would you like some more wine?"

"Yes. Thank you. *'The ball loved Flick/ His hands were like wild birds.'* It's such a sad fucking poem. But the way you read it, you transformed it, like there was this animal in a cage, and he might still be burning to be free, somewhere, so there was this hope."

"Updike really put that one together."

"It was you, Craft. I've read Updike's other stuff—it's okay, I guess. And that's being pretty generous."

"Well, I don't know, there's *The Centaur*. But that's not important now."

"The line about Flick's hands, those are your hands."

I went to an Earhart Hockey game the next night. Lila was there, catching up with two former cheerleaders, and visiting with her old coach, Mrs. Newton, which was how she was addressed by adults also. Lila looked at me once, and I tried to express with my eyes that this was goodbye, but Mrs. Newton caught my gaze, so there wasn't time for Lila to see it and understand.

3

My wife divorced me without warning on my fortieth birthday. So there was that. An old sore, but somehow it still determined all the waking hours of my life.

Until Lila called me, and I predictably accepted her advances, I hadn't touched a naked woman in seven years, that's counting the last year or so with Megan, my wife. Part of a death cycle, woman to man to man to woman to man, unable to think of her body like fruit, then his body becomes oppressive and stupid.

Bright and early the morning following my one-sided tryst with Lila, my department chair and best friend, Tim Conroy, poured me a cup of coffee, like he always did. He was a bartender in Paris for a few years, ages ago.

"Craft, you know I would never mention this to anyone."

"Oh?"

"But I just can't be around you unless you know that I know about you hand-jiving the Bell girl."

"Hmm. Yes."

"Good for you, Craft."

"Oh? How's that?"

"Energize your life, man. Stella used to tie me up. Lightly. You know that. And Viv, well, sometimes I think she's going to give me a heart attack."

"Tim," I said. I looked into my coffee cup. A red push-pin was floating, still. "I'm afraid this is just the beginning of a kind of nightmare. A nightmare that starts off with convincingly pleasant carnality."

"Yeah, I hear that. But don't get all careful and scared now. And don't take any bullshit about this. Cause I'm telling you, it's out there now."

"How did you find out?"

"Oh, everybody knows. I think I was the last one. Nobody tells me anything, man, never have. I have to get everything from the kids."

"Oh, yes. The kids," I remembered.

I was teaching "Richard Cory" that day, the poem by E.A. Robinson, *One calm cool night Richard Cory went home and put a bullet in his head*. Well, Robert Zyler, a boy in my seventh-period class, lost his father in a freak accident the day before he was to begin high school.

If only that horrific non-fact were true.

But no, young Robert's father plunged off the roof of their house (which was built on a hill, putting him sixty feet up), the day before Robert was to begin high school, and this tragedy was explained to us, the beloved Earhart High Faculty, as the equivalent of an after-school special, a riding mower tipped over, crushed him, the perils of lawn care and the family's struggle to cope.

Oh yes, and young Robert played the trumpet. He was outstanding—in eighth grade he earned a spot with the high school orchestra and played a large portion of a Miles Davis solo from "Kind of Blue," right out of the blue, at the Christmas Concert. No one understood why he played it, but you could hear about six or seven people sobbing. The orchestra director, Thomas Ortiz, waved his arms around, trying to get him to stop for the first minute or so, and it became clear Zyler was going off script. Ortiz gave up, because the audience was riveted, caught off guard, confused and moved.

I was waiting for my classroom phone to ring, beginning with the beckoning death-toll voice of the assistant to the principal, Patty Wagner, her pious disgust; then it would be the gallows shuffle into the office of the Lilliputian big man, Dr. Dan Fillman, all of sixty-four inches, to discuss my perfectly legal indiscretion with Lila. But sixth period ended, and no voice from the wall had come. My last class filed in: Keisha Settle, Melanie Roarbach, Eddie Flome, finally Robert Zyler just before the bell. They had read "Richard Cory" the night before for homework. I always made them do a page of notes and ideas along with the reading. I asked them to think about: *The way the speaker describes Richard Cory's suicide, perhaps the speaker is someone who lives in the town, has some special interest, but can we say for certain that the speaker is moved by Cory's death? And what does the speaker's voice intimate and indicate about how Cory is perceived in the town? What is Cory's life worth? To Cory? To the speaker? To the town?*

The discussion was vigorous. Some highlights:

1. Like, it says he was "imperially slim." Maybe he kills himself because he's an imperialist, like a rich parasite. -*Morty Spezzio*
2. That's dumb. Sorry. I mean, he's "always human when he talked." Cory isn't a phony. He's on some whole other trip. The point is probably that nobody knows anything about it, and so everybody guesses, like the paparazzi. -*Sky King*
3. Envy is the worst. You can feel it on the page. -*Keisha Settle*
4. It's right here, "So on we worked, and waited for the light." The light is heaven, and you have to work in life until you get there. That's what all the town's people are doing. Not committing suicide. -*Natalie Stockard*
5. Look out! -*Eddie Flome*

The bell rang and my cheek was sliced open by the edge of a horn, my knees buckled, and my forehead cracked against the linoleum. The -*ting!*- of brass on cheekbone was shockingly audible, even with the school bell clanging overhead. I saw Robert Zyler drop his trumpet and snap a pencil. I could almost see the image of the boy's dead father hovering above his head—then I lost consciousness.

The hospital—I have no memory of being there until I woke up. It was a sun-drenched day, a great surprise, I thought, to be alive, yes, although I couldn't think of much in the way of something tangible, something propelling me to keep moving out of one day and into the next, except my job. I took it as a good sign though, my being able, still, to appreciate a lovely morning.

In the bed next to me was a balding, slender man about my age, his countenance projecting calm and health, if not consciousness. The nurses hung a small whiteboard on the bars of his bed, his name in red marker—IVERBE. I taught English for twenty-five years, taught e.e. cummings all twenty-five of them, only to awaken in a stupor and see something like that—and suddenly I discovered I was on no pain medication whatsoever. A wave of a thousand ultra-thin needles on my cheek screamed out, and I started laughing so hard I opened up my stitches, blood came pouring out, well, trickling anyway. Iverbe turned to me, opened his eyes and smiled, faintly, and a little voice inside me whispered indecipherably, like a gnome or demon. But the things it was saying were true, I knew that. It scared me to death.

"Say, friend, what is your name?" I said to my roommate, testing reality.

"He can't talk right now, sir. He suffered some serious trauma and just needs to rest."

"Nonsense. That man is wide awake."

The nurse paused and turned to me in a full character break, her face shifting to become a brand new person, one who decided to speak instead of filling the air with familiar sound patterns.

"Well, he doesn't really feel like talking to new people right now. Are you going to give me a hard time?"

"I simply wanted to say hello to my roommate," I said.

"All right, go ahead. Just don't let the doctor see you doing it, because he *forbid* anyone from agitating Mr. Iverbe."

"Does he have a condition that's agitated by greetings?"

"It's not appropriate to discuss his condition with you. Listen—"

"I'm not trying to cause a problem. I'll be very discreet."

"You do that. You don't have to listen to Dr. Kingshit Jackass dress you down in front of everyone. He's got terrible breath. I think about it when I eat. You need a new pillowcase. Lean forward."

"Yes. It won't stop oozing," I said.

"Like I haven't heard that before."

I felt the urge to run down to the gift shop and buy the nurse flowers and dark chocolate. She was my age, more or less, and I liked the way she said *pillowcase,* as if it meant *spinal cord.* Her eyebrows and abundant nose hair reminded me of my great grandmother from Manchester, England, who smiled at me whenever I was lost in thought.

"I'm Craft," I said, and waved to my roommate.

He pointed at the sign, so he at least knew he was being identified as the name on the whiteboard.

"Can you believe that sun shining? December wearing May glasses. You don't happen to have a hammock over there do you?"

This man, Iverbe, looked up at me, and his eyes sucked my beating heart out of my chest. I thought I was looking straight into the sun, but free of the excruciating glare. He pulled my whole being from my throat, and I hung suspended in the middle of the room. We paused there together, out of our bodies, and exploded through the ceiling into a vacuum. I know it was a vacuum because my lungs didn't work. The seconds-old memories, my voice, the sheets, my thoughts, were rendered ludicrous, dirt crumbling in a stiff breeze.

"My boy. Florida. The Mouse. Comfort him."

The words boomed around us and floated. They penetrated my inner ear, but Iverbe's mouth hadn't moved. Yes, I'd absorbed a blow to the front and back of my skull, so there was that stain of doubt cast over the supernatural origin of this strange sensation. I didn't know what was happening in that room, but I was there, witnessing. The man had my attention, like he was in the window of a burning building.

"Comfort him," again, the words, again, his still lips. "A beast waits. It knows. It's awake," the voice said, permeating my sore spine.

I had options, but they all seemed to include immense courage, and so were automatically disqualified. No, I did not simply nod as if I'd just received his awful message clearly—which I had. I raced away from his piercing consciousness. I remember the feeling of an opaque shade being pulled over my eyes before answering, but I can't say just who did the pulling. I fear it was me.

"A boy you say? So you have family then. That's good. Will they be visiting?" I said.

And with that we were back in our beds as if nothing had happened. Iverbe looked out the window and shrugged. He turned back to me with a sadness I'd only seen in the mirror, before school, on those days that almost drive away with the rest of you.

He looked down, shutting his eyes tight, and began mouthing words and rocking. I couldn't make out the words, not for sure. *No one? No more?*

"Can I help you in any way?"

He groaned and thrust himself violently against the back of the bed, raised to about a hundred twenty degrees.

"I'll come back after they let me out. How is that? We can talk."

He agreed or disagreed with a wave of his hand. I'd just about convinced myself that this was the right course, that I would actually return and glean something, and provide a service for a fellow injured soldier. But he fell asleep sometime in the early evening, an hour or so after I got the okay to go, and didn't wake up again.

4

When Tim Conroy picked me up from the hospital to drive me home, the hospital staff and I had every reason to think Iverbe, my roommate, perhaps a sorcerer, was still alive, his vitals strong. Leaving that space, the room of the summons, allowed me back into my whirlpool of a life; and in particular to a recent sketch of Lila's—of me, in my kitchen the night she came over, a nude. I sat slouched in the beaded passenger seat of Tim's piebald Tercel, going over the hours. It was chilly and clear outside, and I left the window down to let the air strike against my sewn-up gash, which stung, but the cold wind relieved a hot, deep pain of knowing I could never pick up these pieces of my life.

The night with Lila that inspired her drawing of me, after she dozed off, satisfied, I sauntered to the kitchen to cook some eggs and sausage. I often cooked naked in the middle of the night and was scalded and singed in the worst places. Lila walked in, saw me and convulsed in laughter at once, this grotesquely beautiful and jagged gesture of elbow jerks and gasps. It was a direct contrast to her lissome underwater movements in bed with my finger on her clitoris. She slipped and fell, all the while laughing and rubbing what would become a giant purple bruise. Then she caught her breath.

"The fury you're cooking those eggs with, Craft, with your pecker swinging around like that."

"I think it's doing more bouncing right now. It doesn't really have enough rope to swing."

"Quick! You got any decent paper?"

She ended up using some blank poster board and a thin Sharpie I had sitting around. I'd never seen someone draw that way, so quickly, without pause or hesitation, it looked like she was playing the violin. When the toaster bell rang, the sausage brown, the eggs fluffed, she stopped, and there I was on the thick glossy paper, a figure of some beauty, unrecognizable to my eyes at first. Something familiar emerged in the posture, frantic and slumping, which made me weep for the first time in years. I was so grateful in that moment. I didn't think she'd go home and, say, hang it directly over the pink canopy bed she'd had since she was six, for her mother to find. I couldn't predict her actions—I only knew the girl, not the woman-child.

"Craft, old pal, I'm retiring next year, otherwise I'd quit," Tim said in the car, snapping me back into the present suckhole, the cold wind on my face as he took a risky left turn on a yellow-red. "But the shitheads are going to fire you when you get back to school. I was in fuckin' meetings all day about it."

Tim offered me a cigarette, which I declined. I'd anticipated his words, almost exactly, in the parking lot waiting for him to pick me up.

"For perfectly legal conduct. Tenure?" I reasoned.

"The Bell girl fled to Peru, they think."

"Really? Fled?"

"She didn't tell anybody, just left a note that said, *Gone to Peru*."

"So what? I'm responsible?"

"Well, the parents are saying you preyed on her, got her drunk and, you know, took advantage."

"As in sexual assault?"

"They're saying Peru is her reaction. They're saying, you know, a literal and figurative escape. If she actually went. I had to talk them out of a suicide theory they were working on. The drawing of you kind of upset them, to put it mildly."

Lila had written a title on the back of the drawing apparently, one which I thought lacked subtlety: *Mr. Craft, Flaccid, December 10th*.

"So she renders her nude subject sympathetically, the man who allegedly just forced himself on her, and then flees to the jungle? What is this, Conrad meets D.H. Lawrence?"

"I hear you, but man—that family built the library, the new gym, and they bought all those video cameras everywhere. The hallways are full of 'em."

"Can we get in touch with Lila?" I asked.

"No. They've exhausted the usual channels apparently. I fought like hell for you in there. I said it was crazy what they were doing, that they were way the hell off base with their logic, but—"

"But burn the witch."

"Hey, Bunko, I started spiking my coffee second period this year. I'm gone in eighteen months. I can't wait to get rid of this piece of shit and ride my bike everywhere, man, fuck my wife all the time. I'll never leave my little square mile except for Paris."

"Tim," I said, but stopped.

I looked up at my second-floor brownstone apartment, my doors and windows, sinks and rugs, clogged drains, countertops, the rooms that held Megan's and my life together briefly. There had been fire up there, but not much naked rain. Tim lit another cigarette and I snatched it out of his hands, opened the passenger door, and stamped it out.

"I'm sorry," I said.

Suddenly it felt like walking upstairs and unlocking the door, switching on lights, and brushing my teeth would be a lie, of what kind I didn't even know. An urge came over me to gather what I could and pack my ancient Subaru (Tim and I were vying for oldest living non-refurbished car, Tim's Tercel was at twenty, and I was only two years behind), and drive into the night, find a motel hours away, for drug fiends and petty thieves, wake up and drive again, any direction—but I could only choose one, which would of course *make all the difference*. I shut the car door and leaned into the open window, gazed at Tim but chose not to tell him about Iverbe. It's not that he wouldn't have believed me—he would have. Whatever had just happened with this man, this entity, had transpired beyond the realm of the spoken word, and so I said nothing.

"Hey! Don't hang your head, Craft. And don't watch the ten o'clock news tonight. Nothing good about you."

"Tim, you know I don't watch the ten o'clock news."

"Goodbye, partner."

I turned away from my friend, who could care about me, but couldn't come with me anymore.

"Craft," he said. "We were pretty good, you me."

Staggering up to my front door, I tried to control a cough, as if opening the door to a room holding my own wake attended by six people. Home again. Turning the lock and wrapping my hand around the door knob, the scope of my failure overcame me. It was as if I was seeing it all at once.

My ex-wife Megan taught in our department, though I knew her first as my student, from my second-year teaching. She was a decade younger than me to the day, a happy fact she pointed out when she turned fourteen in my class during the first week of school. It was impossible to keep my mind off her, how she spoke, the ease of it—she carried it in her back pocket. She could have been a cultivated thirty, or older even, but she still maintained inexorable qualities of a young girl, listening to Madonna in headphones when I wasn't looking. I may have been a new teacher, fresh out, but my life, the sum of it, felt laughable by comparison. I reread *Lolita* just so I was square with myself about my intentions, to immediately recognize anything I said that smacked of Humbert Humbert lust. It was damned difficult for me to match wits and composure with Megan each day in class. She commanded hers like a dachshund, and when she wrote: *"e.e. cummings is creating a new American language for a future where war is ludicrous, love is unhidden, and sex is mysterious art,"* I believed her, despite departmental charges of plagiarism, and I had to find a place, close by, but out of reach, to put my heart.

When Fillman hired Megan ten years after she left my class,

and it became public knowledge that we were seeing each other, that is, spending time fulfilling various mutual and now legal fantasies, the whole school got behind what was perceived as a great love story, a kind of sweeping epic, inspiring, until she screwed three other teachers, one P.E., both of them dripping with sweat, I imagined. She tried to seduce Tim, too, but he said no thanks, that he wouldn't allow himself, though recently divorced from his wife (our colleague, Stella), to penetrate any ex-students or present colleagues in that orifice ever again.

That everyone in the school knew of her philandering, and that I chose to stay with Megan, altered the way I was perceived at Earhart beyond repair. It didn't strike me as horribly shocking, and at night in bed, when I lay there alone with my thoughts, I didn't really disapprove of what she'd done. The fact that she screwed them fewer than five times each and tired of them so quickly softened the automatic ego blow that comes with discovering your wife nearly choking in a cock parade. I never fully embraced the concept of monogamy with Megan to begin with—it seemed to sever far too many outlets, blot out too many realities, perhaps even chances to live. I was so much younger then. Since I only practiced fidelity in action and not theory, I would say it's a viable interpretation of our never-quite-love to say I was just as unfaithful as she was.

At first the pity and disdain that was directed toward me from the faculty, now that I was the cuckold, made my job nearly impossible. One lonely Friday night, though, I swelled myself with wine followed by I don't know how much brandless drugstore *Irish Whiskey!* and fell down the stairs of our building, landing on my back in the street. I could only lift my arms and wiggle my fingers at first, but I knew I still had use of my legs, just not at that moment. I pissed myself, at first feeling disappointed and self-pitying, followed quickly by wet acceptance. No one walked the streets, no noise except the ever-present hum and chink of the colossal Anheuser Busch Brewery in the distance. It was just me and the changing traffic light—green.

It took hold of me, there on the pavement, the idea that I had been set free, to be pathetic in the eyes of many, yes. But Megan's generous, loose panties just took my interior world, my conscience and lack thereof, and projected them onto my reality. If she needed a particular brand of human heat, who was I to deny her? Who was she to deny herself something she wanted, perhaps needed, especially when the only thing stopping her was adherence to something that only holds value if you value what it stands for, which we did not?

I never took any lovers, not because I was married, but because all I wanted at the time was Megan, or at least the idea that Megan would thrive enough to connect me with her own growth and relative freedom, and would therefore keep me around to fuck, drink, and grade papers with. The only appeal I've ever aroused in women has been from the hovering ones, pointing, at the edge of some cliff.

Tim beeped his broken horn halfway down the street, again bringing me back my senses, the present, and I watched him drive back to his full life, leaving me holding the previous day's *Post Dispatch*. A small story, but on the front page nonetheless, the headline, "Metro East Third Grader Trapped on Terrorist Watch List." He was a typical-looking eight-year-old, blond with balloon cheeks and a rabbit smile. There he was, an alleged killer, little Brandon Murch of Waterloo, IL, and I couldn't even manage a chuckle, because something—that switch that if flipped used to cause a guffaw to slip out—had simply gone from me. The joke was dead. I felt the titan, Chaos, its teeth and tongue, so real, draped over everything, as it no doubt always had been. How was I coming to the party, or the wake, so late and so sober?

This strange man, Iverbe—his son was somewhere, suffering. Who was he? Why on earth—or beyond earth—did he need me? To what beast had he referred? How could I help anyone? These things now mattered. Something mattered again. In the instant I walked across the threshold of my front door, I knew I mustn't think anymore. I'd spent my life asking questions, most of them rhetorical, not even my own, mindless, through a can and string tied to nothing. And the endless cogitating, more a nervous reaction to life than genuine contemplation. But suddenly, even though very little was understandable, my life seemed on the verge of forming a confederacy of fractured parts that if assembled properly would, potentially, unite as a broken being.

I burned to bend time backwards, hear my brief exchange with Iverbe again, Iverbe and I, lifted out of ourselves, his voice slowing my mind, his message ringing in the air between us. *My boy. Florida. The Mouse. Comfort him.* I sat down cross-legged, as Megan had taught me long ago, nudged the flesh away from my sit bones, closed my eyes and thought of my spine, waited until I felt it running from the ground to my brain, let my eyebrows relax, and there I was again, in the hospital room with Iverbe, in and out of my mind. *A beast waits. It knows him. It's been awakened.* Instead of ignoring the man's pure being as I had in the hospital, the way I'd drunk in his words and removed myself, this time I listened and nodded, alone.

I put on my pajamas and mashed my pillow under my neck as soon as the sun went down. At first light, I would drive a thousand miles to Orlando/Kissimmee/St. Cloud well rested. My savings would buy food, gas, and every-third-night at a Motel 6 or its equivalent for six months if need be. I'd decoded what Iverbe told me instantly at the hospital, though I pretended to understand nothing. Walt Disney was the spoonful of sugar in my medicine, of course, planted in front of the television on Sunday nights. Then I grew hair on my chest and pubic region, as many of us do, and doubted his usefulness, or at least his relevance to me. And now, I just needed to sleep to find out if the possibility of actual change was real. If I could just awaken with a feeling other than emptiness and futility, then my next move would be clear.

Squirrels were screeching at each other on a branch outside the window next to my bed just before the sun came up. No dreams of my imminent journey, or of the ghost of Iverbe, who was still flesh and blood in my thoughts—just ordinary dream confusion, running and fear, opaque symbols, sprinkled with moments of recognition. Like every other night, basically. But I felt something else—unnamable to me then—when I arose for the day's first bladder relief, something that seemed like each action had its own tiny purpose, its own little contribution to an actual destination.

I walked directly to the kitchen and ate a Clif Bar in five bites. Two jeans, two slacks, two polo shirts, two flannel shirts, two T-shirts, penny loafers, seven pairs of socks, seven pairs of jockey shorts, Timex, rest of the Clif Bars, wallet, glasses, travel coffee cup, baseball cap, glove and ball, toothbrush, toothpaste, fleece pullover. Coffee and the rest could be found somewhere other than St. Louis.

The Subaru scratched its way to life almost immediately. It was mild and damp outside, no poisoned black snow piled on the sides of the streets like old, cold Decembers of yore. This day, the week before Christmas, was going to dry out and sit right in the middle of perfection, the way only a traveling day can, through southern Illinois, the corner of Kentucky, over the Smoky Mountains in Tennessee, the great length of Georgia, ending with a test of conscious strength to finish the job—straight into the Orlando/Kissimmee/St. Cloud early morning night.

5

Once I merged onto Interstate 64, I fell into a trance, or what I imagine true meditation to be. I was no springtime youth going west, but rather a fractured fifty on the horizon, freshly unemployed and unwound, and so my dashboard compass read east. I felt my hands on the steering wheel again after seventy miles of hovering on the ceiling of the cab and stopped at a gas station near Mount Vernon, IL, to feed the car and get proper directions. It was with purpose that I did not use Internet-generated navigation, because in no way did I know what I was doing, the excitement of that—the satellite maps that I'd become accustomed to might have sullied the purified air in the cab, jeopardizing my new and barely containable, frantic and focused desire to help another human being.

I walked into the food mart feeling almost at ease, certainly light.

"What about this day we're having, the billowing clouds," I said.

"Yeah. I'm inside, working, so."

"Could you tell me the best route to Florida?"

"Nope. No maps. Don't sell good. Probably got 'em at the Flying J though."

To think that a few days ago, I might've, in some drowsy waking state, silently corrected his grammar, and felt vaguely virtuous doing it, as if I were even a remotely significant or dignified guardian of language. No more. Luck was mine, back on the highway, a full tank—one mile to Interstate 57, toward Memphis, which sounded to me like a reasonable path to Florida. Something was turning, and I realized what I was feeling was the elusive rodent, luck, which I had trained myself to think was a myth, just a stupid misunderstanding of the universe. But now, *what stupid? Luck stupid?* I laughed, *I was stupid* after all, how marvelous, I thought, how liberating. A flesh-and-bone imbecile with luck on my side, driving steadily, sixty-eight miles per hour to Memphis and beyond. Peter Gabriel, the Genesis incarnation, one of two tapes in the glove compartment (the other Vivaldi) sang strangely, as if part machine, the way I liked him to, familiar, and I decided I would play it the entire way, this Genesis, this robot angel, all twenty hours, or however long it would take me.

The tape player went down near Marion, IL, only fifty or so miles later, not even through "Foxtrot" once, eaten and shat out, and I immediately began questioning everything. The usual. Shouldn't I at least have a soundtrack for this odyssey, and shouldn't I interpret the malfunction as a sign? Or was there a better way? Mark the journey with the coming and going of local radio stations' call letters? Or silence? Anyway, I had to make a decision. To play the radio would bring the outside world in, and this quest seemed so insular and irrational. I had wanted total control over the environment inside the car—control—ranked third in the top ten forms of hubris. No control for the controller in this life, especially over the addiction to control. It was a difficult decision to drive with the Subaru's engine as my only aural companion. No call-in hate machinery. No Christmas preachers. No NPR. No Led Zeppelin retrospectives, just the hum and scratch of burning earth blood. For this I would need a new highway. Interstate 57 had held such promise, but it was fool's gold, like almost everything.

While I was upbraiding the tape player in my head, I saw a sign for I-24 to Nashville. Yes, *Nashville,* not Memphis, this was the way, not through the home of the blues and African spirits blown and picked and electrified, but through the home of country music, a much more appropriate signpost on the way to the Wonder Bread magic that Disney conjured. *I-24, it'll be you, me, the Subaru, and all my goddamned thoughts to torment me.* Twenty-four hours was, perhaps, all I had before the spell of purpose wore off.

A handout I gave my sophomores many years ago …

How The Great Smoky Mountains Became Smoky

Before Selfishness came into the world, which by any pedestrian study of history you can well imagine was a long time ago, the Cherokee were happy using the same hunting and fishing mountain lands as their neighbors. But all this changed when Selfishness appeared in the hearts of the tribes, and men began to quarrel.

The first quarrel of the Cherokee was with a tribe from the east, something to do with the young eastern warriors looking for a good time with Cherokee women. Lovers began pairing off, much to the chagrin of the Cherokee elders. The chiefs of the two tribes met in council to settle the quarrel. They smoked the pipe and quarreled for seven days and seven nights.

The Great Spirit grew cross because people were not, under any circumstances, to smoke the pipe until peace had been reached. As He looked down upon the old men with their heads bowed, He decided to show the tribes something, something that would make them remember to smoke the pipe only when making peace.

He turned the chiefs into grayish tubular flowers we now call "Indian Pipes" and made them grow wherever friends and relatives have quarreled.

The smoke from their pipes, puffed in breaths of belligerence, the Great Spirit left hanging over the mountains until all people of the world learn to live together in peace. That was how the Great Smoky Mountains came to be.

This Cherokee oral tale (that I took the liberty of embellishing slightly) was part of my first-day-of-school shtick from the one year I taught sophomore English, which was a disaster. The myth, while working as an introduction to creation tales, was also intended to be a thinly veiled marijuana metaphor for them to think about. If they were going to sit around and smoke grass, which I knew large numbers were, I could at least suggest they do it as a means of experiencing peace. Years later, I hoped, they might replace it with a sober peace, as if I knew anything about it. But these sophomores ended up turning it into a Young Hot Lovers vs. The World allegory, a sort of abridged *Romeo and Juliet*, just wildly out of context.

At first I really was excited to teach the curriculum, Greek Mythology, Sophocles, even *Beowulf* I thought would have its moments, Chaucer, for the tea-drinking set, yes. But this group of kids' hormones all seemed to find a new gear on the same day, which appeared to be the first day of school, and they could barely sit still all year. They began passing notes with reckless abandon, and when I intercepted them, which was often, I discovered they were all having sex with each other. It was madness. I'd never had any real discipline problems in my classroom besides isolated cases that I eventually broke down with equal parts deranged intimidation and a thousand second chances.

I knew that if it got out that my sophomores were in one another's pants, my class would be the front page of the school's tabloid conversations. I found it unsurprising and sad that so many of my colleagues seemed to thrive on student gossip, following their young, nubile lives like *People Magazine*.

"Craft, did you hear about the Mustiff kid?"

"He's not my student. I don't know him."

"No, I know, but did you hear about what this kid did at Jenny Randall's party?"

"Did he kill himself?"

"Jesus, Craft. That's awful! A terrible thing to say."

"Did he?"

"No! He did not."

"Did he kill someone else?"

"No."

"Then we're about finished, I'd say."

I had these conversations for years until I'd been around long enough to finally get a reputation as a prick, thank God. This time, I couldn't help it, the kids were dragging me into their personal lives, and via their myriad letters I knew graphic details about their bodies and desires. I had to admit, at least they were putting some effort into their physical descriptions of each other and the acts they were performing, or planning to perform. Much better writing, I thought, than pandering "Romance Novels," aimed at the lonely, the broken down—nooky scenes for people who don't remember what it's like to have a lover, which sadly included me. I could almost remember, though.

At 3:00, stomach filled with Clif Bars, I hit the Smoky Mountains. I suppose there are grander American vistas, greater peaks, but there is something to be said for these mountaintops painted with gray puffs and dense green. I was no longer missing Gabriel, or any sound for that matter. I returned to that place over myself, on the peeling Subaru ceiling, while my hands drove, guided, it seemed, by someone who knew where he was going.

6

Chugging up the mountain at thirty-five miles per hour, visibility decent, maybe fifty feet or so, I saw a black Monte Carlo with one of those chrome turbo engines sprouting out of the hood. It had always been my experience that inside these vehicles (this sort of "improvement" being popular in my youth) you could find a particularly joyless kind of macho fop. I often hoped to be surprised, to find the layer under the pompadour shell, exposing a deep well of emotion, capped with a wariness of explicitly feeling, but I never did. The car howled and swerved behind me, flashing its lights, though curiously the driver left the horn silent. The last image and sound I recall before I skidded off the side of the mountain was a young man, twenty-five or so, with thick lamb-chop sideburns and jet black cropped hair leaning out the passenger window, brow furrowed with what, in that instant, looked like concern.

"Sorry," he said.

"You—"

"Sorry," again.

The Monte Carlo burned its tires around a sharp turn and was gone. The crash was—the speed of light entering my eyes, a giant pow-symphony of metal and horns, a spraying of glass against my forehead and face, the top of my head, too, like buckshot. An ancient pine tree bent my Subaru like a boomerang, saved me from falling a thousand feet. I pulled the bottom of a coke bottle-sized chunk of glass out of the top of my head, just where my fontanel had been as a baby, looked in the unscathed rearview mirror, met myself there, smiled, swirling—dying, I thought. My eyelids closed.

No time went by—I tell you it was instantaneous when my hands sprung open and my neck stiffened and I lifted my ringing head.

"What is your name?"

"Father?"

"Is your name Craft?"

"Yes?"

"Craft."

"Yes."

"It's okay."

I saw him, this man in front of me, and for the briefest moment I was happy, three inches beneath his chin. Just like they said, the angels had come for me. It was all right, I thought, forever. I started weeping uncontrollably, my voice became my mother's, and her mother's.

"It's okay, Craft, you're okay. You've been in an accident."

"No accident."

"Yeah, an accident. I think you're going to make it. No bullshit. But don't move your head, it's got a big piece of the windshield wedged into it. You're in an ambulance."

"God."

"I do this all the time. Don't worry. I'm pretty good at it."

Where had the time gone? I'd been unconscious, beyond sleep, many times, but even when unconscious there is at least a distant awareness of time passing in the body, our little silent, screaming hourglass, from which we built clocks. I submit that I died in the ricochet spider web of the windshield, climbing the Great Smoky Mountains at 3:45 p.m., headed southeast—and arose, to live again.

I looked deep into the paramedic's face, his mustache, half-shut eyes looking out the window, a gaze really, as if he were on a train crossing the French countryside, with interest and awe, and a fresh memory of a girl he met and kissed.

"Am I going to die?"

"No, I told you, I bet you'll live."

"How much would you bet?" I said.

"Oh, no, no I can't."

"How much would bet on me living?"

"No money. We're almost there."

Then darkness. This time, time passing, time crushing peanut shells under its giant boots. I could feel it in the tingling sensation of anesthesia. I was still alive.

Waking up from the surgery about seventy-two hours after they finished sewing the very tip of my brain back together was not easy to do. I reeled myself back into my face, in slow motion, until my rivers were filled with blood again, instead of the infinite vacuum. It had taken twelve hours for them to pull out the chard of glass, according to the doctor they flew in from Knoxville to perform the operation. So kind, to fly in that way, and to stay until I'd stabilized. I'm sure he wanted to be with his family, or someone other than an evaporating man clinging to his life. Apparently the shard had become lodged in the shape of a fishing hook.

"The problem was, as long as we stayed on the surface there, I knew we'd be fine, but another ten to fifteen millimeters, and we're talking about a lobotomy. Well, not really, I'm sorry, sometimes I forget and speak to patients the way I speak to other doctors. When I get tired I mean, and I'm fucking exhausted. They roped me into two more surgeries since they already had me here."

"How am I? The brain?"

"Oh, fine. It's fine. You're okay, Craft. I thought I told you that straight off. Like I said, I'm beat."

"It was that close?"

"Oh, yeah, it was very tight, very tight. In there, you know, you get in there, and you have to slow your fingers down. I imagine a snail, a kind of healing snail that just glides in and absorbs the problem."

"Yes," I said.

"You have to slow it down, man, otherwise, you lurch at all, like I said, ten millimeters or so."

That he framed my consciousness metrically frightened me

into exploring existence ending in death, no door, no light, not even darkness. Cycles of sun in front of us and behind us, full of numbers and near misses. Midnight? Then nothing. How many times had I asked this question in one way or another, disappearing and pointless? But I had something. I had just, a few days ago, died and returned, wheezing back, choking back. Lying in the ambulance underneath Al's face at sunset. What my return proved or didn't prove did not matter. I was proof. I was alive.

In a chair next to my bed in what I thought was the next morning, I found Al. He was reading a *National Geographic* with a reproduction of a Neanderthal on the cover, which asked the question, "Is this guy our father?" Al looked up and nodded, and I wept again, washing my eyes.

"You're awake, Craft. That's good. They said you've been in and out, well mostly out, for ten days."

"I don't recall. Ten days?"

"You look okay bald. Like the guy who played Gandhi, you know, but with a donut habit."

He coughed and I coughed in response, which turned out to be a terrible mistake, in terms of a frisson of suffering. I sincerely thought I was connected to a high-voltage battery, shocked and frying.

"Tell me your life story. Quick," I said, "I need to listen to something or my eyes are going to burst."

"It's okay to cry. I usually feel better afterward."

He'd been a starting strong safety for the University of Tennessee Volunteers but had suffered a mental collapse on the field after ending the career of a star Florida Gators tailback, his leg snapped in half with only the skin keeping it from landing ten feet away from his arms. The Saturday before, Al had broken the Ole Miss quarterback's ribs, which in turn punctured a lung, and a decade later, that poor guy, he said, still wasn't breathing correctly and might not ever again. Two bad weeks. The analysts in the booths and back at the studio said both were clean hits, ferocious and clean.

"A rulebook for a game says I'm not to blame. We're talking about a guy not walking right, ever, and another guy with one decent lung. That's how I thought about it anyway. I made my body into a weapon and destroyed them, man. Cut 'em down. On purpose. Forget that I didn't know they'd get hurt. Forget that shitty argument. Keep it real simple. My objective was to hit the man as hard as I could. Two men. Hit the man."

He had been a committed Christian since he could speak, up on Jesus, in the choir, proud to attend the rare Tennessee small-town church with "both black folks and white folks praying and singing together." He was positive there was a Christian way to look at his situation, a hundred Christian ways maybe, to draw meaning from his transformation into a flaming sword on the field, but he no longer cared to try to solve Jesus's parable, if that's what He was up to. His disaffected manner was why I believed Al in the ambulance when he said I'd live.

"Everyone's saying, hey, God is trying to tell you something. Are you listening? God is speaking to you, directly to you, Al. You're special, Al. God loves you. I couldn't hear anything except those two guys screaming in my head. And I didn't want to forget it. Every part of the sound, the air coming out of their lungs, the crack of Zack's ribs, Ricardo's femur, his voice was like a newborn, I wanted to remember all of it. I know it's the kind of thing they tell you to forget. Everyone says, Al, you answered the call of Jesus. You received His message. You're saving lives. I can see their point of view, me getting this job driving around like I do. It's not that way. I see people die and I'm less of an asshole. I see people live and I'm less of an asshole. You should put the TV on. Look. Jeopardy."

I watched for a few minutes, and I couldn't think of any of the answers, not one. Dr. Jakroy from Knoxville said, apparently ten days ago, that I might have trouble thinking clearly because, he said, "Your brain needs to sleep like a dog for a while." I didn't see the simile at first, but I could appreciate the beauty of a sleeping dog, and it calmed me to think of my brain that way. But until Jeopardy came on, I hadn't considered how I'd been affected by the crash. I'd blindly assumed that I'd awoken in more or less the same state as when I left consciousness. On television, Javier, an accountant from Tulsa, swept through the Shakespeare category, each question in the form of an answer increased my anxiety, my emptiness, my lack, ringing in the center of the little sphere I'd envisioned my mind to be. Finally, Javier wagered everything on the last square on the board, the second Daily Double. "Answer: Two of the four plays in which a ghost appears on stage."

My mind was blank. I wept again, being an old English hack. Shameful, I thought, such an easy one. Javier smiled with equal parts confidence and avarice, right into the camera.

"What are *Richard III* and *Julius Caesar*." He punctuated it like a spiked volleyball.

"Yes," Trebek said. "Also correct would have been *Macbeth* and *Hamlet*, 'Murder most foul, as in the best it is/But this most foul, strange, and unnatural.' We'll be back with Final Jeopardy, and perhaps another quote, right after this."

"You okay, Craft? You might need some more painkillers."

"I need to get to Orlando/Kissimmee/St. Cloud."

I took a quick deep breath, as if it were the moment before submerging myself under water, and tried to force my body to sit up, but I was met immediately with vice grips on my elbows, with gentle, firm give. Al lowered me again onto my back.

"Hey, man, you didn't just get a little concussion, you dipped a glass nacho chip into your skull."

"I have to go."

"Come on, Craft. Take it easy for a few weeks. Then you can fly down to Orlando."

"Or Kissimmee/St. Cloud. I'll rest when I get there."

"Hey," he said.

A scythe seemed to cut across my corneas, and I saw colorless, transparent light in Al's eyes, or rather behind his eyes. Stillness. I didn't know what was happening to me, or to Al, but I was frozen, and so unable to clumsily flail around at finding out.

"Craft, do you remember calling me *Father* in the ambulance?"

"I don't remember speaking," I said.

"Yeah, it was weird, your lips didn't move, but I know you said 'Father,' because it came out perfectly. It took me back for a second, like it was this moment, I don't know."

"I know the kind of moment you mean."

"You're way older than me, so that's impossible, but for a second it made sense. Weird."

"Yes."

"We can talk about it in the morning. I'll call and check on you."

"Wait, Al, Final Jeopardy."

It was ludicrous: "We're going to give you a line from a nineteenth-century novel," Trebek softly barked, "and we want you to name the work for us. Give us a title. '*My two natures had memory in common, but all other faculties were most unequally shared between them.*'"

"My God, that's so simple," I said, but without finding the answer between my ears, I reached to grab my hair, a gesture I'd repeated thousands upon thousands of times in my life, mostly in the classroom, and this time found a firestorm of bald, scarred skin. I called out to something, or nothing, in that instant, some entity or lack of an entity, to everything I didn't know. The one thing I did, being alive, with or without purpose. I might have *yipped* into the sheets, like a rodent might.

"Yeah. Ouch. You gotta watch out for your habits and tics."

"Al, do you think you could find me a glass of wine?"

"Nope. I'll call you. Don't worry. Oh, here's your wallet. It was in the tree that split your car in half. Your suitcase is in the john."

"Ah, it was a *strange case* indeed, but of whom and whom? We'll start with Geena," Trebek snipped, coming back from a commercial.

7

Out my window, the waning three-quarter moon hung lasciviously low, as if a great weight were pushing its face down, into the earth's crotch, between continents, somewhere in the South Atlantic. I felt better an hour or so after Al left, something about having my wallet reassured me, my driver's license, I was still officially who I was. It perked my spirits just enough to do something brave and idiotic. Megan had taught me "breath of fire," from her yoga practice, to help me stay awake grading essays at two a.m. It aided me considerably, so I incorporated it as the last step of my procrastination routine before the bimonthly ritual of marking up ninety 4- to 6-page papers. I also found, experimentally, that "breath of fire" had a sobering effect when I had chased the deceitful heat in whiskey, caught it, and no longer wanted what I'd caught.

I began slowly, gently pulling in my abdomen as the staccato breaths came and left. I increased the speed of the breaths and the force of my abdomen each time my body would allow it. After maybe five hundred to a thousand breaths, the thought entered my mind that I could completely nullify the cutting pain in my head, neck, shoulders, knees, and feet, the general feeling that I'd been the target of a giant cartoon safe.

Something in my chest began lifting, but not against gravity, and not up, just lifting, rising. I opened my eyes and felt sure that my body was now immune. The machines were shockingly easy to detach. Freed from medicine, I stood up, walked to the bathroom to pick up what was once my father's leather suitcase, my only evidence of his being other than myself, and put on the looser of the two pairs of brown slacks I packed before leaving what was my home. I felt as nimble as a retired hurdler.

Completely contrary to the way I was raised, I tried all my life to avoid growing too attached to articles of clothing. It's tempting to allow yourself to believe that a certain shirt or pair of slacks can soak up all the experiences a person has while wearing them. I watched my mother brazenly embrace such superstition. But for me, through the years, Sperry Top-Sider Gold Cup Penny Loafers took nearly every step, right or wrong, hurtful, wise, or otherwise. Water-resistant two-tone leather, genuine deerskin lining, this particular pair worn-in eight months, optimal. I put them on, and like knowing I still had my wallet, I felt my entire life rush into my feet. I walked out the door, just a calm breeze blowing on burning hot coals.

Unnoticed as I leaked out the automatic doors of the hospital, my imperviousness to pain lasted only until I began breathing normally again. I nearly collapsed but caught myself on the side of a trashcan.

The Indian man, perhaps my age, behind the counter at the liquor store across the street from the Chattanooga hospital looked up when the sleigh bells rang, and I hobbled inside. His eyes fell on my orange plastic bracelet, and I immediately assumed he thought I'd escaped from the psych ward.

"I'll take that Jameson right behind you there and a mineral water, please."

"You don't look okay. Are you okay?"

"That's why I'm buying the whiskey, friend. Please."

"No. I don't think—"

"God is chasing me."

"Whiskey, all right," he said, his wrist collapsed forward, hand open to me. "But God does not chase."

"Well, I'm running anyway. Keep the change."

"You shouldn't walk far. Go back to the hospital. My daughter is a doctor."

"Could she give me a ride to the bus station?"

"She's working in the hospital."

"How about you? It must be about closing time. What do you say?"

"I close in two hours. For the doctors."

"All right, I understand."

"Buy this herb. It costs three dollars."

"What is it?"

"It's from India. Eat it. I will open the package and you eat it. Now. Yes. Keep eating."

"All of it?"

"Yes."

"Which way to the bus station?"

Sticking my thumb in the air, walking backward on the side of the road with the whiskey bottle wearing a paper bag like an apron, was the closest thing I'd ever experienced to prayer. I'd always been able to spot what I thought were beautiful approaches to prayer in others, singers, carpenters, painters, actors, waitresses, poets too, but I had, subconsciously, written it off as impossible, or perhaps deceptive, for myself. But on the side of the road, it was *please, please don't take me now.* I was wheezing and unintentionally allowing saliva to leak out of my mouth and nose, on five pulls of whiskey, thankfully, which would grant me a little time before it wrapped itself around my entire body and constricted again.

The first of the pickup trucks to stop had a wreath with a red bow tied to the grill. The driver, about my age, asked if I'd give him enough gas money to fill up the tank, which was past E. I eagerly agreed and opened the passenger door.

"Headed?"

"South," I said, "and east," putting one foot on the cab's floor.

"No, no, in the back."

"There's no one sitting here."

"I don't know you. Get in the back and give me sixty bucks."

I backed out of the truck and sat in a heap on the side of the road. Two more pickups stopped and I waved them on. One's passenger seat was open, but the likelihood at that time of a similar exchange seemed strong. I lifted myself to standing, but the suitcase was heavy in my elbow and shoulder, even with the few light items I brought. My arms felt skeletal, or like I had cardboard shoulders.

Suddenly I was on the ground again, collecting my breath. I saw a discarded cinder block painted yellow a foot in front of my face. It looked like it had been part a patio wall. Then I saw nothing. Again.

8

My first thought, even before waking, while still enduring scenes in my increasingly ghostly dreams, was that someone had used my jaw instead of a bottle of champagne to christen a ship. I recalled the image of the cinder block I'd seen before losing consciousness and decided the reason I'd been able to see it so well was that I'd fallen on it, leading with the (glass) jaw. I touched my face and was surprised at a few things. One, that it didn't hurt too badly if kept completely still. Two, that I was *not* lying in the street or in the dirt or a ditch. Three, that next to me was a beautiful woman in the driver's seat of a van. Four, that there was a golf ball-sized wad of peppermint gum in my mouth that when I instinctually bit down caused my jaw to pop. Pop. The surge came slowly, like the seconds between the detonation of TNT and the actual explosion. I repressed the guttural sound that rushed up to my throat. A gush of tears warmed my neck and clung to my chest hair. I clenched my hands around my throat with the intent of stopping my esophagus from collapsing, but the gesture was really just symbolic.

"Hello-oh?" she said. "Do you know where you are, drunk bloody man?"

I spit out the gum and stuck it to my wrist.

"You can put the gum in the Starbuck's cup. I'm done with it. I clenched your teeth together a few times to chew it up. Your mouth smelled like an open sewer."

I said nothing. I felt safe looking at her face, intent on the road, blinking, applying Chap Stick. She looked like a Vandella.

"I know where you've been. I see that bracelet. But it looks to me like you should still be there."

I nodded.

"You need some Tylenol?"

"Yes," I breathed.

"Can you swallow without water?"

I nodded.

"Can you remember how you got here?"

"No."

"I'm Sherhonda."

I nodded.

"And you're Craft. I know that much. What else do I know? You've never had sex with a black woman, though you find them beautiful. And you admit you've always been a little nervous around beautiful black women, but not anymore, not tonight. What else. And you're caught between (quote) The Lord and an outhouse."

I wondered who it was in my drunken, impervious stupor that had told her these bullet points of my situation. Her recitation sounded like me, but foreign, like the feeling of having an old friend you haven't spoken to in years give you the old jokes and a punch in the shoulder. But not only are the jokes no longer funny, they seem to take on a pathetic allegorical quality, or a tragic play within a play about your life, abridged.

I was overcome with a rush of my eighteen-year-old salacious self, a drunken, self-conscious sponge, in my dorm room, masturbating and reading a standard college check list, and *by God, I would read it in its entirety*, to make up for lost time—and out of a lack of something better to do. It was the labyrinthine chaos of *Finnegan's Wake* that planted the seed that because I believed I understood certain passages on a schizophrenic level, I ought to become an English teacher, as a tribute—and for summers off.

"So you ain't got no use for Jesus, huh?"

"I can't remember having one or not. Did I say that?"

"You said Walt Disney was your guy. I guess you won't remember I'm driving to Valdosta. You'll have to find a bus to get to Orlando from there. This van belongs to the church."

I inferred that if it were her van, not the church's, she'd drive me all the way to Orlando/Kissimmee/St. Cloud, but more than likely it was just one of a million little facts that slip out in conversation. Maybe she wanted me to know it was a holy vehicle, or that the reason she picked me up had more to do with her role as a representative of the Valdosta Church of Christ than with kindred feelings for a broken traveler.

"You're crazy, you know that? You jumped in front of the van, waving your arms around. Now you're all making me reevaluate the meaning of shit again. I just settled on some things last year too. Asshole," she smiled.

"Why?" I whispered, but she ignored me and continued.

"The front of the van just touched you, just barely. And you just sort of fell back in slow motion with the biggest, dumbest smile I've ever seen on a man's face."

I wanted to sleep, obviously safe now with Sherhonda, but some agent in my mind blocked the tunnel back to the refuge of hibernation. All I could do was try to move as little as possible. Without medication, I felt bound to time, awake. The headlights gobbled up the gray, white, and yellow of the road. In that forward visual trajectory, in the middle of the darkness beyond the end of the air illuminated by Sherhonda's headlights—excuse me—the Valdosta Church of Christ's van's headlights, I saw a figure with a spherical center, a sort of mandala with strokes of ultraviolet stretching like tendrils to the sky, into the ground, around us. I raised an eyebrow and winced.

"I'm hallucinating. I'm listening," I said, correcting myself.

"Huh?" Sherhonda said.

I was stuck in the air beyond the windshield, drawn into the pure, still, black center of the mandala, which seemed to somehow both lack three dimensions, yet possess an *inside,* or a *through.* Sherhonda didn't appear to notice it.

"I know you're a more or less all right guy, because you asked if I minded before you said what you said about sex and black women and the rest of it. Wasn't any way you were going to pull anything anyway. I'd kick your ass so fast—I wouldn't need to, I'd just slap your stitches and that'd be that. Those are fresh, I can see that."

Music I didn't recognize, contemporary-sounding, big harmonies and beats, felt like a vapor around us, amplifying sound through my blood. I broke my gaze out the windshield and saw Sherhonda putting her jacket of CDs back under the seat. I gazed again and the mandala was still there, ultraviolet tendrils, the center sphere that now seemed to be producing the music. I could have seen anything, projected any meaning onto that form, out there in the distance (that was really only an illusion of distance), but what I saw felt like an answer, or a well-timed question. An end to my string of beatings at the hands of strangers and pupils.

"You like this music?"

I nodded.

"Let me tell you something personal, since you brought it up and I'm never going to see you again. And this is something I bet you can understand, teacher man. I think Jesus did more harm than good as a teacher. The rest of what he did was good. But he should've settled on carpenter or fisherman, you ask me. I know he died for our sins. I know all of it. I know. And I know you can make him whatever you want, you can make him Love, and you can make him your conscience, give him the keys and all that, but what he wanted from people was never gonna come. And don't tell me I don't have hope for people, but the hope isn't Jesus. You know why? Because Jesus, as smart as he was, should've known that there isn't a teacher alive or ever lived who can teach walking on water to everybody. Which is what you sure as shit better be able to do if you're going to love all your brothers, every last one. Sisters, shit. You'd turn into a vegetable, or a homeless addict. He picked the wrong animal to teach that love line to, as good as it is. I'll keep going to church, though, and driving the van. I love to sing."

I nodded, not knowing what I was agreeing with exactly.

Perhaps just that I had confidence that Sherhonda would keep her word and continue worshiping at Valdosta Church of Christ and driving the special event van. Maybe I was acknowledging that I had no idea what I actually thought about Christ beyond his iron-clad hold on the role as central-character-number-one in the culture, and I didn't see that changing. I knew we sure wanted to be saved, and maybe He knew the actual saving would come much later, after a miraculous honing of the species allowed life to flourish in lieu of boundless masochism. Or maybe there was no saving to be done. Maybe I just hoped Sherhonda would sing sometime before we arrived in Valdosta.

9

I was born a quick healer. My hair once grew furiously, thick and plentiful, two hundred thousand ultra-thin stalks of corn. It could have been the decades of half-smoked Tareytons resting in the ashtray with a fresh one already lit, squeezed gently between my fingers, that and the conveyer belt of handwritten essays, that slowed my powers of restoration to a crawl. But even in the immense pain caused by the potholes that Sherhonda seemed to have a special talent for finding, I recalled the mandala vision clearly, and I was still convinced that if I simply found a way to stay alive the next few days, that I would be, if not all right, then at least spared further bludgeoning, and maybe even my life. The dive the Subaru took off the cliff was the last of it, or so the ultra-violet tendrils seemed to say anyway.

I told Sherhonda my tale, from the point when a bevy of consequences had become impossible to ignore, in some larger context. She put on a mix she made while I talked, which she said helped her concentrate. She was a rapt ear, filling in details of my life with intuition and razor-sharp analytical skills. She would've aced my class.

But it actually felt more like I was speaking to someone who knew everything God knew, and was a much better listener. A few examples:

1. *I bet you lost your cherry at like twenty-one or something, huh …*

True! It had been a hypocritically principled choice. Although I'd performed novice to intermediate cunnilingus (and everything "below" that on the sexual scale of the young) on five of my classmates in the School of Education (what the boys called "Surf City"… two girls for every…), two of the young women more than once actually, and had fellatio given to me by six gracious young women, four serious and orderly mother figures from class who held their ponytails behind their necks, and one bluesy-eyed vixen from the business school who treated my humble tumescence like a microphone—oh yes—and one male English professor, the drunkest but not the worst night of my young life (we'd stayed up all night discussing Whitman, what did I think was going to happen?), that is all to say I didn't *sign the deed* until graduation day, with my neighbor from the house where I grew up, Randa, five years older, broad shoulders and powerful thighs, a chain smoker, a softball player. As children she threw rocks at me as hard as she could, which evolved into pinning me to the ground and slapping my face until it turned tomato red, which came to its full flowering that sunny day in May, Columbia, Missouri, 1980, in the bathroom of my shared apartment while my small family party barely hummed in the living room. Our mothers had played Knock Rummy every Sunday night for thirty years. That's why Randa was even there.

2. *You're lying about your wife. Ain't no man alive didn't want to kill somebody when he finds out she's messing around, her, him, or both.*

Yes. I went as far as to craft a plan to murder my wife, Megan, worthy of Poe, I thought. After I found out that she'd propositioned Tim Conroy, from Tim himself, I told him I was going to kill her, and could he please speak well of me after I received my lethal injection.

"What is it, Tim?" I said. He looked skeptical.

"How are you going to do it?"

"I'm going to shoot her, of course, quick, in the head, plead insanity, change my plea back to sanity and ask for the death penalty, because it would better represent my condition of being so indecisive about suicide—an act you damn well know I could never perform, even with a gun to my head."

"Okay, okay, but I think you should sleep on it. You're not thinking straight. Sleep on it."

"You know what'll happen if I do that, Tim. The same old shit."

"Ah, you never can tell. Change is funny, like the Chinese

fable."

"Which fable?"

"The guy—I don't know, my head's so full of crap. But it has to do with not knowing anything, not being able to predict the future, outcomes, I don't know."

"Hmm," I said, recognizing in that moment that I didn't have the right salt for murder.

3. *Don't even make this shit about that boy in Disney World. It's about you.*

How could it be just about the boy? I was desperate for a binding agent, so there he was, the glue, this exotic, suffering boy living in the manifest vision of Walt Disney. I knew he was out there and real, though, feeling, in pain, completely unexotic, with a heartbeat and bad skin. It was about purpose, the real boy. But the themes were internal, concerned with the self, clash, dichotomy, grasping at straws—nothing groundbreaking. Pure kindness, generosity, altruism, those things come easily only when free of desperation. The scrambling, fearful man doesn't have the luxury. He needs conceits, meanings, symbols, and he hopes for a result, specifically survival, which if watered properly might grow into a life. Or so he must force himself to believe.

Valdosta is the last outpost on I-75 before you hit Florida, our extremity, dangling, obscene. Otis Redding covering Sam Cooke rang like only that man can, calling out to the cracks in the sky, and the sky itself. Sherhonda sang along, and had the incredible sense and taste to sing a supportive harmony, above Otis, but behind him. All she needed was a robe. She already had the sway.

My head was oozing again, though my cheek stitches from the trumpet wound were healing nicely. Unfortunately they were surrounded by the cuts and jags from the tiny pieces of glass that had embedded themselves in my cranium and face. With my eyes closed, I imagined that her husky sweet voice was sealing my cuts, but the song faded slowly, and she turned off the car stereo.

At the front of a small urgent care clinic attached to a tanning salon, she leaned across and opened my door, insistence on her lips.

"Listen, I know who you are. That shit about the missing rich girl you messed around with went viral."

"Don't say that, viral," I said.

"Well, you don't seem to be aware of it. She's still missing last I read on Yahoo News, but I don't know."

"Why did you pick me up, Sherhonda?"

"Cause those people, her family—straight up assholes."

"Well, they must have dropped the charges anyway."

"Swear to me, Craft. You'll go and get your head looked at before you get on the bus to Orlando."

"Kissimmee/St. Cloud."

"I don't want to read about you dying, all viral again."

"I doubt I'd even get an obituary in my own hometown."

"Well, I just think you're having a breakdown. You said you used to be more or less fine, right?"

"No, no, I've always been like this. I've just always been cloistered in a place where half the people are insane. It's all relative."

"What, high school? They're still just kids."

"No, the teachers."

"This kind of stuff, it passes, believe me," Sherhonda said.

"Oh, I do. Everything passes. Everything dies."

"They call them anxiety attacks now. All you have to do is slow down and take it easy for a while. Then you can help this kid, rested, with your head on straight."

"Sherhonda, I haven't done a damn thing."

"What?"

"To help."

"Help the kid?"

"Anything."

"You teach, dummy. Go in and let a nurse look at your head."

"Would you have made love to me, if I hadn't been in this condition? And shorn bald? That is, if I'd been someone else?"

"No."

"Just no? No explanation?"

"Goodbye, Craft."

"Thank you."

The bitter chill took me off guard, watching the van pull away. The man smoking outside the clinic, his considerable girth taut under his mandatory flag-pride T-shirt, exhaled both cigarette smoke and his own frosty carbon dioxide. The night air gnashed its teeth, and mine seemed to scream at my gums, scream at them to just please, leave them alone.

10

Tossing out Sherhonda's concern for my well-being like threadbare dress socks, I opened an ancient copy of the Yellow Pages and lifted the receiver off the phone at the urgent care clinic. No one was at the front desk. Through a small hole in the corner of the ceiling, a band of hornets flashed in and out. A woman in the off-white waiting room was bent over, moaning, a moistened copy of *Allure* squeezed between her bosom and legs. I asked her if she was all right, and she moaned louder, and higher pitched, and it was then I noticed she belonged to the group of American women who, though still middle-aged, had stopped distinguishing between pajamas and all other articles of clothing.

This was a sect I'd had to scrutinize early in life. Somehow they had found in my mother, Patsy, a lifer in customer service at JC Penney, an ear and a face that wouldn't turn away. And so, one by one, like moths (though Mother herself remained neatly put together until moments before turning in for the night) they'd return to the store just to stop by customer service and register a complaint with the nice young lady. When they began telephoning at home, I thought nothing of it. It seemed only natural. When sweet-smelling pink boxes arrived, carried by women in their nighties, I gleefully consumed the contents while my mother willingly absorbed a series of tales: *The Bastard in the Parking Lot, My Daughter Is Never Home, The Pain Has Moved to My Hand, How Does Fixing a Bumper Cost $1000, Blacks, I Thought of Going to the Beauty Parlor but Decided Not To, The Phone Company.* And so I'd lie on the carpet, with a comic book in which I had no interest, listening for the brief and rare moments when my mother's voice would levitate above gentle affirmative grunts and validate their unending hopelessness with a declaration of their value in the world. Sometimes upwards of two hours per phone call, three hours or more if they showed up at the door with donuts and Danishes.

These were the first social critics I recognized as such. The fact that they'd abandoned a loosely-agreed-upon dress code is, for groomed society, an instant signifier of the depressed underclass. But something like that could be interpreted so differently through the lens of a child. What villains, I wondered, cared so deeply about assuring these women a place in Hell on earth? What monster forced them to roam around this way? They seemed to yearn for a better world, at once fair and service-oriented, one that would allow them to wear actual clothing without beating them down so fiercely. I carried them with me through adolescence, tucked away but close by, their scoffs and other choleric inflections. Consequently, I never noticed their residency and considerable influence in my addled adult mind.

"Do you need a doctor right away?"

"Quiet, it hurts," she whispered, humming until she coughed.

I dialed, and Ronald at the AA Action Taxi Service said he'd be "about an hour," that he was just about to have a snack.

"Should I call another taxi service?"

"Why?"

"Because I'd like to get to the bus station sooner than an hour from now."

"Well, from the clinic, you could walk there in about forty-five minutes probably. If you're spry."

It killed me to say I couldn't walk more than a few feet at a time, that there were physical realities in my body that superseded any delusion I had about fool courage. And besides, I'd already played that chip. I needed rest, to be fed, cooked for, possibly sponge-bathed, and to sponge-bathe someone else, often—not that I'd known anything like that in years, or ever, but if I didn't find it, a certain permutation of life, one defined by lack, by inevasible death, was coming for me—and soon.

"Well, I'm the only taxi in town. I got a partner, but he's in a leg cast, can't drive. There's a limousine guy, black guy. Went to

Lowndes High. Basketball kid. He probably isn't too busy this time of year."

"Limousine? No, no. All right. I'll see you in an hour, Ronald."

"I got something in the oven. Could be more like an hour and a half. Maybe longer if my stomach doesn't settle."

"Do you have the limo driver's number, or the name of his service, I have—"

"I don't like to get stuck in the cab in that condition. Nowhere to stop in town really."

"Yes," I said.

"Okay. Yeah. AA Limos."

"Aren't you AA Taxi?"

"Yeah."

"Is it part of your company?"

"No. He works for himself, that guy."

"It sounds as though you have considerable disdain for this man."

"Now goddamn it, what do you know about it?"

"Nothing. But more and more I'm growing curious."

"Who is this?"

"Nobody, a teacher, a traveler."

"You got a pen and something to write on?"

"Yes," I lied. I had the phone book, of course, rendering Ronald redundant, and yet I felt compelled to stay on the line until we'd finished the exchange. But something happened, and I heard the receiver drop to the floor on Ronald's end, a promo for the local news blaring, loud enough for the speakers to distort the anchors' voices. The young woman who worked the front desk returned and looked at me, zeroing in on my hand holding the receiver, as if trying to will it back to the cradle with her mind.

"I'm finished," I said.

I hung up on Ronald hanging there in limbo, signed in for urgent care, and carried the yellow pages, like Moses, over to a chair by a tiny fish tank without fish, just a diver and no treasure chest. The woman who'd been moaning had stopped, and was sitting upright, cupping her throat with one hand, thumbing through her *Allure* with the other.

"Excuse me," I said. "May I borrow your phone? It's a local call."

"Doesn't matter. That's not the kind of plan I got."

"May I borrow it anyway?" I asked.

"If you can find it in this purse. Ever since I got sick, I haven't been through it except to put more stuff in."

"Thank you."

"You come over here, and I'll hold it open for you."

Seams were starting to tear away from the thin metal rods holding the bag together— buttons, used Kleenex, used bloody Kleenex, lipstick, Chap Stick, batteries, dollar bills, sunglasses, candy bars, individually wrapped Halls, post-its, gum-filled post-its, key chains with no keys, hair clips, and dirt—it was taut. The phone, though not in plain view at first, was easy enough to find, sitting near the top of the heap. I dialed and found a deep, direct voice on the other end. I explained my whereabouts, which didn't seem to faze T.J., the independent limo driver.

"I can be there in ten minutes if you don't care that I don't wear a suit."

"No, no, it's not that kind of night. Come however you can, as soon as you can."

"Okay, sir. To the bus station, then that's it?"

"Yes, that's right," I said.

"It'll only take about seven minutes."

"Let's do one quick stop at a drive-through, anyplace with French fries and a milkshake. Seasoned fries."

"Sure. I can do that."

The woman had begun moaning again, two longs and a short, but this time the receptionist came over and asked her to stop.

"No, it hurts," she pleaded.

"You stopped before," the receptionist whispered, "so I'm

going to need you to stop again."

"Okay."

"Okay?"

"I can't," the woman moaned.

"Try please. Try."

"Excuse me," I said. "Why are you castigating that poor woman? Oh, and thank you for letting me use your phone, ma'am."

"You're welcome," she said, picking at her nightgown's loose thread.

"Because I don't think there's a need for that sound. I think someone's being a little melodramatic."

"And who are you to make that assessment?" I asked.

"She's been doing it for two hours. At some point, it's like, come on."

"Why in God's name has she been sitting here for two hours?"

"Because the doctors are busy. Did you just call T.J., the fucking chauffer?"

"Yes," I said.

"Mm-hmm. Are you going to wait to see a doctor or are you leaving?"

"No," I said, not knowing which question I was answering.

"Then you need to leave here right now. Ma'am, stop moaning. Breathe. Stop it."

"I can't," the woman said.

"If you want her to stop," I said, "get her in to see a doctor. Tell them it's urgent, like the sign says."

"They don't listen to me, all right?"

The woman's moaning evolved to wailing. But her pain truly ignited when a hornet, one of the many I'd seen flying near the ceiling, landed on her neck and stung her squarely between the earlobe and collar bone. Already in tears, she began screaming, which drifted over the course of thirty seconds into screaming. I could make out a man's name—Torsten.

The name shocked and hypnotized me, and I suddenly felt there was an audience sitting above us. I had been cast as the pummeled stranger. A downtrodden angel interloper? A harbinger of locusts and broken spirits? I might have been Torsten himself for all I knew.

"Torsten. Torsten. Torsten."

"Stop it," the receptionist said.

"Who is Torsten? Can I call him for you?" I asked.

"He's dead." And she returned to her original moaning, one hand on her throat, the other now covering the side of her neck.

"It's just a bug bite, you're going to be fine, now—" this time the receptionist was cut off in mid-sentence, as if choking, still, frozen. In the darkness of her open mouth I saw myself. What I saw—I'd seldom loved. *Seldom*, perhaps the name of this town, or perhaps even the title of the play. But there were corpuscles, intestines, femurs, and teeth. It wasn't a play, my life, their lives. Those delusions, diversions really, couldn't hold their shape anymore. They kept dissolving into the actual moment. It was squarely into these women's hardships I was limping, holding up my face to the light.

T.J. came through the doors in baggy jeans and a black Georgia Tech sweatshirt, a yellow jacket poised to sting displayed prominently. T.J. had no way of knowing, obviously.

"Get out of here," the receptionist said to him.

"I'm doing business."

"You're a lying fuck."

"Calm down, Brooke. We're leaving. Don't embarrass yourself."

Their eyes now three inches apart, I saw how the tenderness that T.J. must have shown the receptionist—probably not long ago, perhaps cooked her breakfast and lingered over her body with the breeze blowing in through the half-open window—had churned inside her, and how it had morphed into vengeance.

"Go."

"Please help this woman," I said.

"Give me a break. She was here last week for the same thing."

"What difference could that possibly make?"

"Is there a problem?" A nurse appeared through the door with a bark and a twist of metal. She expected her answer (in the form of a question) to bring finality to the situation.

"This woman is ill," I said.

"She can wait her turn like everybody else," the nurse said. The tiny victory made the receptionist smile, squinting one eye at me.

"Let's go, Mr. Craft, you have to get to the bus station."

A professional, T.J. But there was just no escaping hemorrhaging hearts. I thought of Patsy again, how she would audition a new suitor—she called them suitors—every three years or so until one day, when I was sixteen, she stopped deceiving herself about ever loving them. Who knows, one or two might have been men who would've taken a genuine interest in her boundless imagination, her compassion, but she didn't want to orbit anyone but me and Grandma Faust, as far as I could tell. Her allusions to love were ambiguous strolls down memory lane, no names or flesh to fill in the picture. But I'd imagined that she'd truly loved somewhere along the line before engaging my father in a night of confused creation (I never glimpsed even a photograph of him, a signature, an article of clothing that belonged to his face, his hands, his chest). Just his suitcase, this suitcase in my hands, was still with me.

T.J. and I stopped at Arby's and ate in the parking lot, mostly in silence with quick flourishes of commentary. Chewing up seasoned curly fries was a punishing act if I broke my concentration for half a second, allowing my jaw to open, or shift more than a fraction of an inch. So I focused on the night sky, the stars sprinkled heavily over the small town's relative darkness. Someone in the run-down adjacent neighborhood began shooting off fireworks that were in perfect view out the windshield. T.J.

watched the colors separate in the air, strands of firelight, emphatically chewing his Super Roast Beef sandwich, swallowing after each interval of explosions.

"What are they celebrating, T.J.?"

"Drugs probably."

"Would you say Valdosta is a mostly hostile town?"

"Mmm, I wouldn't say hostile, but you gotta be careful."

"Careful of what."

"Where you stick your dick," he said.

"Mmm. Isn't that true anywhere?"

"I don't know. I ain't really been anywhere else."

"What does that taxi driver, Ronald, what does he have against you?"

"Huh," he said, "a lot. His daughter for starters. Like ten years ago."

"You ever consider raising a family?"

"I don't really have any hobbies, so I don't see it working out."

T.J. gave me his *Entertainment Weekly*, which I read cover to cover while waiting for my bus to depart, mostly to distract myself from the throbbing on top of and underneath my skull. I rested my eyes on an obnoxious film review that compared some Oscar-pandering-protagonist-as-martyr-movie to Ingmar Bergman. *Through a Glass Darkly* was discussed at some length. After getting over the initial agitation at this, I was shocked to feel the reference section of my brain had returned to me. I could remember my Bergman period, sitting there, this particular film in quick shots—Karin, depressingly beautiful, her splintering body and soul, and her poor, aroused younger brother, Minus, hurling himself into his sister's madness, literally. And Max Von Sydow, a celebration of austerity as husband, along with her absentee writer-father, cart poor Karin off to the mental hospital, where she believes she'll join God. But we know, of course, she'll be abandoned like everyone else—silence!—they were returning, the things I knew, understood, and misunderstood, for better or worse. I finally boarded the Greyhound, found a seat near the middle of the bus, a window seat, and passed out.

I dreamt of a large man standing behind me, always just out of my field of view, trying and trying to expel phlegm that was determined to remain stuck to the back of his throat. No matter where I went, or who I had arranged to be in a dream scene with or without me, three feet behind was the coughing man, heavy and, even though I couldn't see him I knew, homeless. I apparently slept sixteen hours, the duration to Orlando/Kissimmee/St. Cloud, not once shaken by another passenger, not once touched. But every passenger knew my odor when they got off. I am sure of that.

Stepping off the bus, I saw my reflection, a portrait of whipped filth. On the pavement again, of my own, it seemed, volition. Yet I felt commanded, tied to a string, or perhaps drawn to a magnet. Cueing up behind a half dozen passengers, I held my belt like I had somewhere to be. It was good to see Walgreen's and Starbuck's together, through the parting bus door. Finally, Orlando.

My Sperry's hit a patch of bright green Florida watergrass. I noticed my head had ceased to feel like it was being sautéed. In place of that feeling was an intense tightening, a wooden vice, which blurred my vision, but was far more manageable. The automatic doors shot apart, and I felt a stale drugstore breeze on my dirt and sweat and blood-caked forehead, but as it passed through me I imagined being fresh and cool. I requested eighty dollars cash-back from the checkout girl, the maximum at this particular Walgreen's.

"You can't use the products while you're still in the store, sir."

I'd already swallowed six Extra Strength Motrin before she rung me up, three more in my mouth ready to slide down.

"You have to go outside," she said.

"Do you have a payphone?"

"Nah, they ripped those out like, I don't know, three years ago or something. Where the Bearclaw game is, that's where they were."

In Starbuck's I popped four more Motrin, bought a yogurt and hot tea and sat down next to a skinny, vaguely high-school-aged kid, could've been fourteen or eighteen, that type, on her laptop. When out of school, I never knew kids' ages until I conversed with them.

"Could you please look up a phone number for me, when you have a minute?"

She recoiled at the sight of me (fourteen) after grudgingly tearing herself away from a YouTube montage of cat stunts, the last of which incorporated two trampolines and barbed wire, leaving the cat unscathed, unruffled even.

"Awwwe," she whispered to herself, looking at my face more closely.

"The name is Iverbe."

Nothing in Orlando, I saw on the screen. The kid sat like a statue.

"Kissimmee," I said.

Clicks and a few strokes. "No Iverbe."

"St. Cloud, please."

She found it, one listing, and she looked off to the glass case filled with baked goods and juice, as if sending me there with her mind. Away from her.

Robert and Kaye Iverbe, of St. Cloud, 4040 Lorimore St. #3. My breathing became quite heavy in the dark brown and green swirling Starbuck's, spinning, and spinning.

"Please leave my table now," she said, wisely.

My walk produced no air between the soles of my shoes and the tiled floor. Underwater in all my senses, about to buckle to gravity, my rear found a chair next to a rack of CDs and download cards.

"Could someone please call me a taxi? Please. I'll give you

whatever money I have." I thought I was either going to throw up or lose consciousness again, but this time I held on, taking slow, deep, long breaths through my nose, down my throat (again, a yoga gift from Megan), taking the occasional sip of "Awake" tea. I felt a hand on my shoulder, a large hand. It gave me a gentle squeeze.

"A cab should be here in ten minutes."

"Thank you."

I couldn't see the man who called the taxi; my eyes had become washing machine lenses, rolling and swishing, but the voice sounded like Andy Griffith. Was it Andy, in Orlando, perhaps shooting a commercial with what was left of Mickey Mouse, of them both? It didn't matter anymore, Andy or no. It was the same.

"And keep your money, buddy," he said.

11

4040 Lorimore St. #3 was #3 of a six-plex condo community with sixty-four units. The sign at the front announced pertinent statistics, along with the fact that they were celebrating their third anniversary without major flood damage.

Many would've viewed the complex as a shit hole; boarded windows dappled the buildings, some graffiti too. But the few people I saw walking around looked friendly, and when I sat in a lawn chair on the narrow front porch, I felt a wave of calm that ran parallel and opposite to the seemingly machine-generated pain that I was getting used to. My ankles felt like they were holding my arms together, my fingers keeping pieces of brain from drizzling out of my ears. The familiarity of these sensations should have frightened me, but didn't. A dying hanging plant hung three feet above my face, which I felt the need to nurture.

When Megan and I lived together, she had a viciously stubborn mental block, a refusal to recognize that our apartment was filled far beyond capacity with plant life. I sacrificed two chairs, both beautifully refurbished, one my leather reading chair, just gave them away so we could house a giant aloe plant. I watered them all, and Megan ignored them after a few days of cooing and rubbing their leaves as if they were kittens. I lost a lot of plants to disease and just plain overcrowding, but I never told her to stop bringing them home. We always just made space.

For a moment, I didn't remember exactly why I was at the Iverbe home, which made me wonder if I'd ever known. It was overpowering just sitting in the chair, and a reason felt far less important than simply being alive for this rare moment of recognition, familiarity, the boarded-up windows, the hanging plant, the flatness of the horizon. It all felt like something I'd seen hundreds, thousands of times, a routine. Iverbe's voice came back to me in a groaning howl that seemed to originate in my guts and rattled my skull from inside, like a metal shack on a windy hill, about to be blown over. The door opened.

"Excuse me. Excuse me, why are you sitting on my porch?"

"My God."

Her irises were the color of pine bark, a rasp in her voice that betrayed too much to even consider in that moment. She looked me over with what appeared at first to be an angry countenance, but the softness in her eyes told me she was one of those people who look angry when they're concerned.

"I think you need an ambulance. Okay?" she said. "Stay here. I'm going to call you one."

"No, no, please. Iverbe told me to come here."

Her lips quivered and a flood of tears streamed down her cheeks.

"Are you Kaye?"

"Who are you?" she asked.

"I'm an English teacher."

It took a fully integrated physical effort to rise to my feet and face her. The face I saw, looking directly into her left eye, the both of us standing four inches under six feet, was the kind of face that drapes over a person, a mind, rather than the kind that is the person.

"A teacher," she said.

She put her arms around my neck firmly at first, then they melted, and we held each other for a whole minute—maybe thirty seconds, a time that stretched. I thought of the tears on her face, how they came immediately at the mention of Iverbe, and I was transported again, back to the hospital, the sound hovering over the both of us, the seconds between the lightning and thunder. Smelling the cigarettes and lavender in Kaye's hair, I focused on regaining normal breath and sensed Kaye was alone in the condo. No son, family, or friends. I was now certain that Iverbe was dead.

She pulled her arms back from my shoulders and wiped her face in an act meant to channel poise, but it looked more like she was removing makeup. I wanted to hold her again, longer this time, to let her know that she was perfect, that restraint and composure would've been embarrassing. My knees vanished from the rickety structure holding me upright, and I was on the ground again, my good friend, the pavement.

"You're really hurt. I'm taking you to the emergency room. I'm not any kind of nurse."

Abbey Road played on the way, inside her ancient Civic hatchback, another pure teacher's car, the lining of the ceiling tenting downward, stuck through with push-pins. The harmony on "Because" kicked in very softly. We didn't say anything.

The emergency room doctors were very light on their feet. They cleaned up my face and head, and replaced some stitches on top. Frenetic, expert pinwheels whirled in their eyes, perhaps two days without sleep, a young Indian doctor and a medical student assisting, their hands were soft and quick.

"You look like you've had a bad couple days, huh, sir? You have a lot of different injuries at various stages of the healing process. This one here," and he tapped my scar from surgery, "that's the work of a professional. I'd say a brain surgeon. What's been happening to you?"

"I don't know exactly. I'm trying to understand, though."

"Well, do you have somewhere to sleep, or do you sleep on the street?"

"I'm traveling."

"We could probably get away with keeping you here overnight."

"Kaye? I'm sorry. May I sleep on your couch for tonight?"

"Yeah, yeah, you can stay with me for tonight. That's fine," she said to the doctor, "I'll take him. I don't think he's dangerous," she laughed a little, "he's an English teacher." They didn't respond. "What's your name?" she said to me, and I realized the formality hadn't yet occurred.

"Craft."

She touched the top of my hand.

"Craft. Okay, Craft."

"Thank you, Kaye."

"My son is gone, not missing, but gone. I don't know what—"

"Yes. That's why I'm here. I'd like to help you, not that I can help you, but try to, find your son, if that's what you want. That's what Iverbe asked me to do, to help. I'd like to. My mind isn't working properly."

Kaye dropped her chin to her chest and two sobs escaped.

"I'm sorry, could I ask you to please finish this conversation on the way to your car? We need to get the bed ready for the next patient. Hannah will wheel you out."

In the parking lot, it was unmistakable that Kaye and I were together, that we were walking facts in each other's lives. She strode with determined, loud steps back to the Civic, like she was holding in those spring-loaded snakes that pop out of mock peanut jars. And I hobbled along beside her, bald, determined to continue moving under my own power.

What else was there then, but to get into her car and decide what to do? About her son. About everything. About the next five minutes. As soon as the act of deciding anything was even possible, we would. I could feel the desire in both of us to confront the morning. Just a week before it'd been a scramble to fill the day with reasons to wake up. Something was simple again.

The Honda started like new, as if with age it improved, all the dents and rust. She said I was welcome to take a bath when we got back. I thought of sponges and her hands, and had to force myself to remember Iverbe was freshly dead. She turned off the music and leaned her head over the gear-shift, into shared space.

"Did you teach with Robert a long time ago?"

"I just met him. Robert. I didn't know his name was Robert."

"What do you mean you just met him?"

"Days ago."

"Were you there when—were you there on Monday?"

"Monday—I don't know. What day is this?"

"Thursday. Robert died on Monday."

"I'm sorry. No. I didn't know until the doorway, your condo. I'm sorry."

Kaye returned her head to the driver's side, put the car into gear and zipped out of the parking lot onto the wide streets.

"I was in a hospital in St. Louis for another injury. A student attack. Robert and I shared a room."

"Student attack? Well, he was from there, around there. Originally. He woke one morning two weeks ago and told me he needed to go home alone. I said okay, you know, I trusted him. He was always on a mission. That's what he was like."

"How did you meet?"

"Ten years, nine years, ten years ago. I was doing a lot of coke—I'm sorry, I don't know what I'm saying. I'm out of my mind. I don't think I can talk about this."

"It's all right," I said.

Kaye brushed her hair out of her face and rolled the window down all the way. The sirens from a passing ambulance awakened my dormant head wounds, though I didn't ask her to roll the windows back up.

"So did you talk to him much, was he able to speak?"

"Yes, just a little," I said, "but it was very potent. I can't describe it right now. I'm sorry."

"He told you to come here?"

"Yes," I said.

"Everyone thought he was crazy. Went crazy. Maybe you have to be crazy to go crazy. I don't know."

"I don't think the word has any meaning anymore. It's an abused word. One of many I'm afraid."

"English teacher, huh?"

"Sorry, it's an incurable disease."

She seemed to get distracted putting out her cigarette in the ashtray, and we smacked the median and bounced back into the lane with a quick swerve.

"I forgot I was driving. Sorry about that. How's your head?"

"Recovering nicely, thanks."

"So you seem all right, Craft."

"No one's ever said that to me before. How do you mean?"

"I don't know, normal I guess. Nice."

"No one's ever said that either."

"I'm going crazy. I need to see my kid."

Kaye wiped her nose, which didn't appear to need it—an old habit rekindled perhaps. It was difficult to resist reaching my hand over to her shoulder.

"The police will find him, I'm sure."

"I didn't call them."

"Oh. But what is he, eight, nine?

"He's seventeen, but younger kind of, you know what I mean?"

"Seventeen? How is that possible if you met Iverbe ten years ago?"

"What? Oh, Iverbe is—was, his stepfather."

"Yes, of course. How long has he been gone?"

"Three days—he left in the morning, right before I found out. He called yesterday from Texas. That's where he said he was. He was drunk—he doesn't drink. He said, 'Mom, I'm all right. I'm really drunk in Texas, Mom. I love you.' And he hung up."

"Do you believe him?"

"I always believe him."

12

It's possible that I became disoriented when Kaye and I walked through the front door, seeing her fossil of a Shih Tzu, older than her son, she said, in perfect geriatric health. I bent down to greet the little gentleman, and he shook my hand like an old, bereted man in a Parisian café.

"That's Garcia," she said.

We hadn't gone inside when Kaye found me on the front porch, but the instant I crossed the threshold and craned my neck to look into the kitchen, I spotted a collector set of hand-painted Beatles plates on the wall over the sink. Four more sets in the living room: the complete American presidents wrapping around three walls, a circular cluster of a Disney film set over the TV featuring *Twenty Thousand Leagues Under the Sea, The Swiss Family Robinson,* and *Old Yeller*, a colorful Space Program set starring the usual cast of national heroes, and, of course, American Landmarks, among them the Redwoods, Hollywood, The Grand Canyon, Mount Rushmore, and my instant sentimental favorite, The Arch. The rush of déjà vu, or the obliteration of linear time, or the melding of waking and dreamed life, poked me in the eyes, causing a few tears to stream down my cheeks. The tips of my fingers tingled, and I was lost again somewhere between what I thought of as my life and whatever it was I was living in that moment. I knew this place, this woman, that gnarled plaid couch.

Garcia sniffed at my bandages with interest, careful not to disrupt the doctor's work. He sat down, nodded and inspected the window with a huff.

"He's seen some shit," Kaye said, noticing my gaze at the Shih Tzu.

She fell back on the couch, like she had a thousand times, and evaporated from the room. Her light just turned off, and immediately I knew my cue, as if I were an expert on her electrical wiring. *An hour to herself, no more or she'll get lost, give her an hour to decompress—that usually works.* Only after planting myself on the toilet did I remind myself that there was no *usually* between us, there wasn't even an *us* a few hours ago, but I couldn't make that fact matter. I hadn't had an *us* in so long, it only took the briefest eye contact and a few kind words.

The year they gave my ex-wife the sophomore honors class, the last of our three years, she joked about the karmic imperative of having an affair with the next new-hire English teacher who was also an Earhart alum. Man or woman, she would not discriminate, she said. The worst fight we ever had was over a former student of mine, Carisha, the only girl in honors who was bussed in from the city that year—one travesty among many others, da-da-da, as we turn and turn in the widening gyre. After we did *Call of the Wild*, Carisha became the fiercest interpreter of every work that remotely interested her, *Romeo and Juliet*, Robert Frost. But everything by the pilgrims, especially Jonathan Edwards's *Sinners in the Hands of an Angry God*—and oh, an excerpt of Cotton Mather's *Remarkable Providences*—made her get up from her desk, arms waving, finger pointing, her voice bouncing off the windowless walls.

"That's the reason why y'all fucked up! Fuckin' people up! Motherfuckers like that saying God's in his ear."

"Y'all?" someone protested.

"Y'all white people. Yeah," she nodded for emphasis.

Did I rein this in? No. Luckily, for the sake of relative harmony in the classroom, there were two white students who were early hip-hop enthusiasts, De La Soul was their group of the moment (they made the CDs for me when we had a conversation about music and I told them I listened to jazz and folk), and they shared Carisha's critiques of the colonial writers and supported her claims that the language and perspective assumed racial, cultural, and spiritual superiority.

"It's like he thinks everyone's a piece of shit," Steve Diekman said.

"Can you imagine if this guy was your dad?" Thad Bull added. "And my dad's the biggest dick in the world."

"Why you teach this shit, Mr. Craft? You're telling me there isn't something better to choose from?" Carisha demanded.

"Well, the thinking goes something like his perspective is essential if you're going to understand the spiritual and moral motivations of the characters in the literature of the period. Mather's views were the governing morality, the intensely rigid morality that allowed things like the Salem Witch Trials and inspired characters like Hester Prynne. It helps us define and understand what's going through characters' minds when they're calling someone wicked. Hell was a very real, functioning place for them. You'll get to all this junior year, but Mather and some of these other good time Charlie's are the scaffolding."

"Let me ask again. Why are you making us read this shit right now?

And when a few other students started to find courage that transcended their psychological need to be average, anonymous, and indifferent to literature, when they began shouting out reactions, blazing with ignorance/wisdom—*Death of a Salesman* really pulled it out of them, a recession was in full tilt—I lost control of the class. In other words, there was no longer a need for control. It was the only time I ever really taught, actually guided a collective love of books, poetry, taught anything besides paragraph structure. For a sustained amount of time anyway.

We almost came to blows though, Carisha and I did, bumping chests over Mark Twain, to the point where she said he was a "racist fucker." No, I explained, he just found it more effective (and fun) to ridicule, mock, characterize, endear, just make them laugh like hell so people would really take a look at something. Fundamentally, people want to be in on the joke.

"I guess maybe," she said.

Carisha had a dog at home, a tan poodle, Rosa Parks, who

was already five when Carisha was born. After earning an A- the previous year in my class based on the content of her essays (though often bereft of key elaborations), the quality and earnestness of her contributions to class discussion, and the show-stopping, bring-the-house-down "process speech" in which she taught the stiffest, squarest male in the class, Jamie Dahlem, the Palongo African dance, which she learned from an aunt who lived in Memphis, she got an F first semester from my wife who, instead of finding a way to engage her, to bring out the obvious powerhouse that she was, failed her instead.

"What is this? *F* for Carisha? Did she miss a test? Did she not turn in a paper?" I said.

"As a matter of fact she didn't, and not only did she fail to turn it in after I reminded her again and again, she openly refused."

"Why?"

"Because she's defiant."

"I can't believe I'm listening to you call a student *defiant* like that, like one of the assholes we work with."

"You don't like *defiant*? How about *mutinous*?"

"Mutinous isn't a synonym of defiant. They're only loosely related."

"Fuck off, okay?"

The kitchen in the brownstone inspired claustrophobic takeovers of the mind. I remember willing my fingers off the plate drenched in Italian dressing and surgically removing my vision of smashing it on the countertop.

"Maybe you're handing her a reason to defy you. Did you consider that?"

"Craft."

"It seems to me that you're intimidated."

"She's not your student anymore."

"Is she having trouble at home? Did you even ask her?"

"I gave her plenty of time to get over it," she said.

"Get over what?"

"Her dog."

"Oh, no. Rosa Parks died?"

"Yes, Rosa fucking Parks died. Jesus, here it comes. You're about to bore me to death with morality. I don't know how you can stand yourself."

It was always troubling when Megan happened to be wearing the tight scoop-neck T-shirts and skirts that flaunted her perfectly thick legs when we engaged in *Who's Afraid of Virginia Woolf?* It rendered my best points and phrases limp.

"How could I have been so wrong about you, all this time? Don't answer that, I know, I'm an imbecile."

"Self-righteous horseshit! You're full of shit and you know it. You advertise yourself as the misanthrope virtuoso teacher. You're just a depraved depressive with no staying power. You know how easy it is to fool children into thinking you're somebody?"

"It's impossible, actually. They know immediately. Why do you think you have weekly clashes with the girls in your classes? They smell your empty lust and they despise it."

"I fuck other men because you're not there. If you're going to be in another room, I wish you'd take your tiny dick with you. Save us the time and the mess."

She took off her heels and tossed them into the center of the living room. I knew it was a challenge to take her on the floor, the antidote we'd used for a hundred such glasses of each other's venom. It's not as if I didn't hear the whisper from my flagging loins, but the voice of futility drowned it out with truth.

"You don't know what Rosa Parks was to that girl, and you should know, Megan. You could have given her a C and discussed a plan for improvement."

"She didn't deserve it. *Grades are the worst things for kids anyway.* Your words. So who cares?"

"That quote doesn't support any argument you're making. It's completely out of context."

"Oh fucking stop it!"

"It could be her future. She's trying to dig herself out of a mountain of shit," I said.

"You said futures are bullshit, you said futures are the biggest line of shit we sell these kids. You said now is what we ought to be teaching them, and *now* she gets an F, because she's in my class and that's what she earned."

"You're heartless."

"Yeah? Well yours isn't that great either, it just flares up occasionally, which is worse for us all. Believe me."

"You're jealous of her."

"Why, are you planning to fuck her in five years, when the statute allows?"

"All right, Megan. If she'll have me, yes! Are we through?"

"Dead. A corpse."

"Good," I said, which was the first word of truth I'd spoken to her in a year. We would never have children together. That was our gift to the world.

Looking around at the myriad knickknacks and child figurines in the Iverbe condo, whose presence emanated a debilitating psychological weight, I let my eyes drift to the dying sympathy floral arrangements gathered in the corner. The most prominent was in the image of the classic shit-eating grin of Mickey Mouse. I walked over and read the card.

"From the whole family here in the Happiest Place on Earth, our deepest sympathies for your loss."

Kaye caught me, crouched down next to Garcia, gazing at the combination of painted carnations that constituted Mickey Mouse's face.

"We all got jobs at the parks after he quit teaching," she said. "It was a part of Robert's vision."

"Yes. I see."

"Did he give you the 'Walt talk' in the hospital?"

"He alluded to him indirectly."

"Twenty-five years of teaching. He was good. One day on my lunch break—I was an office lady—I get pulled away from my desk by the sophomore principal. In the hall I see my son standing there stricken, which is something he just never is. I run out to the car, and Robert's prostrate in the back seat, muttering, gone somewhere in his mind. Never went back to the classroom."

"Twenty-five years. I know that number well."

"Something changed in his eyes that morning, but I just kept trying to put it out of my mind. I didn't care about his job or mine. I was sick of it. You know office ladies. Vicious. I just wanted to make sure he'd feel cared for."

"He did, I'm sure. Do you have any guesses at your son's destination?" I said, remembering my purpose.

"I want to show you something."

Kaye whipped around and walked with frantic purpose up the stairs into what appeared to be a small bedroom. She returned with a burgundy-colored spiral notebook, which caught the brilliance of the bare bulb above the stairs and emitted a sort of wavy, red aura. Kaye's eyes, at that wonderful seventy-five degree angle, looking down upon me, seemed to offer this as evidence, but also as arcana.

"I found this yesterday, under his bed. A handwritten play," she said. "It's astonishing. Look at the way each letter is exactly the same size. No mistakes either."

Before I lay my fingers upon it, I knew everything—*time present, time past, contained in time future*—just like Eliot said. And so the lack of surprise when opening the cover and seeing her name there, all symmetrical and full of Ls, my genuine expectation of seeing what I saw, that was the real shock:

Burgundy Five Star

An Unfinished Play by Lila Bell

I smiled broadly at the sheer fact that this was happening. What in Hell and on earth was she doing? And how had a part of her ended up here?

"There's an address on the back. Los Angeles."

She looked down at a pile of Duke's dirty sneakers, jammed under the sofa. I held Lila's play in hands, and I could see from the wear on the outside edge of the notebook how often she'd flipped back to read what she'd written in a previous session. Her writing always had an equally unsettling and alluring calculation, action by action, one phrase at a time.

"Kaye, I—this girl," I said, but the phone rang and the musculature of Kaye's face changed completely. Invisible streaks shot out from her hair as she seemingly covered the fifteen feet to the phone in two strides.

"Hello? Are you safe? Why did you—right. I hear someone screaming. How long? I love you. Bye."

A cuckoo clock I hadn't noticed struck midnight, sending the bird into a chirping fit above our heads. Kaye's hands met a gush of tears on her face.

"Is he all right?"

"He says he is."

"Should I take you to the airport?" I asked.

"I'm broke."

"I have about two thousand dollars left."

"All right, let's go."

My testicles hung like paperweights in my jockey shorts. The blood in my veins was lead. The urge to weep pooled in my spine. I wished that I'd known Kaye's nightgowns and socks by heart.

"Me?" I said.

"What?"

"Both of us? To Los Angeles?"

"Yes."

After a brief pause, we happened to follow a nonspecific impulse to move quickly, in opposite directions, and slammed our shoulders, spinning our noses to point directly at each other.

I catapulted my dry lips to hers, my hands from cradling either side of her jaw line. I could not stop my chest from pressing against her panicked softness, where I found, in her breath, an imprisoned lover, mother, a woman who would rather lose her life than wait for it to be stripped from her again.

Part II

Burgundy Five Star

Burgundy Five Star

an unfinished play by Lila Bell

with scene prefaces by H. Craft

Characters: LILA, 21, wears a hearing aid, pretty, short, blonde, verbal, ill

NINI, 42, her mother, an older twin, somehow Southern, against all fact

INTERPRETER, 40, stout, assured Aymaran Indian of Peru

SPIRIT, 80(?), tiny, Aymaran medicine man, silent, content

DIANE, 47, Lila's sister, tall, angular, blonde, coifed, proficient, seething

PIGMAN, a hideous creature

YOU, 17, Lila's brother, invisible though addressed, the audience (of one)

Preface to Scene One

Now and always, it may be said that there are two sorts of people. And though we know otherwise, the temptation is great to present two boxes and attempt to fit each and every soul into one or the other. In any case, this is my contribution to the fallacy. When it comes to the unveiling of some great truth (after living years of an equally great lie), there are:

1. Those who are engorged by the specific thrill that truth brings—the liberation of mind.
2. Those who take great umbrage…
   a. in the form of steadfast denial.
   b. in the form of (foolhardy) romantic vengeance.

I've fallen consistently into 2-a throughout my life. Lila Bell falls squarely into 2-b. As I am inextricably linked to the particular giant lie in question, as her one-time teacher and recent halfway lover, it is my charge to deliver some lifelike portrait of the author, and the play, *Burgundy Five Star*—a self-portrait, a body, that is, the pages on which it is written. They cannot be separated—pages and body.

To begin, then, is to look into the mirror where Lila stands. What is missing from this face? What is there to shed? What is at war? Does it have love to offer? What do the eyes see, and fail to? What do the ears hear and miss between the roars and murmurs of the world?

The mirror reflects a scrunched up, freckled face underneath curly blonde strands. She's tucked herself under the Hollywood sign, framed by the bathroom window. It's synthetically powerful, and she catches herself gazing up at the iconic letters as if waiting for them to rearrange themselves—YOLDOHOWL. DOYLWHOLO. Like all places of destiny, it feels to Lila more like a distant memory than a first arrival. Her eyes shut tight and her ample lips have been reduced to a tiny, flexed, colorless oval. The toilet fills up again, and the showerhead's droplets mark the seconds.

This bathroom is to be her composing studio. She's living with a man ten years her senior, Morely Loney, whom she met days ago, picked up really, at a coffee klatch. *He fits the profile,* she thinks.

A. Older. Preferably 10 years. A good distance from actual youth is imperative.
B. Marginal employment. Nothing vested. Nothing to (really) gain.
C. Consistent but not paralyzing consumption of drugs and alcohol.
D. Once had lofty expectations, but not too recently.
E. Somehow desirable.

It bothers the barometer in Lila that she actually constructed such a profile. But then again, *why?* Morely is perfect for her purpose, and so the profile is justified. She is, after all, on a mission, or maybe it's more accurate to say she's answering a call. Anyway, crusaders and missionaries don't have the luxury of considering others, or love.

Her reflection now reveals scheming eyes, wide open, the tip of her tongue protruding through the lips, the pink of blood underneath.

Drip. Drip. Drip. The married couple with a ten-month-old in the adjacent duplex has a hunger for arguing in circles at high volume. The wall between Morely's place and theirs seems substantial at first glance, but the couple's voices are the type that boom and blast through thick concrete and closed windows, and hover distinctly over the white noise of traffic.

"What is that—*do you want me to throw out your sandwich?* Never mind I know what that is! I hate it!" the wife says.

"We were supposed to be hanging out, Helly. Like having a good time! Wine and figs and sandwiches, feeling snappy and peppy. I made them with avocado."

"I took a nap. I was exhausted."

"I know. Life exhausts you. I know."

"You're a dick. A drunk dick right now."

"My time is expendable to you. I live with it. Just like I live without sex," the husband says.

"You think that makes me want to fuck you? It doesn't. It makes me want to go back to bed."

They're no George and Martha, but their tone and pitch scrape the inside of Lila's ribs the way Richard Burton and Elizabeth Taylor seemed to delight in doing in *Who's Afraid of Virginia Woolf?* I steered Lila to Albee all those years ago, ninth grade, the first of our four years together in the classroom.

It was right after *Romeo and Juliet*, she wanted something modern, *something still sort of old but really American*, she said. I gave her *Death of a Salesman*, and she cranked out a scalding three-page analysis of Willy Loman as the apotheosis of the pawn in the chess game of the rich. Each paragraph began with a chess move as a topic sentence, and proceeded to identify how the scene in question epitomized how the rich wanted the rest of us, just so, broken and delusional, beyond repair or ascendance. What convinced me most was that it sprung from a fourteen-year-old's perch of ludicrous affluence, and so carried credibility. She simply listened to her family speak, and so came to understand royalty. I directed her to Albee next, and she went home that night and watched Liz Taylor hang herself out there, screaming all the way to drunken sleep. She was in my room the next morning, an hour before the first bell, before my quart of coffee even.

"Craft, that was disgusting. Just sickening. I couldn't take my eyes off it."

"Mmm, great performances, though I could have lived my

entire life without ever seeing George Segal's work. He's still alive, too."

"I was shaking, and I thought I was going to puke, but I never did. It just like stayed in my throat, like bubbling. It was worse than vomiting."

"I think you'll find a great many things are. You should read it, to pick up on the little things he's doing."

"I wrote a play last night, or most of one. I fell asleep at my desk."

"Last night? What about?" I said.

"About a girl who only exists in her mother's mind. And they hate each other."

"Kind of derivative, but it sounds promising."

"What's that mean, like copied?" she said.

"Oh, I'm sorry. It doesn't matter. Everything's stolen. Or it would never exist."

"Hey, not bad. I can use that line in the climax, the mother could say that."

If I didn't have a great deal of personal stock, involvement, blame, pain, and interest in what happened on and off the page as a result of the new play, I would be swelled with self-congratulation for attributing this work to those days, my class, her first attempt, eight years ago, similarly penned in a single night on the pages of a spiral notebook. While she was at Earhart High, I read a dozen of her plays, spent my lunch hours and study periods with her in my classroom dissecting them, but really each other. Each play understandably was a pastiche of the playwright flavor of the month, whomever's canon she was consuming. I read four Albee knock-offs, a Beckett (technically sound), a Sam Shepard (a disaster), two Jean Genet's (some wonderfully biting individual scenes in each), a Pinter (no heart), an O'Neill (never did get the tone right here), back to Miller (a success), and two of her bread, butter, and jam—Tennessee Williams. I asked her if she had any interest in reading women playwrights, but I was embarrassed at my inability to name any when she asked for a recommendation.

"That's all right, Craft," she said, "Tennessee is enough woman for me—for now."

She sought my praise, and I gave it willingly. It cost me nothing. In fact, the mere thought of passing those years without Lila makes me wince on top of the wincing that was actually taking place, the fruition of my identity as the cuckold manic depressive. But if there's one thing I know how to do, it's to extract good passages of something and hold them up for acclaim to make it appear that the whole is a complete success. It's exactly how I justified continuing to live.

In regards to Nini, the mother character in scene one of *Burgundy Five Star*, I met with the real-life inspiration in October of the year I had Lila in class. I feigned concern about Lila's apparent isolation among the other students in the hope that I might calm the flutter in my chest region over my precocious little scholar. The thinking went something like this: *If you meet the mother, Craft, you'll see Lila in a healthier context.* Looking at it now, I realize the grand self-deception that was taking place, a deception only made possible by the panicked pull of the need to love. I wanted to know how it was possible that this girl existed in a corporeal state and ended up waltzing around my classroom in headphones, as my ex-wife had, when the other students had gone.

Does Lila have many friends? I planned to ask the mother, whom I'd envisioned as a polished, plump, ridiculous aristocrat. Furs possibly. But instead, a version of Lila herself, aged twenty years, walked into my class, wrapped in a kerchief pointing down at a low neckline. She sat in an empty desk and giggled. The likeness stunned me stiff.

"I'd completely forgotten what these desks feel like. Like little cages," she said.

"Yes. It's a bit like the zoo. Something not quite right about it, but you feel like it's more or less good they're here."

"Oh, you're a funny little man. No wonder my daughter never stops talking about you. She was obsessed with Dudley Moore at the age of seven. Strange bird, isn't she!"

"I'm afraid I'm not a good judge of strange."

"Still, though, there's something about her. Driven. More like the men in the family really, although I guess you might say the women are driven in a different direction."

"I'd like to meet her father," I said.

"Stepfather. He's driven also—well, no, he's a conniver, which is different."

"Yes, I know the distinction well."

"What is it you wanted to talk about … I didn't get your first name."

"Craft will do, Ms. Bell."

"Bell-Weathers," she said.

"I was just concerned—not concerned, but—"

"Because she doesn't have any friends? She does. She has one, Laurel. You can imagine what she's like. Braces bigger than her teeth. Bad skin. At least she's not fat—or poor. To think she's a cheerleader—well, a hockey cheerleader. You know the difference, I'm sure."

"That's good," I said, "that she has a close friend."

"Well I didn't think so at first, of course. But then I remembered those girls in high school, the ones that were part of a pair, and you never saw them apart from the other, or with anyone else. I suppose I was that way once, but she moved away. Estelle. We used to share boys without them knowing that we knew."

"I see."

"Wicked," she said and laughed. "Would you like to have a drink somewhere? Is it mandatory that we stay in this bunker to talk?"

"I shouldn't."

"Why?"

"Well, I can't say, exactly."

"As an English teacher, you ought to be able to say something about everything."

"Alright then. Grading," I said. "I'm quite busy."

"I wouldn't worry about Lila. I'm sure there are loads of sad cases roaming the halls, parents out of work, illiterate, just dull. And the bussed-in children from the city, no fathers, barely mothers to speak of. I see it at the downtown library. I read to them one Saturday a month."

"Quite well, I'm sure."

She stood and removed her kerchief, folded it, and daubed her forehead.

"It's important, as you know, to read to the children. Goodbye, Craft. It's too bad—well, goodbye."

Theater is about *change*. For Lila, this play, though blasphemously or brazenly imitative of a smorgasbord of her influences—take your pick—is a chance, finally, to be everyone at once, influences and interlopers, family and enemies, every voice vibrating and caroming around in her brain's darkest matter. All of this for the sake of one reader, whom she has not met. And to be sure to change her audience of one forever, she must continue to check the mirror to see which pair of eyes has elbowed its way to the front, looking out and back at her. Wanting, as everyone does, to be recognized, fully.

Back in the duplex bedroom now, through the door, she detects Morely singing a credible version of *Just Like a Woman*. That his deep voice is partially swallowed by the drip of the showerhead and hum of the air conditioner is of little consequence. She knows the words. There is only, now, to put pen to paper.

SCENE ONE

We begin in a St. Louis penthouse dining room, old furniture, contemporary art, one of a few buildings in the city with a well-paid doorman.

LILA, 21, her silhouette, up left, thick in leg and slender in torso, on the minus side of sixty inches tall (this is key), walks downstage like a whipped equestrian horse. Her black bodysuit reflects the light.

Spotlight, a face, a birthmark in the shape of a penis mushroom, as she calls it, high on her cheek. Purple eye-makeup, pink lipstick. She turns profile and something red and plastic bulges from her ear. A hearing aid.

LILA's hands hang, heavy, clumsy hands, they hold something, a doll. She stares at the Strawberry Shortcake in her hands. She chokes it.

LILA pries her own hand off the doll's throat and throws it on the ground in front of her. She steps on its face, considers spitting, but backs away. She considers spitting again, but instead wipes her bangs to the side.

NINI enters from up right, a 42-year-old version of LILA, wider, slower, two inches taller, with hands and arms more fluid in their movements, like an old bathing beauty—whereas her daughter jabs and whips, NINI flutters and sweeps. NINI's eyes always seem drawn somewhere, in a gaze to a vast, distant landscape that seems to alternate between fireworks, helicopters, full moons, and her own reflection. The mother and daughter's faces are stunningly identical.

NINI walks over, a foot in front of her daughter and waves, a clownish wave, pretends to brush and floss her teeth. She fixes a single strand of hair, fluffs her eyelashes, all in front of LILA's face as if in a mirror. NINI's pile of blonde sits atop her head like golden yarn. She actively admires it without movement. Satisfied, NINI walks down center to another mirror, one that exists only in YOUR eyes.

NINI: Lie?

LILA: Don't call me that. [*LILA shuts her eyes, goes through half a sun salutation, freezing in upward-facing-dog. She stays there, completely still.]*

NINI: Lie?

LILA: Don't call me that, please. *[NINI slips onto the kitchen table, on her side, as if she's the main course.]*

NINI: You've been gone. I forgot. I'll think of something else to call you. *[LILA pushes into downward-facing-dog, hops to standing, finishes in mountain pose. It seems to neutralize her. She bends into a squat, slowly bunching herself into a tight ball.]*

NINI: I've got the club coming tonight. *[LILA opens out of the tight ball and pretends to fiddle with her hearing aid.]*

LILA: I can't understand what you're saying.

NINI: Oh stop it. The surgery was a success. It's your imagination.

LILA: Aren't you a little drunk for your book club?

NINI: I'm not drunk. Not really. No. But I didn't read this one. Tonight I'll just be agreeing with everyone, so my neck might get sore from all the nodding. Did you get Motrin? Did you see the note? The Motrin and eggs note. I forgot to put them on the order.

LILA: You never read the books. No, I didn't see the note. Why do you say shit like that—I didn't read this one—which one did you read?

NINI: I don't know, a few of them, half of a half dozen. The one about the horse and the country doctor.

LILA: Why do you bother? Book club. *[LILA situates herself in wheel pose, her head upside down, hands and feet on the floor, an arched bridge.]*

NINI: Well, it's the only way I can get another human being to come here and pay a visit, you know that. You've told me that at least eight times in the last year.

LILA: Once. I hate that shit, using shit like that against me later.

NINI: Why do you want to go pulling scabs, Lie? Leave my club alone. Oh, sorry, I haven't thought of another name yet.

[NINI slides off the table and walks over to her daughter, appraising her form. NINI sets her glass of brandy on LILA's stomach, as if she were a table. LILA swats the drink off her body and stands, NINI's eyes on the spilled drink.]

LILA: Stop it. All of it. The whole routine.

NINI: Oh, how about Li'l Captain? You remember.

LILA : You're drunk.

NINI: I am not. *[NINI walks back to the table and positions herself atop again, reclining.]*

LILA: I hated that name. It was an insult. Look at you.

NINI: I am not drunk, and it certainly was not an insult. It was affectionate. I'm just lying on the table because my reflection makes me look about six inches taller, and it's capturing my attention at the moment. But I don't really mind being short. How about you, Captain? Does it still bother you? *[Lila picks up a fashion magazine and puts it down.]*

NINI: All right. What came after Captain? Oh yes—Flower, your coat-hanger years.

LILA: Where's Reggie? I'm just asking.

NINI: He moved out yesterday, Lila. I suppose he's moved in with her now. Now there, I said your beautiful name that I gave you. Almost a flower, but a girl instead.

LILA: When? With who?

NINI: Whom. A week ago. A new one, I don't know her name.

LILA: Yeah right, you don't.

NINI: Paula I think. Paula, she's very smart you know, very smart. That's what he said about her once, very smart this Paula. I suppose she goes to the dentist and gets her fangs whitened. Maybe she whitens them herself. I wish I had fangs. *[NINI flops onto her stomach.]*

LILA: Are you upset?

NINI: Yes. Don't I look upset?

LILA: No. What are you going to do? *[NINI sits up and inspects her empty drink. She wants to refill it, but she'd have to get up.]*

NINI: Keep volunteering my time for the children. Oh, I'll find another man someday, things being the way they are. Then another, maybe, if I'm quick about it. But probably not more than two, I imagine. It shouldn't be difficult. I'll just open my mouth and the liars and narcissists will come running. Isn't that right? Could you freshen my drink?

LILA: If we're going to sit around and go through all the horrible shit I've said to you, it'll be one of the worst psychotic nine-hour episodes of our careers. I don't think the book ladies would like it either. [*LILA takes the glass from her mother and fills it at the bar in the wings.]*

NINI: I'm upset. I'm upset about it. He's actually living another life now.

LILA: I know. It was just a matter of time, until he had his own money.

NINI: Oh, I really don't want to have to start talking to men again, all the ones I could barely stand the first time around, before they got divorced. [*LILA walks over to NINI, helps her off the table, and guides her downstage. NINI doesn't resist, but seems to stiffen, not suspicious, just glassy.]*

LILA: Nini, look.

NINI: Hmm?

LILA: Look out there. [*LOOKS looks out into the darkness, but not at YOU, at HIM.]*

LILA: Can you see him?

NINI: I don't see anyone.

LILA: Right there, in front of the television.

[The backdrop comes alive with lights. There's an animation of a hideous Pig Man in a reclining chair watching cable news.]

NINI: Oh, yes. How dreadful. I don't know that room … Where is that? *[NINI peers along with her daughter, her eyes widen for a split second in recognition. She crouches and vomits, immediately composing herself as if it were a sneeze. The animation disappears. PIG MAN, a real person, enters up left, replacing the animation. He takes a reserved, empty seat in the audience and watches silently.]*

NINI: Hand me a towel, dear. I'm in need. [*LILA gives her a napkin.]*

LILA: Why didn't you tell me about Him?

NINI: Uncle Lev told you?

LILA: How could you?

NINI: First Lev marries that fat farm girl, then he betrays me to my daughter. He knows I won't tell your pappaw that he told you. I wish he'd never been made partner. Then he would have moved to New York, where people just disappear.

LILA: Forget Lev! How could you do it?

NINI: To have you of course.

LILA: He kills actual human beings.

NINI: Oh, not anymore I'm sure.

LILA: He's a murderer, Nini.

NINI: Those were different times, Flower.

LILA: They were good people he killed, just people trying to do normal things. Like for their kids, so they wouldn't have to live on dirt floors and work twenty hours a day like they did. He killed a woman in Chile with a baby.

NINI: He didn't tell me anything like that. Nothing like that. [*The mother and daughter look into each other's eyes. Something is happening to their faces. They are trading expressions, somehow, shifting between each other, trading eyes.]*

NINI: Stop it.

LILA: You stop it.

NINI: Please stop it.

LILA: I can't.

NINI: Don't ask me to.

LILA: Please. I'm dying.

NINI: Lila, he mostly just made phone calls.

LILA: What's wrong with you! Get mad. Be something.

NINI: But I'm not mad, and you know it. *[LILA crumbles slowly onto the floor, her hands over her head in her mother's vomit. She faces YOU. She speaks to a distance now.]*

NINI: Lila, your mother isn't the little captain you are. *[LILA is crying. NINI immediately seems more comfortable, nursing tears, a better role for her than being interrogated. LILA recoils from her mother's hand.]*

NINI: There isn't a place on this whole big earth where people aren't killing each other.

LILA: *[softly]* You don't have to breed with the ones doing it, go around making new people. Murderers shouldn't make new people. They should stop. It's the least they could do. But he couldn't stop. You know why? Because he's psychotic and found lunatics like you to take his seed.

NINI: Oh, now— *[LILA pushes herself off the floor and looks down on NINI. She begins to slowly circle her mother, predatory, placing one foot softly down after another, stepping over the vomit.]*

LILA: There are nine of us, all stitched up with cold, calculated murder in our veins.

NINI: I told Lev not to put together a file! He asked me and I said absolutely not. I just want to kill him.

LILA: Nine of us! I've already talked to six. They're made of shit. They're monsters. Except this sweet kid in Florida. *[LILA points at You.]* The rest are just his pig litter and they don't even know it.

NINI: Oh Lie, you're just fine!

LILA: Oh, but listen, *Mother*, the eldest seed is a woman older than you. Diane. My spine shakes thinking about her. She still lives with The Old Pig. I haven't talked to her yet. I can't. It makes me sick to think about. Guess where her mother is, the one the pig actually married. Guess.

NINI: Flower, stop!

LILA: Removed from society. Watercolors and pudding.

NINI: None of this matters! [*The strings holding NINI together are tearing, which she seems immediately aware of, and stiffens in response.]*

NINI: But it doesn't mean anything for you. Think of it. What does it matter? Did it matter before you knew? Simply free yourself of it.

LILA: I think about killing people. I've been thinking about it since I was eight.

NINI: Now, Lila, that's the sort of thing you should have told me about.

LILA and NINI freeze. Light moves down their bodies, illuminating their legs and feet then back to their faces. PIG MAN rises in the first row, climbs onto the stage, placing his hands, gently around NINI'S throat. Neither LILA nor NINI sees him. NINI notices a slight discomfort from his hands on her neck.]

LILA: You think I wanted to get doped? You think I didn't see what it did to my friends? We stopped being friends because I wasn't doped and they were. It was like being doped, not being doped. *[Agitated, NINI tries to pry PIG MAN's hands from her neck now. He easily keeps her locked there.]*

NINI: You're a gentle little flower. It's the culture, honey, not you.

LILA: Impalements. Everyone I meet, I see them run through. But it's the moments right after the blade goes through that really stick in there, hours, whole days. Mouths drooped open, blood spit trickling, licking, tongues smacking, trying not to choke. If I had the slightest personal justification, I could kill somebody. Do you understand that?

NINI: Now that just compounds a problem. I think we're both very upset. *[PIG MAN moves his hands down, holding NINI around her waist. She twists, but it's still just a strange, constricting feeling.]*

LILA: You're not that upset.

NINI: I am, Flower. I just don't have a way of showing it that appeals to you. [*LILA walks, feline, over to NINI and positions her face in front of her mother's. NINI tries to avoid it, left, right, left, but Lila follows it intensely, nose to nose, until NINI gives up and shuts her eyes. PIG MAN releases his grip from NINI, takes a few steps back.*]

LILA: Do you ever think about killing yourself?

NINI: Never.

LILA: Of course you don't! You're the center of the universe.

NINI: Now you're just being unfair.

LILA: I'd have killed myself if I were you. I'd at least consider it often. [*NINI opens her eyes, suddenly smiling.*]

NINI: That's because you're a good little captain.

LILA: You don't care about anything.

NINI: Well, I don't know about that. All the same, I'm happy you were born. We eat well, don't we? And you can talk to me in your cruel way, and I listen. I try to say things that'll be helpful to you when I can. You can let loose that brain of yours on higher order concerns while the other children worry about internships. Just think, if you were middle class, you wouldn't even have time to worry about your hideous mother. [*NINI stands and undoes two pins. Her beautiful hair spills around her. She shakes her head, rippling waves of blonde. LILA looks younger now in her posture, rubbing her feet together on the floor. She touches her chin to her shoulder.*]

LILA: You let me twist. Look at me.

NINI: You're just fine and I believe you know it.

LILA: Nobody will get near me, unless they're some passive-aggressive predator. And I'm so desperate I let myself be taken. I just stopped repeating that pattern a few months ago. [*NINI turns and faces her daughter, clearly pleased.*]

NINI: Lie, it sounds like you're seeing a therapist. Are you in therapy? You're talking about patterns and things. Anyway, they're all just boys. You've grown up into a sexy little civic-minded young poetess. It's a lovely thing to be at your age.

LILA: I'm not a poetess. I don't write poems. I write vomit and bile in spiral notebooks.

NINI: No love poems I suppose?

LILA: Wrath. Hate. Disgust.

NINI: Same thing. Flower, I'm just not that concerned about you. [*LILA begins to reach a hand out, shaking.*]

LILA: You lied to me, Mom.

NINI: That's why you'll always be a little captain. You think that's a crime. [*LILA rips her hand back. She stands slowly. A sick, false, smug grin comes over her face.*]

LILA: Oh, yeah? I quit school.

NINI: Oh, now that was just stupid. You're going back and finishing. And speaking of stupid, your Pappaw came over to drop off the venison and you know what he saw? He saw that wonderful nude drawing you did of your old grammar teacher. He's going to get that poor little man fired.

LILA: What!? How did he even know who that was?

NINI: Well, I told him of course.

LILA: Why would you do that?

NINI: You know I can't hide anything from Pappaw. That reminds me, tomorrow I'm taking your suggestion from a few months ago and making an appointment with Dr. Jahana to *get spayed*, I think those were your words.

LILA: Stop it! Stop it! Stop dodging me! I know what you're doing! [*Suddenly, LILA notices PIG MAN is there, in the room, not just the projection from before. She's horrified, breathing and squealing, backing away, pointing in shock.*]

NINI: What is it? Haven't I entertained your every notion in this conversation? [*NINI shakes her head in feigned confusion, erasing what she needs to from her mind.*]

LILA: [*in sheer terror*] He's here ... now ... with us ...

[*There is a furious knock on the door. LILA screams. PIG MAN walks backwards, as if on slow motion rewind. Before exiting, he stops, turns to YOU and points.*]

LILA: *[also to YOU]* I'm sorry! *[He backs offstage. LILA shivers. The knocking grows maniacal, as if a dozen hands are bloodying their knuckles a few feet away.]*

NINI: It's just the Barbaras and the rest of them coming to gossip. Calm yourself now.

LILA: I have to leave you, Mom.

NINI: I think you should stay. We'll get massages and talk about flying you back to New England to work things out. [*LILA walks offstage, still shaken with fear. NINI is left alone, the lights growing slowly dimmer. She looks at You, although she has no idea You're there.]* You should go somewhere and write me a poem that makes me cry. About being orphaned. We'll have a real mother-daughter long-distance cry. Isn't that good advice? Yes. I think you should. *[NINI walks to the front door, somewhere offstage.]* Barbara! Juliet. Regina! Kim Lo. Harmony. Gertrude! Maude. Barbara again! Jennifer. Dot. Barbara! Tell me you all loved the book. No! But the writing was so rich! Oh, I can't believe I'm hearing you say that. No, I just can't believe it. I'll make tea! Earl Grey or Oolong?

[The lights fade.]

Preface to Scene Two

If Scene One asks one essential question: *"What is Lila going to do about this Pigman?"* then Scene Two attempts to answer, *"What is Lila going to do about Lila?"* But, to inch forward, as is often the case, we must leap back.

According to the playwright, the father specter in the play, given the countenance of swine, originated in the form of a one hundred thirty-five pound box of files, sent UPS, from her godfather, Lev Weilerman, a partner in Lila's grandfather's firm, the legal behemoth, Bell Higley & Williams. She'd always believed her father was Guy, a Frenchman she'd never met. Legend had it he played guitar in provincial cafés, flopped in one-room apartments over grocery stores, over women, finally over twenty-one-year-old Nini one night during her year of European travel. According to her mother's tale anyway, she awoke at dawn, tripped over a few empty wine bottles, stuffed her backpack, fixed her hair and caught a train to Lyon, pregnant with the beginnings of what would become Lila.

Decisively not so.

One of her mother's ex-lovers of that era was the very same Lev Weilerman, who remained an ear for Nini's confessions even after the pivotal heartbreak she dealt him. Lev Weilerman who would one day debunk a Bell family canard.

"I still don't understand it," a single-braided ten-year-old Lila said to Lev on the eve of her mother's wedding to her soon to be stepfather, Reggie. "You're the only person she talks to, like *talks to,* without the whole weird voice thing. That accent."

"I told you. She didn't want to marry me. Your Pappaw had a way of voicing his disapproval without using his voice. She didn't like the thought of that struggle. I didn't either, but you know, I was young and arrogant. I thought I could have handled it," Lev said. "Anyway, it's old shit—stuff."

"Like I'm going to let Reggie tell me what to do."

"No, I suspect you won't."

"I asked Nini a hundred times to help me find my father in France. 'Let it lie, Lie,' she says and laughs. While I'm standing there pissed off."

"Some people don't want to be found."

"Gee, thanks for the support," Lila said. "How can you even come to the wedding? Won't you just be standing there, like wanting to puke? I know you still love her. You could make her better, just like, decent."

"The real question is how many times are you going to make me endure this conversation, sweetheart? She didn't want to look at my face every day. Straight from the horse's—your mother's—mouth. How simple can it get?"

"Don't you hate Reggie?"

"No," Lev said.

"Don't you think he's full of shit? I mean like extra full of shit."

"Full of shit—they teach you that in fifth grade now? Good grief. Go read some kind of girl detective book, will you? Give me the delusion of pigtails."

At the first moment it was socially acceptable to do so, long enough after being made partner, after his seldom-thought-of god-daughter had flowered and flown, Lev bought a classic American convertible and retired from the firm to begin training for the minor league equivalent of the senior golf tour. But before turning in his set of office keys to the firm, he made a decision to obliterate his famous professionalism and take the notion of *right and wrong* into his own hands. Admittedly, it was shaky ground for Lev, a dogged relativist. He'd mastered the art of tilting compromise vastly in the firm's favor for the better part of his life, much to the chagrin of fucked-over souls everywhere. Driving out on the rural routes, though, somewhere between St. Louis and Columbia, Missouri, his Jewish atheistic morality—or maybe it was mortality—struck him with the high hat of a thunderclap. He'd couldn't have been further from *it* no matter how far he traveled, how many strokes under par he could descend. With the wind gliding over his Ray Bans and into his five-inch curly locks, and barely a drizzle leaking from the clouds, it was clear that it wasn't too late, not yet.

The box of files Lev sent to Lila could have doubled for a coffee table. It was mummified in clear packing tape and was far too heavy for Lila to even lift into her communal house in bucolic Vermont. Amidst the sonic barrage of a dance-centered playlist and someone vacuuming upstairs, no one had heard the knock on the door from the portly UPS man. Unable to rope any of her roommates into helping with the heavy but brief task of carrying the box inside, Lila sat down on the stoop and chipped away at the layers of tape with a spare house key. She knew she could easily walk back inside to the kitchen and find some knife, probably dirty, in the sink. But there was an undeniable pull originating from the innards of the box. And the option to go back into the house, into the noise of young women, their bodies everywhere, the smell of lunch hanging in the air—it was suddenly off the table. After ten diligent minutes of working the key through the tape, what she found first was a piece of yellow legal paper with the handwriting of a man who'd never married.

Dearest Goddaughter,
If it can be helped, no one ought to walk around imagining a lie as big as the one I've been at least partly responsible for resting at your feet. Now, at your feet, I'll lay the truth. You know how good the firm's P.I.s are—hell, half of them are ex-intel—so you can trust the veracity of this box's contents.

This is hard truth, my dear. Aside from the fact that I love you and care deeply about your happiness (and I know I've blown that most of the time), all I know at the moment is that living a lie unwittingly makes for a tragic end. I'm gambling here, out of love—and some regret too. I regret never becoming a father myself I suppose. I did have the chance, a few times. I regret disappearing from your life for long stretches, years at a time, when you might have needed our effortless conversations. I regret a lot of things, but just like the sages say (to whom no one listens), I only regret the shit I never did. And some more cheap wisdom from a favorite poet of mine, "Don't let the bastards get you down."

Yours in God and all,

Uncle Lev

Lila inspected the stacks of paper and file folders like pieces of raw meat, and the image of the man crystallized. It'd taken her three hours of digesting the innards of the box before she finally vomited for the first time, and then she cried. And as she read on, she couldn't keep down a glass of water without Tums fizzing down her esophagus. Her father, it seemed, a Bart Plowman, for a vocation, designed brutal traps that led people to various bottomless holes of silence. *How to Make People Disappear!* He co-authored the playbook of death. He was, you might say, the offensive coordinator—or if not quite that high up, then at least the quarterback coach. Bart made his share of plane trips to South America over the years to talk logistics with Pinochet's and Videla's men. It was a rich time for a man with his talents and tolerance for the effects of his brand of pragmatism. On-the-clock targets were erased and a few persons of interest were fertilized.

Reading up simultaneously on the victims of Bart's plots and the mothers of her siblings, it became impossible for her to distinguish between it all: victims, mothers, victims, plots, beds, victims, brothers, graves, sisters, victims. The eldest daughter, Lila's only half-sister, Diane, was the sole legitimate heir. Diane was the only offspring to grow in Bart's shadow, with her mother down the hall somewhere, fading away, for a few years anyway, until she vanished, too. She read of a much younger woman, Kaye, who gave birth to Lila's youngest half-brother, Duke—she cried again.

Lila fell asleep next to the box sometime between sunset and midnight, and when she awoke with the back of her head against pink painted concrete, she fixated on Orion, hanging above her, a flashing ache in her skull. One of the girls upstairs was talking through the open window, on her phone.

"I should know by April. I know right? Grad school! Fuck! So if not Yale then Columbia, because I have like a hundred friends, but they're all in Brooklyn, but if not Columbia, then Michigan. I know, right? Michigan? But this guy, Sade, came to visit his girlfriend. I don't know, one of those little grandmas with the little sweaters and pearls. I know! I hate that! Anyway we were at this party, and I see him and his girlfriend who I'd seen on campus, like in a shawl, always sipping something—"

Lila thought of the girls in the house, how at least half of them must have walked right by her corpselike body, never bothering to help her inside to the couch. It took another week, digesting ten or so pounds of the box per day, before she made one of the easiest decisions of her life—to change her future, her present, and her past with a simple change of mind.

In Scene Two, set in the Peruvian jungle, we find Lila after leaving school, then her mother, then me. The mission that emerged for her: to wrestle the father specter to the ground and to rise up victorious with blood on her face. On her guided tour she was promised *primitive life* that the brochure promised, all for the low price equal to one of her college courses.

Her gargantuan trust fund gave her great flexibility in terms of programming her wanderings through her own consciousness. So it was easy enough to book the flight out of the country, to Lima, to connect with the tour bus, to connect again with a boat cruising down the Tambopata river into the beating heart of the jungle. It was especially easy to leave her family to speculate about her whereabouts, safety, motives, and general state of mind. Granted, she'd never had to be more than a room away to feel isolated and wholly apart from her family's constant one-upmanship and frequent declarations of their value as a dying breed of high gentry. But, to hear Lila tell it, they'd always been there next to her, in her thoughts, playing the counterpart in some sophist dialectic. To burn through the voices of her Pappaw, her mother, her stepfather, teachers, and classmates, it was clear to Lila that she'd have to strip it all away in a place that couldn't give less of a shit about the might of Bell Higley & Williams, and the loneliness she carried *in and out of days,* as Maurice Sendak so succinctly put it.

I, of course, received the fateful phone call from Lila, a simple invitation to coffee, that led to the end of my longstanding employment at Earhart High a week after she received the box from Lev. Part of me, the part of me that was conditioned to seek the best outcome, still wishes she'd told me about the box, about its weight, all the layers of tape, and all the blood inside. We'd have had all night, with our coffees, to sit and marvel at life's surprises and tragedies. But she let me flutter there, zipping around her light and never comprehending the source. Maybe it was the years away from our impossible brand of mentor-protégé that made it possible to keep me outside, to make me another piece on her board—a benevolent stop on the way to higher, more perilous ground.

The way the appeal to reason evaporates amidst a stubborn mind leads me to believe whatever paltry attempt I would have made to persuade Lila to return to school, perhaps seek counseling, keep a journal, etc.—all of that would have confirmed my ineptitude. She'd already plotted the map before she somehow unearthed my unlisted home number. We should have never seen each other's parts, shouldn't have kissed on my Turkish rug with our eyes closed. To refuse her, I'd have been a prig. To receive her, I became the manifestation of spineless lust. Presented with two options to fail her, I chose one. Either way, she'd already booked her head on a flight out of society, out of every web of expectation. She awoke in my apartment, the sun creeping, forgoing the lazy morning conversation I'd presumed would be the order of the day. Instead she slid her jeans over her hips and walked out my door and down the brick steps to her mother's ticketed Audi parked in front of a fire hydrant. She was already in Peru.

SCENE TWO

Darkness everywhere. An Aymaran Indian flute plays sustained notes, scaling up and down, whirling into and out of each other.

Dim lights on a jungle floor, deep in the heart of Peru alongside the Tambopata river. Palms and dense forest provide a canopy. A boat is beached, half off-stage left. As the flute fades, the lights go up.

LILA enters from stage right in her black bodysuit, her eyes and forehead blackened with mud. She walks entranced downstage, covering her eyes from the lights.

Loud laughter from off-stage right, screams and howls that provoke rounds of intensified laughter in response. LILA fiddles with her hearing aid and looks off-stage in the sound's direction. She smiles briefly, seeming to remember something.

Two Aymara Indian men, one large, INTERPRETER, the other almost in miniature, SPIRIT, enter from stage right, laughing wildly and slapping each other on the shoulders, back, and legs. They catch their breath, then the large man makes an indecipherable animal sound, accompanied by a series of hand gestures and pantomimes that send the tiny man into near convulsions.

LILA: Sounds like you got what you wanted, from the gods. The celebration.

INTERPRETER: *[still laughing]* What's that? Oh, Jaqi. Oh, man. What did you say? *[The two men break down again.]*

LILA: I said everyone's very happy. They must be celebrating the Tambopata—that it didn't flood.

INTERPRETER: Everyone knows it's going to flood in a day or two. Because of you. *[SPIRIT leans into INTERPRETER and speaks. We don't hear it clearly—we never do. Just the intonations and rhythm of the words. He only speaks to INTERPRETER, only looks at INTERPRETER, or at a fixed point that causes him to look up just slightly, teeth glistening in the moonlight.]* He says when an outsider comes in and leaves with the head on fire, the river always floods two to three days after. Depending upon the size of the flame.

LILA: Well, I don't want to leave. I'm not finished—

INTERPRETER: *[suddenly intimate]* We have spoken about this.

LILA: I'm not ready to face him.

INTERPRETER: We have spoken—

LILA: You spoke to me about it. I didn't say anything. When I tried to say something, the midwives threw scalding water on me.

INTERPRETER: You were told not to speak. *[LILA kicks at a giant palm leaf, paces, then approaches INTERPRETER, her lips pointed at his ear.]*

LILA: I was doing well. You said I was doing well—I've only been here a week! I'm—I'm aware.

INTERPRETER: Aware of danger, yes.

LILA: See! That's aware. I'm engorged in— *[She's nearly climbing him like a tree.]*

INTERPRETER: You are not engorged. You are groping in the mud, very much like a legless frog.

LILA: But isn't the mud, like, holy? *[He gently shakes her hands off of him.]*

INTERPRETER: You are in a desperate stupor. You narrowed your attention out of necessity, that is all.

LILA: What! No, no, that's bullshit. After the dance, and the roots, and the vision, you said I was seeing clearly.

INTERPRETER: It was dawn's mirage you saw, not dawn. *[LILA crumples on the ground, head between her knees. SPIRIT speaks to INTERPRETER.]*

INTERPRETER: He says you take affirmations of tiny things to be … how do you say it … all-compassing?

LILA: Encompassing.

INTERPRETER: Yes, you encompass nothing. You have done very poorly at listening. You are … a deaf person.

LILA: That's not my fault. I had an undiagnosed fever and lost half my hearing. *[INTERPRETER speaks to SPIRIT and the two men rip up again, echoed by a wave of laughter from the celebration off stage.]*

LILA: Are they celebrating me leaving?

INTERPRETER: Yes. That's very good, very perceptive.

LILA: Why are they doing that?

INTERPRETER: You have used up your stay with us.

LILA: But why?

INTERPRETER: You were not invited! Yes, there was a boldness in your act of escape, letting the boat return to the surface world without you.

LILA: Right? That's what I thought.

INTERPRETER: This is why you weren't thrown naked into the jungle! Do not think the idea did not have support. *[INTERPRETER, all of the sudden, leaps into the air, spreading out his legs like wings. He lets out a great bird noise that sustains itself perfectly even after landing with a seismic thud on the stage.]* It is a great triumph whenever we can take on the burden of an outsider and send them away alive. Your head is on fire, and our ways of putting out the fire are useless to you. But you are in a different state now. And you will leave this way.

LILA: That's good. That's got to be good. *[SPIRIT speaks to INTERPRETER.]*

INTERPRETER: You have, he says, the wrong measuring device. You cannot be truly spoken to, because this device is planted very far up your asshole. We would have to cut you open and remove it, but the man who had that task is dead five years. There is no replacement for him. The young people don't have the stomachs for it anymore. I do not blame them. I do not either.

LILA: I can't—I can't go back. Not yet—

INTERPRETER: Again, you are not going back. Because you do not see this, you must leave. This is very basic.

[An Aymara couple, young, 20 or so, enter from stage left. They

pass by the beached boat and we see they are mostly naked, caressing each other, their mouths interlocked. They move downstage next to LILA while groping and moaning in exhales. A foot away, the young man lies on his back and the young woman straddles him, moving up and down at a pace so slow, movement is almost undetectable. Her back muscles flex and relax, flex and relax.]

LILA: Should we leave them to their—Should I cover my eyes?

INTERPRETER: The music is about to start.

LILA: I mean are they going to just keep at it with us standing here?

INTERPRETER: This is the place they go. It is the place they decided on when they saw each other, and we are interrupting that place and their moment. The only reason they have not asked us to leave is because of him *[points to SPIRIT]*. There is no point asking him to be somewhere other than where he is, when he has known where he will be. The book is written.

LILA: Well, I want them to stop it.

INTERPRETER: Maybe they are doing it for you.

LILA: They are?

INTERPRETER: No. I told you why already. It is the place where they do what they have decided to do, and it was determined it was the right time. But for you, it might be they *are* doing for you. What do you think of it?

LILA: I think they're enjoying themselves. I'd say from the angle of her neck, she's definitely enjoying herself.

INTERPRETER: This enjoy, this enjoying, this is redundant. *[SPIRIT speaks to INTERPRETER. The young woman astride the young man vocalizes wildly, a shotgun blast of Aymara words, punctuated by heaves and squeaking noises.]*

[SPIRIT produces a small yellow-tailed woolly monkey and hands the animal to INTERPRETER. He presents it in the direction of LILA.]

LILA: I saw one of those on a walk yesterday.

INTERPRETER: This is the same k'ellu monkey you saw.

LILA: Yeah. Hi there, little fella.

INTERPRETER: Break its neck.

LILA: What?

INTERPRETER: If you break its neck, you are welcome to stay here.

LILA: That's disgusting.

INTERPRETER: Your assessments are not important.

LILA: I don't care about cultural norms or whatever the fuck.

INTERPRETER: You are the sick one. This animal will show you how you are sick.

LILA: I won't. *[LILA looks out past the lights now, at You.]* You wouldn't do it right? For the answer? How much would you change for the answer? *[She waits. INTERPRETER also has turned his attention to YOU.]* Should I do it? *[She drops to her knees, shaking her head]*

INTERPRETER: Then you are already gone and you will take your burning p'iqi *[pointing to her head]* with you.

LILA: But you said it yourself. *[pointing to her eyes]* You said my nayra were okay, it was the jinchu that were the problem. *[LILA grabs her ears. She flexes her hands, tearing at her ears, then stops, out of breath. Music rises, drums, flutes, and singing. INTERPRETER hands the woolly monkey back to SPIRIT who tosses it into the brush. It scampers off, unfazed.]*

INTERPRETER: *[to SPIRIT]* What? Oh yes. He says your words have no uma, no water, just air. You cannot do what they do without uma.

LILA: All right! *[The young couple's ecstasy is increasing, their voices now in unison.]* They're not *enjoying* themselves. They don't know what enjoying is because it's like breathing or something. Right? I get it. I'm not a complete idiot. You don't know what it's like. You get to stand there all wise and half-naked. There's quiet! Real quiet for you! I can't even hear my own thoughts—I have to run them through some kind of filter! *[SPIRIT and INTERPRETER share the briefest of glances, rip up heartily, and regain their composure quickly.]*

INTERPRETER: I do not know what you are saying now, but it is very sad. *[INTERPRETER scoops LILA off the ground and takes her in his arms. They kiss, slowly, the parting of their lips even slower.]*

LILA: Was that goodbye?

INTERPRETER: No. It was the proper way to end it. *[He releases her dispassionately. LILA sinks away from him, her head and shoulders hanging on her chest.]* You are not ready to know the meaning of defecating. You must connect to your bowels. *[The young couple thrust slowly now, reaching the end, or as they say, the bridge. They collapse on each other, appearing to have passed out. The music is now blasting. SPIRIT sits down on stage and weeps in his hands.]*

LILA: Why is he crying?

INTERPRETER: Because you are leaving. He is a serious man. Even though he knows you could not be helped, the human in him weeps for you.

LILA: Don't make me go! You were there! The midwives gave me the root and danced with me and said I was a moon woman, a phaxsi marmi! A phaxsi marmi! I cried when you told me, it was so beautiful!

INTERPRETER: The moon is a giver of death, also. I told you that, but you were not listening.

LILA: But death is good, right? Not good, but you know what I mean. They were smiling. Doesn't it come back around and fold into one thing?

INTERPRETER: Wrong! They were not happy to greet death, only smiling in recognizing you for what you are.

LILA: I'm a good student! I'm learning.

INTERPRETER: You do not teach also. You are like a cloth. You sop only.

LILA: Stop it! Just stop it. You all hate me! Hate us all! I hate us too okay! I get it!

[LILA suddenly grows concerned about the collapsed young couple.

She inches towards them, inspecting them for signs of life.]

LILA: Hey! They're not breathing!

INTERPRETER: Not in this moment.

LILA: Aren't you going to help them? Isn't he? *[LILA gestures at SPIRIT, now weeping audibly.]*

INTERPRETER: Tomorrow they'll breathe again. You will not see it. They will show you no more of what they do. *[She grabs her hair, perhaps to keep it attached to her head.]*

LILA: Should I do what they do? How they do it? Is that it? *[SPIRIT gestures for INTERPRETER to come close. He does.]*

INTERPRETER: You cannot do what they do. You are empty and full of leaks. You are a leaking person. But it is very sad because you have nothing to leak, so there is only dead air leaving your holes. What they do is full.

LILA: Just tell me something good, one thing. Just—

INTERPRETER: This *good* of yours—

LILA: Please! *[INTERPRETER nods, considering.]*

INTERPRETER: Your dreams are in the sky, because you left them there.

LILA: Oh. That's so sad!

INTERPRETER: Sad is, for you, the same as this—good—of yours.

LILA: Did he say that? I want his answer. *[SPIRIT, silently weeping now, exits stage right.]*

LILA: Get him back here. I don't want your evaluation. I want his.

INTERPRETER: They are the same. You are the same.

LILA: But, my father, I have to face him and you said you'd help me!

INTERPRETER: I did not say this. I said you will meet him. There is no help. *[LILA walks over to the boat and puts her hand on the bough.]*

LILA: Well, do you say goodbye or is that redundant?

INTERPRETER: Yes, we say goodbye. But not until you are

gone.

LILA: You said I was already gone.

INTERPRETER: I say lots of things. It is my name. Interpreter.

The lights fade. The faint chop-chop-chop of a helicopter floats on the breeze.

Preface to Scene Three

To interpret Lila's banishment from the Aymara as another part of her design, considering the axe-wielding imposition of her will upon the likes of her mother, then me, is to take a definite position on her character—that of the manipulator and erector of a monument to self-justification. I offer a gentler treatment, though biased and soft in the head, I'm sure. There must be something particularly satisfying and emboldening, always being on the inside of opportunity and privilege. But perhaps there is something freeing, seeing those once inexorable identifying qualities torched and pitched aside in the name of attempting to live. Was there a new Lila yet? Had one had time to form? What lasting vision of her time with the Aymara would become central to her mission? It seemed to Lila that nothing of import would come to her without first reconstructing the stairway to ecstasy she'd seen in the jungle. What great mental time could be saved if she could merge bodies the way the young couple had—with great effort, yes—but with such assurance of the imminent ecstatic bounty! The sheer amount of time was staggering.

Lila likes Morely's duplex, likes the chill of the hardwood under her diminutive bare feet, even if her soles turn charcoal, coated with equal parts canine and human hair. She'd taken an architecture class and had gravitated to the California Craftsman style. It seemed to embody the swaths of America with welcome mats, the dark wooden beams and ample porches. The unassuming rectangles argued for the good life, friends laughing round the table at 2 a.m., driving home in Volkswagens and Hondas, rather than the promises that forty-foot ionic columns make about the stiff, vicious power that dwells within.

She watches Morely in the shower through the translucent curtain—without his knowing—and the way he efficiently cleans his ass, never lingering but unafraid to do what needs to be done, allows the idea of *the future* to seep into her cortex. Wouldn't he look good, walking down the hall, cup of coffee, tousled hair, waking her for yoga and a fuck or vice-versa? The very thought of such sweetness is an unwelcome guest, though, and her hands grab at her gold strands as if trying to rip the notion out before it embeds itself in the womb of her brain. Catching a glimpse of this action in the mirror, she realizes she is in two places at once—she has conquered time inadvertently. She is watching and living, breathing, watching, considering, watching, moving, split not down the middle but into identical eggs of consciousness, one in the physical world and one in the anti-world of the mirror. It explains the hours she'd spent as a girl in front of her own image, lost in her own oversized pupils; and no one had ever told her of the danger in there, of getting lost.

One particularly vile St. Louis afternoon, sleet on the streets and cafeteria chili in the hallway air, I found Lila in my classroom with the lights off, her head down on a desk. Flipping on the lights, at first glance, I thought she was dead; and I felt a trickle of urine soak through my boxer shorts.

"Lila? It's time to wake up."

"I'm awake, Craft," she said, though her lack of perceptible movement would have made it plausible that her voice was originating inside the loud speaker over her head.

"I jump out of bed in the morning. Put my headphones on, write in my journal. But now I think it's more like a habit from when I was a little kid. It doesn't feel the same. She's starting to sound empty or something."

"She?" I said.

"What? *It*, I mean. It feels empty. So I don't really wake up and my head is still dreaming really confusing dreams." She lifted her head, holding her hands over her eyes.

"How are they confusing?"

"Like, people being demeaning. A big circle of demeaning. In one—one of my mom's country-club friends has like nineteen cats—and she makes me scrub a floor with actual shit, cat shit, everywhere, like with three paper towels. And I can't do it, of course, but I can't leave until I figure out a way to get it clean."

"Yes," I told her, "I used to dream of treading water, sometimes in a lake, sometimes the ocean. Either way, boat after boat would speed by, filled with boys and girls, students, laughing, waving to each other. Waving to me, kindly—it was as if they thought I was out there struggling by choice. I'd always wake up before I became too tired to keep my head above water. But last time I had the dream, I got so tired, watching the boats, and I slipped under. I looked down and there was a submarine full of people, about fifty feet down. I swam down, but the farther I descended, the more resistance I felt. And I could tell the people in the submarine—I could see them through the portholes—I knew they'd seen me and were rooting for me to make it."

"Yeah. And?"

"That's it. That's how it ends."

"What's it mean?"

"Nothing, I suppose. Just drowning" I said.

"This is why I trust you, Craft."

In Morely's bathroom, the mirror growing a frame of steam, her hands knotted in her hair, Lila knows what must come next. It has to come off—all of it. Her blonde, Vermont-elite college side-swipe, suggesting the easy disinterest of privilege, was permitting a counterargument to gain traction: *Just leave it alone. Go back and finish school.* Yet the giant box of files from Lev had taken up residence in every room of her mind, demanding so much space that she trips over it no matter what else she thinks of. She simply can't walk past without digging in, if just for a moment, for more validation that something must be done to expose the being that made her and, consequently, what we tolerate in the name of hemispherical dominance, cold comfort, and cheap bananas. But what would keep us all from shrugging and returning to our phones to see who has wondered aloud how it's already next year, how they'd just gotten used to calling it last year, and who has agreed with their bewilderment over the passage of time?

The clippers rest in a basket on a shelf over the toilet under an extra roll of toilet paper and replacement razor blades. She checks the medicine cabinet for shears and comes up empty. She'll have to use the office scissors, until it gets short enough to go electric.

Her hair drops onto the floor as if guillotined, and Lila keeps her eyes off the littered, checkered tile to maintain her resolution. The clippers glide over her head, revealing a lunar surface of a scalp, winding and hilly. Morely turns off the water, rips open the curtain, shutting one soapy eye, pauses, breathing her in, and nods his head. He wraps himself in a towel and stares at the hair carpet for a moment. His eyes drift up to Lila's face, searching. Having heard her mind eight hours a day over the last week, he knows there'll be no real answer in her explanation.

"I bought a gun from a kid trying to sell me dope," she says.

"Oh, man."

"I can't do it without a real gun," she says.

"Just last night we agreed—fuck. *You, sir,* are not a man of your word."

Morely, though not particularly godlike in stature, exudes the kind of ease, wearing just a towel, that has brought a steady stream of women stumbling through his door and falling onto his Japanese platform bed. He runs a hand over Lila's freshly shorn scalp and shakes his head, sighing atop the closed wooden toilet seat. He could always run her out the door, he thinks. It wasn't as if his oft-impaired initial judgment of women hadn't made similar actions necessary in the recent past. What was her name, Cassandra, screaming into the phone at her roommate—stolen money, infestation, coke, the electricity had been turned off again, could she stay there a couple weeks?

Lila's eyes in the mirror, glancing off the glass toward Morely, are unlike those of the women he's known in their sheer commitment—and then there are those tiny spirals in her large pupils of course. He thinks about how she'd chosen him that afternoon, just a week ago, undone by time now and spread out into three years' worth of anything he'd experienced before. The flophouse coffee shop gargled a glut of men pretending to work or read. She drifted straight to the signal emanating outward from his head—*game for something, open to suggestions.*

It had all become so easy for him, over time, so gray with splashes of taupe—four shifts a week as assistant manager of the gourmet liquor store and deli, amply supplemented by the monthly jaunts to and from Humboldt County, stocked with twenty pounds of medical cannabis. Here was something else entirely, out of a parallel existence.

The first morning they awoke together, Morely recognized his total body soreness as equal to the morning after a car wreck he'd had in high school. Finding the bottle of Aleve empty, he shuffled outside in his robe to smoke.

"Hey man," his neighbor, Tom, said, on their shared porch, whittling what appeared to be a turtle, "I could hear you last night. Well, not you exactly, but ..."

"Oh, okay, yeah."

"I mean, that's cool that she's enthusiastic, this girl, but—"

"Tom, just don't."

"Helly wanted to call the police, man."

"Ah, your wife is nuts," Morely said. He dropped his cigarette to the ground and stepped on it.

"I know. I know. I finally got her to do her breathing exercises and sleep for a couple hours. You woke up the kid, man. Well not you, but you know ..."

"Don't give me that, Tom. I'm about to deck you, you know that?"

"The walls are cardboard."

"No shit, and I have to listen to your public service announcement on the torture of marriage every goddamn night."

"That's my life, man. Shit, Morely."

Tom looked at the turtle and sighed before throwing it into the street. Morely shook his head, jogged to the street to retrieve the turtle, and placed it at Tom's feet.

"It's a project, we're working on something, could be a while."

"I hate you sometimes, man. Project. You know the last time I was laid?"

"Your birthday."

"Which is coming up again in three weeks. How long's this going to last?"

"It's her call, Tom."

"Days?"

"Her call."

What is it about the mirror, Morely thinks, that takes the swirling danger in a person's eyes and cubes it? That in conjunction with the shorn scalp of a woman is enough to blow up any dam. Now there is a gun somewhere in his house, a living condition he'd managed to avoid despite his status as a low-grade outlaw. He wants to hurdle Lila's bald head, streak out the front door and run, testicles flopping, back to the fork in the road that landed him here, then take a hard right. But it's no use—there are too many synaptic forks to remember, so many of them charred and scorched by vice.

Most of the girls Morely grew up with in Bakersfield learned to shoot. A date to the range was the equivalent of bowling or a movie. It was another way of accepting your locus on the map and being from somewhere. He'd had to listen to so much Merle Haggard and applaud for so many girls who could obliterate a target as if congenially dominating a game of barroom darts, that it finally broke him. He swore off the whole lot for good. No more girls with guns. But now, a captive in his own bathroom, he imagines Lila aiming a handgun, a completely different kind of creature, and whereas before the pistols and semi-automatic rifles in the hands of women had simply depressed him, now the thought burns inside from his neck to his ribcage. Absurd, grotesque, Lila, like a Girl Scout eating raw meat.

She tugs gently at the bottom of Morely's towel and softens her cheek muscles, something Morely wishes she wouldn't do. He knows he is being manipulated, and it irks him that he can't get out in front of it. She is too much. He can't deny that having a program again has forced him to remember the foggy idea of a genuine life pursuit rather than just the series of paths of least resistance. Morely drops his towel, the bathroom bulbs shimmering and burning him out of his body, whisking him to the ethers where Lila resides, where their nakedness together is their source.

Morely's scruff of a dog saunters into the bathroom, flops on the cool tile, and raises his brow to his guardian. And though the dog has taken to Lila and appreciates the prolonged scratches and two-mile hikes through the hills, he remembers life before her. He prizes Morely's happiness above his own and can't help but wish the now-bald girl in the bathroom would find a reason to walk out the door and never return.

SCENE THREE

Lights up on a big Japanese platform bed, center stage. LILA's sitting upright, legs under the covers in a sweatshirt, in mid-sentence. MORELY, hairy, paunchy-athletic, 30, at peace in white briefs over the covers. 70s Miles Davis plays softly on an Ipod docking station on the nightstand next to MORELY. A shaggy black dog/alter ego, Mosely, lies on the floor in a huddle next to him.

LILA: It wasn't anything you were doing. It was—I don't know. You were fine, good, really good, and I turned off all the noise in my head. It just wasn't … it.

MORELY: I just don't think I can do it any slower than that. *[MORELY reaches over and turns off the radio.]*

LILA: Hey! What are you doing? Don't turn that off.

MORELY: I don't know what I'm doing, Lila. There. It's back on.

LILA: It has to be slower, and go for longer. How much time do you need before you're ready again?

MORELY: I guess—

LILA: I was thinking this time we could do it Western for longer, sort of embrace the fact that we still have all these sexual filters—

MORELY: Right.

LILA: You know, connected to the poison in the culture, like really fuck it out. And then, before you let it go, we wait for the point where we connect and go East. Get down to work. What? What is it?

MORELY: No, I hear you.

LILA: What's the problem?

MORELY: An hour probably. I need an hour, I think. You want some orange juice?

LILA: An hour! *[MORELY turns off the music again.]* I just said keep that music on.

MORELY: It's disorienting. It was cool during, but now it's confusing me.

LILA: Leave it on!

MORELY: Fine! Do you want some juice or not?

LILA: No, tea maybe.

MORELY: I don't have any. *[MORELY tousles her hair and walks off stage left. The dog rolls onto its back.]*

LILA: Not juice. I don't know, something, but not juice. Water. No, yes, water. *[To herself]* Uma.

[MORELY returns with two glasses, one orange juice, one water, and a giant Milkbone, which the dog takes in his lips as if being handed a glass egg. LILA sits in a wide-eyed daze, staring through the window at the tall grass in the back yard.]

MORELY: You all right?

LILA: Yes, yes, fine. Three times ago, that was the closest. And I knew it, and I became conscious of it, then it was over.

MORELY: Three times ago—wait—you were going crazy three times ago. You sounded like a raccoon killing a poodle. You sure you're okay?

LILA: Stop asking me that. I'm fine. I want to make a plan—I'm trying to talk to you, obviously!

MORELY: Okay. I don't know. We're doing all right, I think. We're on the path, right?

LILA: No. I lost focus. That's not how they do it—all caught up in themselves. It's like they obliterate themselves. And the ecstasy, it's directed, not vomited. It's not right at all. Have you been listening to anything?

MORELY: Listen, believe me, I admire this project. And I'm thrilled you asked me to help you out, but I think your idea of, you know, *the desired result*, it's too narrow. We're not in Peru, you know, next to a river with vegetation and Mayans. It's L.A., you know, it's just going to be whatever it is.

LILA: Aymaran! And what do you mean by that that?

MORELY: What?

LILA: Turn the music off!

MORELY: You just said—fine. *[Far too gently, he switches it off.]*

LILA: Narrow? Desired result? What is that—*be whatever it is*? You said you were a serious man. A *serious man*, you said.

MORELY: Cut it out.

LILA: You said, *don't worry, Lila, don't you worry about a thing.* And why do you need an hour? *[LILA kneels on the bed, drawing inward. She could tilt either way—back to MORELY's arms or to attack position.]*

MORELY: All right, all right, you're right. I said I was up for it. Listen, I'm just having a great time, I mean, I was just sitting there in the coffee shop, minding my own business. And here I am thirty-six hours later—

LILA: Oh, now you want to do a recap? You're wasting time!

MORELY: My back's sore, my neck's all cockeyed. It's a hell of a feeling! It's just hard to share your goal, you know, exactly. But you're right. There's a goal. You laid it out, you know, so to speak. *[LILA leaps to her feet atop the bed.]*

LILA: Goal! I'm not in middle management. It's an expedition! *[pointing to her head]* This is wrong. I was wrong.

MORELY: Poor little rich girl.

LILA: Is that supposed to hurt me?

MORELY: It's supposed to make you see yourself right now.

LILA: Do you honestly think I haven't spent my whole life thinking about being a poor little rich girl? Do you think I don't know that you and anyone else can call me that at any time, over anything, and that's supposed to be some kind of final word on my being!

MORELY: I'm trying to tell you—you want everything when you want it, and that's not how it goes, whether it's consciousness expansion or getting off or the weather or taking a shit. And yes, I think money has a lot to do with it.

LILA: I looked at you and thought, for once, I wouldn't have to slow myself down. It's oppressive, waiting for people while they belch and pick their asses. But you wouldn't understand that, would you? Ass picker!

MORELY: *[chuckling]* Listen, listen. Let's get some sleep. They sleep in the jungle right?

LILA: I thought you were different. I thought you were here. *[LILA points to her eyes.]* I really am stupid. Why couldn't I have known I was this stupid earlier?

MORELY: It wouldn't have done you any good. And I am different, and that's the last time I'm going to defend myself. I'm committed to your project. It's something worth trying, which is more than I can say for just about anything else.

LILA: I can see now, he'll cower in the moment. He's fucking worse than me.

MORELY: Who are you talking to?

LILA: This is why nobody does anything about anything. It's too much to count on anyone.

MORELY: Lila. *[She dismounts from the bed in one motion and grabs at the floor for her leggings and a T-shirt. MORELY moves quickly to her, places a hand on her hand that's holding the clothes.]* Come on. You're going to ruin the surprise.

LILA: I don't even care to know what you're talking about.

MORELY: Tomorrow my friend, well, not my friend— *[LILA pulls away and dresses in a whipped-up frenzy.]* but this guy, kind of a psychotic type really—anyway I work with him sometimes, and he's giving us his helicopter for the day.

LILA: What do you mean giving us?

MORELY: To fly, dummy.

LILA: Who?

MORELY: Me.

LILA: You fly helicopters? *[She stops dead in her tracks.]*

MORELY: Yeah.

LILA: You're a pilot?

MORELY: Instead of medical school, yeah.

LILA: *[Clearly touched]* Pappaw used to take me up in his

plane when I was a little girl. Then he just stopped. This is a beautiful gift.

MORELY: I just want to show off.

LILA: No, that you would—this is ... *[Shifting now, putting something together, LILA cackles, her face to the ceiling. MORELY's seen similar such swings the past few days, but this one causes him pause.]* This is perfect!

MORELY: Well, I take it that's a yes?

LILA: *[To somewhere else now]* Ha! Just like Los Desaparecidos! Oh! Oh, your little girl is—

MORELY: What? *[LILA climbs atop MORELY, wide-eyed, her hands on his shoulders, squeezing.]*

LILA: Are you ready yet?

MORELY: Yeah I guess so. What was that you were—

LILA: I said are you ready?

MORELY: Are you?

LILA: Ready is redundant.

MORELY: Don't get cocky.

LILA: Concentrate.

MORELY: I'm sorry about the poor little rich girl.

LILA: Forget it.

MORELY: No, I had it wrong. You're an angry little rich boy.

LILA: This is why I trust you. *[She pulls his face into her hers. Their mouths touch.]*

MORELY: You're lucky I'm open-minded.

LILA: Concentrate.

MORELY: I'm concentrating, you concentrate.

LILA: No more talking.

MORELY: Just find your nothing place in your head and don't you worry about me.

LILA: You have to meet me there.

MORELY: I said don't worry about me.

[A quick fade to darkness. A spotlight on LILA's face. It holds there, then darts between their faces. Time is passing in their countenances.

Their gazes are through each other.]

LILA: Okay, okay, I can see it!

MORELY: I see it, too.

LILA: See it?!

MORELY: Oh my God, I see it.

LILA: It's unbelievable.

MORELY: I actually see it.

LILA: Keep concentrating. It's folding around us.

MORELY: I don't want to look at it.

LILA: Don't be afraid!

MORELY: It's death!

LILA: Keep concentrating.

MORELY: Oh, it's opening up!

LILA: It's enormous!

MORELY: It has a mouth!

LILA: No—it's an eye!

LILA screams. The Miles Davis sustained note returns, fusion in the darkness again.

Preface to Scene Four

With the wind of some form of love at her back, the new Lila finds it shockingly easy to lift Morely's heavy arm from her chest, push herself to sitting and fully awaken, not spilling with doubt and dread, but glowing with the butterflies of an imminent performance. She traces her hands and fingers over her body, half under the covers, finishing at her soft, stubbled head, which sprouts the promise of renewal, the first new golden threads popping through. She picks up Morely's phone and calls a taxi.

On the toilet, knock-kneed, she writes in her journal—which will eventually find its way into my hands and onto these pages. It's the first entry written directly to her brother, Duke, and should, perhaps, serve as the prologue to the play:

Duke,

When we are children again, I'll terrorize you with pillow stories of chainsaws and kitchen knives, cocaine dealers, the undead, nuns beating each other blue in cornfields with their severed limbs.

When we are children again, the moon will seem closer, like something we're aware of all the time, like a crush, before you ever have a lover.

I'll wear my heart on the front of my bike, round street corners shouting my eyes, where I've just come from, what just happened—it won't take you five seconds to know how your wind will blow and be blown.

When we are children again, I'll say goodbye a hundred times before shutting the door.

You'll see me slap a girl in the face, hard, sending her spinning back and off balance, because I don't want to learn a lesson right now, because her mouth, the shape of her mouth when she said that shit—what does she know about my little brother.

When we are children again, I'll point out your faults with a sharpened red pencil, pacing from the door to the window, about to punctuate when you tighten your grip on a hockey puck—but no, you think, and let it drop to the carpet.

You'll leave for the summer, to study outer space, to blow apart dams or something, to find her face her laugh her glasses her braces, to leave me lying around in sweatpants, mouth hanging open, unshaven legs up the wall, fuming at the door to your empty room.

When we are children again, I'll make scrambled eggs on Sundays while the house is asleep, with chopped spinach, just to watch you pick out each green fleck.

I'll make your girl cry, the one you might just love with the curls and brown skin, he thinks you're kind of stupid, he told me, it's a good thing you're so cute, I'll say, as if being helpful, to test us all, what we can all withstand, just in case you love her.

Lila dresses, a tank top and jean shorts, sneakers and sunglasses. In the bedroom, Morely snores softly, on his belly, satisfied unconscious. For the first time since she can remember, she feels light and agile on her feet. She scratches out a quick drawing of one turtle mounting another, sticks it on the refrigerator with the caption, *slow love*. The taxi is already waiting outside—she trots over, slides to the middle of the backseat, and gives the address of The Pinnacles School, off Mulholland Drive.

The cabbie guns it through the canyon, keeps going to his nose and coughing. Approaching the restrained yet still ornate, crested gate, Lila rolls down the window and informs the uniformed guard the she's here for a student tour, *Hildegard Brunsen*, she says. The security man, black and stout, probably ex-police, cocks the walkie-talkie over his mouth, obscuring the back and forth. She hears, *yes Mr. Plowman, yes, a student tour, no, okay, Mr. Plowman*, and a chill raises the hair on her arm perpendicular. *It's happening, the beginning of interloping*, she thinks.

The receptionist, Ms. Ramon, is a perky young brunette whose T-shirt stretched tight over small breasts must drive the boys wild. Back at Earhart the principal's secretary, Mrs. Lang, was constantly chewing sugarless candy, matching patterned cardigans to patterned, tapered slacks, and checking the stiffness of her nest of hair. O California. Ms. Ramon looks out on a faux waterfall with metal fish that appear to be defying gravity, leaping through the water, up, up, and into the sky.

"Hildegard? We don't have you down for a tour. Did you make an appointment with Admissions?"

"Someone did. They just told me to be here at 7:45," Lila says, feigning boredom.

Ms. Ramon stands up behind her half-moon desk and gestures to a pair of boys who could've just walked out of a Beat Generation coffee table book—one in a sweater vest and tattered trousers, the other in all black, T-shirt and jeans. They amble over with Starbuck's cups, all caffeinated smiles.

"You boys free first period?" Ms. Ramon asks.

"Why, do we look free?"

"Not anymore. Hildegard is here for a tour. We don't have any reputable guides available, so you'll have to do."

"You can trust her to us, Ms. Ramon."

"I'm not going to interpret that."

The vested boy pivots from Ms. Ramon and looks directly into Lila's eyes, bowing just slightly. He is rehearsed, but sweet, she thinks.

"Welcome," the boy in black says.

"I'm Charles, a Jew, that's Kiram, half Indian."

"What year will you be, may I ask?"

"Junior," Lila says.

"Wait, how old are you?" says Kiram, always first to speak after Lila. The boys punctuate each other like rubber balls and ready hands.

"He's asking because there's something about you."

"Was that rude? I apologize, sort of."

"Boys. Seriously," Ms. Ramon says.

"What?"

"The tour," she says, "this is official school business."

"Don't douse the fires of the young in the name of officiousness, Ms. Ramon."

"Or quash curiosity."

"You only have 45 minutes," says Ms. Ramon.

"Do you wish us to be paper dolls or men of flesh and substance?"

Ms. Ramon is now on the phone with someone who doesn't understand directions. She is understanding—or her understanding is indisputably authentic-sounding.

"Fifteen," Lila says.

"What?"

"You're fifteen? Where are you from?"

"I just came from Peru," Lila says.

"That explains it, Charles."

"The eyes."

"Not exactly the eyes," Kiram says.

"Facial musculature."

"The sideways glance."

"That's it. You read any Bolano?"

"He's Chilean, Charles. She said Peru."

"No," Lila says.

"Peru, huh?"

"Where should we start?" Charles asks.

"Quad," Kiram answers.

"So it shall be."

Ms. Ramon hangs up and sighs, answers another call.

"See? All in good time, Ms. Ramon."

The swelling morning rush of teens and teachers peaks at 7:55. Lila and the boys sit beneath an oak in a triangle formation, picking out faces for assessment. She tunes in and out of their Kerouac Laurel and Hardy routine, happy to have the cover of their company. Once class begins, Charles and Kiram summon her to follow them on the long cut through campus, one that would take most of the day.

What if, she thinks, instead of the rehashing of Lila and Nini's scenes, she'd come home during breaks in college to find Duke shooting the cosmic breeze with charming fools like these boys? She squints her eyes, chasing away the question at first, before returning to it. Might she be different altogether, her whole *central problem* replaced with another, one far warmer, solved with long hugs and attentive conversation. But here she is, and she knows Charles and Kiram are an impossibility in Duke's world anyway. At the wrong-side-of-the-tracks high school in Kissimmee, this Rosencrantz and Guildenstern could never exist. The kind of symbolic soft rebellion the boys had been perfecting since middle school, no doubt, is only available to the wealthy, who risk nothing by sticking out their tongues—they're not biting the hand. Already having acquired the language and customs, they know that hand will pat them on the back and send them along to the hubs of the gentry, the arts, and more ass than they can possibly handle.

Lila smiles all the same—their impish eyebrows and skinny chests.

"He's digs men," Kiram announces.

"I haven't acted on it. Girls fascinate me too much still."

"How exactly is your name Hildegard?"

Lila answers with a glance and a purse of her lips. She takes their hands and swings them as they walk.

"He grifts."

"For cigarettes. Kiram dances."

"For money."

"Yeah, I've heard of that," Lila says.

"What kind of boyfriends do you get with a shaved head?"

"Bald guys?"

"With the pissed-off walk? A future of tattoos?"

"Or bald guys— "

"Like into Moby."

"My boyfriend is thirty," Lila says.

"Makes sense."

"Thirty. What does your dad think about that?"

"Do you like Monk?"

"Charles plays piano."

"I don't know what my father thinks," Lila says, "I don't think he knows. He designs people's deaths for the government, so he's not very interested in my comings and goings."

"Our government?"

"Who did he kill?"

"Should we know that?"

"What could he do to us?"

"Nothing. Not like the people his bosses disagreed with in South America," Lila says.

"Hildegard, I don't know what to say."

"I'm sorry."

"Yeah, I guess that's it."

Lev's box of illumination described in some detail the lives of the people Bart had been responsible for ending. They were unsurprising to Lila, having majored, for a semester anyway, in Latin American Studies: organizers, union men, agitators, but two struck her beyond repair. One was a beloved high-school principal in Chile, running for governor on a leftist ticket. The other was a mother of three young children, the wife of a prominent lawyer who'd disappeared. She'd organized widows' marches and sit-ins that grew to a magnitude that television couldn't ignore.

After his official retirement, Bart had moved into the private sector as head of security for Walt Disney World, where he met Duke's mother, Kaye, assistant manager of the bakery on Main Street U.S.A. in the Magic Kingdom. He'd honed a technique via years of field work in Latin America, extorting sex from local women, barely connected to the events that brought him there. And Duke was born, too. Disney World had always been a place where secrets could live an unusually long life, but whispers and fears of lawsuits and bad press always reach critical mass eventually, leaving Bart with a severance package and a lifetime pass to the family of theme parks, which he despised.

Walking off the main path, mid-morning, Kiram's iPod in her ear playing some discordant, prepared piano number by John Cage, Lila finds her mental construction of Duke again. It is impossible for him to be what she has built, but she can't help it. She'd always felt entitled to write other people's stories, without getting their sides first. She envisions him now, practicing jumping between basic chords on a tinny acoustic guitar, singing *did you exchange, a walk on part in the war, for a lead role in a cage … how I wish … how I wish you were here*. It's terrible and perfect.

The boys lead Lila to an enclave of bushes of trees behind the science building built into a great hill—it appears to be completely out of sight.

"This is where kids get high," Kiram says.

"The Devil's plant."

"Clouds the heart."

"Give me Bushmills and a woman on my arm."

"Beware El General Viejo if you decide to smoke, you know, to fit in or whatever."

"He and his swat team know about the place."

"El General?" Lila says.

"El General, si."

"Plowman."

"Head of security. The good Dr. Plowman's father. She's the Head of School. He's head of the military. They live together up there."

Charles points to the peak of a hill, a colonial two story, the only one of its kind among the modern rustic mansions.

"Sexless harpy that woman."

"Fun at parties, though."

"I want to see her," Lila says.

"You'll see her soon enough."

"I'm sure she'll be pleasant."

"You know, if you change the definition of pleasant."

After a school lunch of Pad Thai and garlic French fries, the three walk out to the center of the football field and choose numbers on which to lie down, interpreting the clouds like an R-rated Peanuts cartoon. Lila thinks to ask them if they'd intended to go to any classes today, but what does she care? They're not even real. They are there just for her, a karmic reward for some intention she'd discovered with Morely.

After a few too many breast, cock, and masturbatory references, she knows they're going to ask her to join them tonight on some escapade. And she'll accept, agreeing to meet them at some coffee shop where she'll never actually arrive.

Lying on the pillow the previous night, Lila told Morely about her plan to case Bart's house. She ignored him when he questioned her ability to be stealthy. Lila's study of Lev's box of files had somehow overlooked that her father had a housemate, that is, his daughter. It all made sense now, his official retirement from intelligence, his move to and from Walt Disney World, and his swan song, joining his daughter to observe the comings and goings of the elite's spawn. He'd always been their Doberman.

Kiram takes Lila's hand in his and points at a small formation. She never had this kind of ease with boys at this age, and so she soaks it up.

"That one there looks like my mother's nipple."

"What's it like having your dad kill people?"

"It makes me feel like I have to do something," Lila says.

"I see."

"We're just the opposite."

"We're obligated to do something … else."

"Bonded over tragedy."

"Dead family."

"What are you doing out here?" a voice barks.

They look up to see a goateed, well-built, sunglassed man brandishing his walkie-talkie like a Taser. Sitting up, letting the boys do the talking, Lila sees an old man by the security kiosk behind the end zone, hands on his belt, head cocked, needle eyes poking right through hers, and she knows.

SCENE FOUR

It's night. In Pig Man's house, TV is on, financial news. LILA walks down the stairs, stage right—she's been looking around for some time. She touches the recliner and wipes her hand on her jeans.

DIANE enters from stage left, holding a remote, a purse over her shoulder. She's forty-seven, lean, tall, coifed, angular, striking. Somehow she is deafeningly loud without making a sound. There's a strange and horrible knowingness in her eyes—it almost appears kind. She switches off the television.

DIANE: Excuse me. What possible reason do you have for being in my house right now?

LILA: Oh. There you are. Here we are. *[LILA motions to the audience, to YOU.]*

DIANE: Who are you?

LILA: There's time for that. But there's not just me. There are seven others—most important is that handsome one right there. *[She motions to YOU again.]* Can you see him? Because he can see you now.

DIANE: Okay, fine. Whoever you are, you need to leave. Right now. *[DIANE looks at the stairs, walks briskly over to them.]*

LILA: He's upstairs asleep. Please—call the police.

DIANE: Maybe I should tell you I have a gun in my bag, so I'd advise you to get out.

LILA: Maybe I have a gun. *[Again, nodding to YOU]* How does it feel to know you're being watched?

DIANE: Leave. Right now.

LILA: Who am I, Diane? Go ahead. Guess.

DIANE: Okay, fine. If this is supposed to be some kind of special meeting, I think you should use a phone and explain your position. Until then. *[She motions to the door.]*

LILA: Guess. *[DIANE motions again to the door.]* Go ahead,

guess who I am. I want to hear your answer. You're not going to shoot me.

DIANE: You have five seconds.

LILA: I disagree.

DIANE: One, two—

LILA: I'll be the timekeeper. Do-you-know-who-I-am?

DIANE: Okay, fine. You want to play? I know there's some little duchess who claims to be my father's daughter who has been checking up on him.

LILA: Word travels doesn't it?

DIANE: My father is very good at what he does.

LILA: Okay. Now here we are.

DIANE: Yes. Now leave.

LILA: Now, the first thing you did upon meeting me was to threaten me, your sister by blood, with a lethal weapon. There's something in that, don't you think?

DIANE: Oh, you have a little persona.

LILA: What does it feel like to meet another daughter?

DIANE: I acknowledge nothing.

LILA: *[Again, to YOU]* And to know he's watching you?

DIANE: I acknowledge nothing.

LILA: What you acknowledge and what you know are two different things, Diane.

DIANE: I am going to call the police. Your life is about to be ruined in a way you can't imagine.

LILA: Please. Ruin me. It's what I want.

DIANE: I don't care what you want. Do you know what you are?

LILA: A problem.

DIANE: A parasite. No. Do you know what you look like to me?

LILA: No, but you're exactly as I imagined.

DIANE: You look like a suicide. I pick them out every time at school, and I go straight to the psychologists, and I tell them, you know, I say, *you know my track record*. Spot on every time. Like clockwork. Mommy's medicine cabinet. I'd say late thirties for you, after it's all worn off.

LILA: I didn't think you'd be so afraid of me.

DIANE: I'd like to see your gun.

LILA: No.

DIANE: You're going to prison, one way or another. Do you know this?

LILA: *[Again, to YOU]* She can't hurt me.

DIANE: Are you so sure? Because I don't think you are.

LILA: I'm sorry about your mother. That must have been too much, hearing the whispers behind your back. I know you have reasons—for being this way.

DIANE: Oh, you poor thing. You're spoiled *and* stupid. That's so very sad. And so young, so you don't even know. *[LILA takes a few steps toward DIANE. DIANE slides her hand into her purse. LILA smiles and leans against the recliner.]*

LILA: Diane, you know, the funny thing is we could start over right now. I could walk into the room again, and you might see me and—and cry. An actual sister. You have one. I have one. Or you could even get angry, scold me, and take me for a drive, try to give me some big picture speech about letting things lie. The truth is, I'd listen. I don't want to be here. I'm here because I'm sick with the knowledge of him. So are you.

DIANE: I bet being original is important to you. How is that going?

LILA: It really is you. All these years. You're the voice in my head. It's always been you.

DIANE: Okay, fine. I'm going to give you some advice now. Run home and say you're sorry for everything. It was all a mistake. This is your last chance. I don't care who your grandfather is.

LILA: You know, I read a story about you. Would you like to hear it?

DIANE: I couldn't care less.

LILA: Oh, I disagree. *[DIANE crosses to the stairs. LILA puts her hand on her hip, holding the object in her back pocket. DIANE clutches a hand on her purse, stops on the first stair.]*

LILA: There was a curly-haired girl named Ashley in a sixth-grade class of a very strict and admired teacher. Ashley suffered head trauma in a car accident as a little girl, and so she had trouble putting things in order. You could tell her to brush her teeth, put on her pajamas, put away her clothes, and go to bed. She might leave the toothpaste on the toothbrush, leave her clothes on, and fall asleep in the hallway. Anyway, Ashley and her class were on a field trip at the symphony in Chicago, and some very comical children in her class thought it would be a good idea to convince Ashley to sneak outside with them. *[DIANE takes a step up, turns her body to face LILA. LILA follows to the bottom of the stairs.]* And she felt so special, conspiring, you know. And they thought it would be an even better idea to send her across the street to ask the men sitting on cinder blocks if they knew of somewhere close by that sold a particular kind of trading card. She'd also become very gullible, you see, because of the head trauma. And that's a reliably funny joke, to children I mean, how gullible a person can be. Just how gullible can she be? Especially with that enormous birthmark that made her face two-tone. How ugly! And gullible! *[LILA backs up a few steps, toward the front door stage left. She turns to face YOU.]* And so she walked over there, and the boys went back inside to a heroes' welcome. And then it was time for the bus to leave. Where was Ashley? Well, no one had to worry about her anyway. Or did they? But after the funeral *and* the investigation *and* the trial *and* the lawsuit you bounced around for a while, Diane. Los Angeles is a long way from Connecticut. It's a good thing The Pig got that security job, so you could keep sharing a trough. But it really is very sad about your mother, the hospitals, then just, poof, gone. What was it like to help him sever her cord for good?

The lights drop out suddenly. Scrambling on the stairs. A gun fires.

Preface to (as of yet unwritten) Scene 5

As the only authority on the work of Lila Bell, I submit *Burgundy Five Star*, unfinished, as her riskiest, most relevant and experimental work. For that alone, I consider it her most interesting—though I fully acknowledge questions may persist as to whether or not the play *works*, or is in the process of working. I admit I have a special need and a personal interest in redefining, for these purposes, the definition of *work*.

To do that, I ask the following: What is the play supposed to *do*? And in emphasizing *do* over *work*, we automatically reach for the playwright's intent, which caters to the play's strength—Change—and before we go any further, make no mistake, no bullets pass through any flesh in Scene 4. All is still possible, on the table, all players alive. But again, let us remember, while we are in the business of justifying existences, this word—Change—is at the central mission of theater. Change, I'd tell the frightened faces who stared back at me each day for twenty-five years. Change in the characters, perhaps. But change in the *audience*, certainly. While the former is impossible to measure in this play without a conclusive scene, the latter would seem to offer boundless potential, considering the playwright's audience is handpicked, an actual boy, actually related by blood, as it turns out, to her.

The nature and depth of Lila's intent, however, officially precludes me from making any other assessments. Now we have entered into the business of life in motion, off the page, family, love—subjects of which I am painfully, obviously unlearned. Sometimes, though, I tell myself anyway, it takes a glaring and monumental ignorance to make a person uniquely qualified to provide a special clarity; if for no other reason than to supply an opposite perspective in stumbling, plain sight. Even fools love to watch the fool fall—but more so to rise up, from something, against something, so that we may leave with the tiniest inkling that we might do the same.

Lila came to me senior year. She'd been working on something based on an amalgamation of Colonial America, a sort of generalized Puritanical backdrop. She was troubled by Miller's *The Crucible,* because try as she might to place her sympathies with John and Elizabeth Proctor, found guilty of witchcraft, executed, she found herself angry at Miller for demonizing Abigail, Proctor's young mistress, the engine of the Salem Witch Trials.

"No mother. No father. Fifteen years old being repeatedly raped by her employer—"

"Well, that might be a bit strong—"

"Would we not call that rape now?"

"Yes, legally," I said.

"Craft, you've never struck me as an ape. Are you an ape?"

"I suppose so."

"It's basic physiology. Fifteen-year-olds don't have the brain development necessary to enter into a carnal relationship with grown men. Especially angry, repressed, horny predators. They haven't even developed empathy. They can't see consequences. The prefrontal cortex barely exists. They simply can't do it."

"Well—"

"Well what? Oh okay, vaginas yes. Brains no."

"I'm following."

"Miller's a brute and a hypocrite is what I'm saying. All anyone in the play had to do is not *believe* the crazy bitch, and the whole thing would have ended with simple humiliation, shunning, shame, for all of them, shared fairly equally."

"Are you making a case for Abigail as a victim?"

"She's horrible, of course. Miller made sure of that. But yes. Yes I am."

"Abigail gets off rather easily, Lila, compared to her victims. Being hanged at the stake is no picnic you know. She just skips town."

"Don't give me that, Craft. Proctor had his precious *name,* didn't he? Where was Abigail going to go? What was she going to do? She had two choices: prostitute or nun."

"You might have me there."

Back at Morely's now, Lila sits on the front porch, debating whether to rip the last page out of *Burgundy Five Star* and attach it to the back of the notebook with the piece of Scotch tape on her finger. She'd printed out the play and taped each piece into the notebook, where its original draft lay. The piece of paper in question is a letter to Duke, written quickly by design, so as to capture a set of thoughts without the calculation of drama. Calculated candor instead. She simply can't allow herself to let her play stand on its own, can't resist the impulse to link her brother's elbow in hers and whisper directly into his ear.

"You done with it?" Morely says, appearing next to her, carrot juice in hand.

"No, but I'm going to send it anyway. I have to start planning, and there's no way I can really finish," Lila says.

"You know I don't think you should send it to that kid yet? Right?"

"Is that something you want me to actually answer?"

"Nope, just going on record again."

"Stick your record up your ass."

"It's liable to upset the little guy, don't you think?"

"I said—"

"All right. Up my ass. I heard you. No need to jump right to penetrating orifices. What is it, 8:15? I just woke up."

"What if I love you?" Lila says.

"Don't know."

"What if you love me?"

"I'm not asking the question. You are. I thought a cop was following me, yesterday. I tell you that?"

"No," Lila says.

"I must have made a dozen left turns—with me every time. I think your old man's got it figured out, been making some calls."

"Probably. And don't call him that. Call him *the* old man, not *your* old man."

"I get it, I get it. Shit though, it's too early in the game for lawyers."

"It's never too early for lawyers, Morely. Never."

Lila rips the letter out of the notebook and attaches it to the back of her play with two-page-wide pieces of transparent tape. She eyes the notebook, the front cover with its diminutive sketches of coffee shop faces, meaningful, overheard sentence fragments, and coffee stains. Her fingers run over the metal spirals, up and down, between the spaces. She presses her palm against the front cover. It feels like it should have a fuse on it, like it should give its own unappreciated gifts at Christmas, like it ought to have its own pullout couch on family vacations, like everyone walks on eggshells around it—except Duke.

Temporary Epilogue

Dearest Duke,

Hi.

If you are reading this letter before reading the play (as I probably would), then I just want to thank you. Believe me when I say I have an Everest of things to say to you, mostly involving how my recent discovery of your existence has, strangely enough, motivated me to rip myself ... out of myself. When I go back in, I'm hoping to add a few things that fall under the general jurisdiction of love. First, though, there is a fifth and final scene to write into this play, which I don't think I'll be able to even begin before getting some kind of reply from you. I'm nervous—you know that line about unringing a Bell (get it? Bell?), it can't be done. But—and maybe this is crazy—more than anything, I'll be a kid watching the mailbox, standing by the window, pacing, waiting for some form of you to wind up in the mailbox (address included on the inside cover).

If you are reading this after reading the play (as I think you are), then you can well imagine I've already lined up a bevy of possible reactions you might have to this work. Each one includes you actually responding in some way (note, again, the address on the inside cover). You've probably surmised that I'm presumptuous, so I'll skip that whole bit. But I did consider, for a brief moment, that it was possible that you might just toss these pounds of paper in the trash, you know, sleeping dogs and so forth. Duke, I'm not saying (exactly) that we're in this together, but then again, here I am and there you are. And Him. Just that fact, combined with the circumstances—well, we're in this, and *together* can mean a lot of things. I'm open to your thoughts on that one.

If you are reading this with a furrowed brow and more than a touch of nausea, just know that the number of people who love you has recently increased by one. That may be problematic, I grant you, but you may also have surmised that I'm not especially shy about giving people new problems if I can reasonably (or not) justify it.

So, what do you think?

Love,

Your sister,

Eagerly,

Always,

Now,

Lila Bell

p.s. The book of stamps included in the envelope should be self-explanatory, right?

p.p.s The $500 was a last minute addition. You know—if.

Part III
The Kingdom

1

Three a.m. and it's hard to believe this shit. A week ago these people were strangers to me. They've fucked up my fucked-up life, which was, at one point, fucked up properly, almost exactly the way I wanted it fucked up, with just a few exceptions—all right, many exceptions maybe, but I had a plan, not a plan, but an M.O., a doctrine. I like to know what I'm saying. I'm industrious and attentive compared to my peers, who don't seem like peers, not the way people talk about having peers—I just don't like that word, peer. It's vague. I will, I think, be decent looking someday, or, at least, have a kind of *look*. I could have ridden these qualities indefinitely.

I'll get my GED—already did the initial paperwork. The whole thing only takes six hours and costs $65. It's shocking more people don't do it. I didn't tell Mom. It'd make her happy for a minute, but I can't tell her. I don't know why. I know why, but I can't explain it, not now, sitting here on my bed, stifling tears, stuffing clean and dirty socks and underwear into my backpack, Iverbe gone—where? The void. Iverbe. The spiral notebook. That lunatic—no, she's not a lunatic. I'm sorry. I'm not sorry. Anyway, now I have to *do something*.

At EPCOT and with my few acquaintances, they said, *Why, Duke? You're throwing your life away! You're not the type! That's what drug dealers do, pimps, thugs!* They wanted reasons, or one good one, so I just told them as plainly as I could. I need to see my life more clearly, and high school turns my eyes to white noise. *Just wait one more year! College!* they said. But I'd been waiting, in graffiti desks, in my own pulse, no-pulse dreamless sleep. I was actively flunking Calculus. There was no change on the horizon—I know—I used to sit there and stare at it for hours, as the sun set.

When it came time for me to join Walt's ranks along with Mom and Iverbe last year, I made it clear it was EPCOT or nothing.

Iverbe thought it was disrespectful to Walt to make a demand like that—which was, by some transitive property, disrespectful to Iverbe—but I didn't see it like that. I knew the other parks would eat me, slowly, piece by piece, until all I had left was an imagined smile.

Split into two distinct themed sections, Future World and The World Showcase, EPCOT is the only one of Walt's parks that doesn't subscribe to the *hub and spoke* philosophy, which is a blatant architectural pander to merchandising, funneling guests through a labyrinth of stores as they enter and exit.

"I'm Disney born," I said to my group of three interviewers. It was Mom's first job. She loved it, had a whole group of Walt friends, a few she knew from her acting classes at Kissimmee Community College. She thought she might audition for the shows at some point. But she says cocaine was making a big comeback at the time, and she got pregnant with me, so she ended up having to quit Walt and school. I think she always knew Walt would call, eventually, back to the fireworks at the end of every night. The whole essence of Iverbe and Mom was their love of Walt. Even before his breakdown, at any mention of Walt, Iverbe would say, *a genius, a man of action, pure and simple.*

"I'm a Main Street U.S.A. kid," I said, laying it on thick, but honest, too, "you know that, from my file there. I just think that gives me the right to at least ask. I want to work Spaceship Earth. It's my favorite building in the world, I mean, I simply want to welcome people to my favorite place, and help them out the door, you know, after they experience it, like a guide, or a shaman. I mean, just think how authentic my smile would be, which is worth something to Walt—authenticity. It just makes sense, but, you know, I'd also really appreciate it."

"All right, son," the old man said, a sort of emotionally neutral cul-de-sac'd grandpa who seemed to be in charge. "You can start there if it means so much to you. Here's your welcome packet."

The centerpiece of Future World (and all of EPCOT for that matter) is Spaceship Earth. It concerns itself with the evolution of human communication, from prehistoric man to the space age. I found out from Teddy, the coolest of the *old guard cast members* (80 plus), that the whole thing was inspired by the work of R. Buckminster Fuller, who Teddy contended the smartest person of all time. He was the creator of the geodesic dome concept, and the phrase, Spaceship Earth. Teddy let me borrow some of his books—I was shocked to find pieces of my own mind on the page, but, you know, infinitely smarter.

"Yep. Bucky got to see it, the year before he died. I helped him on and off the ride. That was opening day—glorious," Teddy said.

"What did he think of it?" I asked, but Teddy was lost in a big smile, still picturing himself with his hero.

The guests all call it *the giant golf ball*, young and old alike, snickering, misunderstanding, thinking they're the first to make the connection, which is an unavoidable one. Even the Disney marketing people call it that now on the website, which is blasphemous and cynical. But truly, it's a grand design for a settlement on the moon or mars, a central building, a gathering place. The uniforms aren't degrading either, just sort of gas-station-attendant-in-space, very blue collar and minimal. Comfortable and loose. They make the girls look boxy, but sexy, taunting you with mystery, what's underneath, waiting. A bunch of good people really, working Spaceship Earth.

Dame Judi Dench's voice greeted me every day in the vehicles. I took the test-ride at the beginning of the morning shift, alone, Dame Judi and me, through cave painting, ancient Egypt, Greece, Rome, the Renaissance, the Industrial Revolution, space. It's wildly optimistic about the future of humanity—I mean, it has no problem whatsoever disregarding the massive bloodshed that awaits future generations. Not to mention the new species of, like, super-sociopathic geniuses with nano-computers in their bloodstreams. But that's what Walt is all about, man—The Future is Good. I've come to need Him, I know this, He knows this. The question is whether or not you can identify His true essence, and then, if you can stomach all that it is, and then, become it. Obviously most of the people who wait in line and ride don't know an asshole from a blowhole when it comes to Walt or Bucky or the future of humanity; they're just trying to make it through the day without losing their kids in the hordes, where they'd be minced and deep fried inside the stiff-battered casing that covers Walt's chicken. Kid strips in red baskets for their parents to chew on while pretending to consult a park map, terrorized.

For me, though, Spaceship Earth (and the rest of Walt's Kingdom really) felt like home from the start, reassuring and warm. I rode it with goose bumps when I was seven, Iverbe and Mom crunched next to me—our honeymoon they called it—Jeremy Irons doing the narration then, a better script, more subtle and open-ended than the one they wrote for the Dame Judi update. But anyone who knew anything knew the real bitch's brew was Cronkite.

"You want to know how it is, listen to this," Teddy said, and shoved headphones and a cassette player in my face one morning before my test ride. I wished that I'd been born a decade and a half earlier. What played was his cassette copy of the original narration, done by Walter Cronkite, the old voice of trust. Ascending through the ride, I flashed in my mind to a clip I'd seen of him pausing to hold back a tear before telling my grandparents that Kennedy was dead. And now he'd passed on to the infinite, or nowhere, the same placeless place maybe. This was the essence of Spaceship Earth, what made it home to me. It was without location, promising the same for eternity.

"Duke!" my shift manager, Vand, said, waving, walking with his usual urgent purpose out of the ride's darkness. This was a few months ago, right before the end of junior year. The park was packed and cooking. When it got like that, guests didn't know what they were even standing in line for anymore. They were just looking for something that appeared organized and would lead to air conditioning.

"What happened?" I said. "Is everything okay?"

"I-uh, talk to you a second?"

Vand always tried to comb his little patch of dark hair straight back, but a natural wave made it poof up into a hair beanie. Every day I worked he'd ask me how my mom was, and I'd try not to think about why he was asking.

"I don't know how to say this, Duke, so I'll just say it. Did you quit high school?"

"Yeah. Last week. You know, it was kind of strange. I thought there'd be some kind of intervention, but all you do is stop showing up. "

"Why did—never mind. Listen. This is hard, because darn it, I like you a heck of a lot, and you do a real good job, real good, really, but you seem to be unaware of policy."

"Should I start shaving? I didn't think the hair on my face was thick enough to worry about."

"Well, yeah," Vand said, peering at my upper lip, "you probably should. Mustache is coming in a little. But Duke, you can't work an attraction crew if you drop out of high school. You're going to have to go to I.F.S. right away."

"Why do I need to be in high school to work an A.C.?"

"The whole image of it. Precedent, stuff like that," he said.

"Wait. What's I.F.S.?"

"Invisible food service. Kitchen work. I can put in a good word for you, keep you out of that hellhole spinning restaurant at The Land. I don't know what they call it now, like Harvest of Plenty, but something else. That damn dog on the ride just keeps barking and barking, and you can hear it in the restaurant, the kitchen, in the john."

This was the only time Vand ever cursed, talking about his

time working The Land.

"You forget it's not real," he continued, "and it sounds like it's got dementia. Used to give me real dark thoughts at night—when I worked that crew. The waiters petitioned to get the thing muted or just turned down. You know how that stuff goes. Yeah right."

"I have to say, Vand, I didn't consider this at all."

"Doesn't sound like you considered anything. But you don't have to go if you don't want."

"No?"

"You could, you know, resign."

"Oh," I said. "Okay, I'll take I.F.S. You think you could get me into America?"

"Done. Wait, why America?" Vand said, alarmed.

"I'm kind of partial to the show."

"Duke, you should really think about going back to school."

"I think I'll just go over and be in America for now. Does Carrie know?"

"She was the one who told me you quit."

Carrie was the first person I met when they assigned me to Spaceship Earth. We started the same day. She had vicious acne and a smile with wings. The hair on her forearms was thick. It planted visions in my head of proportional pubic thickness. She made it obvious, as often as possible, walking side by side on the moving platform, guiding guests into the vehicles, that she thought of me as a child. Seventeen months older was all she was, but I guess I come off that way to some people. I don't know what it is that distorts people's vision of me to the point where I'm wearing pajamas with feet, and a bowl haircut with a red Kool-Aid ring around my mouth. If anything, I feel like a pornographic cartoon when I look in the mirror. I see a sweaty wolf, smoking a giant, phallic cigar. It's puzzling.

I used to imagine sneaking into the park at night with Carrie. We'd undress each other on the moving platform, slip into one of the hard, bright blue plastic vehicles, ride it straight through twenty or so times, fuck like some violent ballet, get a few bruises, smile secretively about it the next day. Or, we would fuck deliberately, trying to stop time as the vehicles moved from cave paintings to the Information Age, the style all depending upon her mood, of course, me being flexible and pretty amorphous. We'd sit and talk in between sessions, letting our parts cool, listening to Dame Judi's soothing, impish, knowing alto, to the animatronics through the annals of time, we'd astral project ourselves to the light bulb stars. It became a default thought in my head, this fantasy, in line for coffee, *smooth moist entry,* at a stop-light, *my finger in her ass crack,* cooking with Mom, *her whispers with a hand around my cock.* It was problematic.

At the three-week mark of thinking only of taking Carrie, Carrie taking me, I felt a wave wash over first my scalp, then my throat—and an external wave of recklessness that somehow permeated my skin and became unstoppable. Carrie was trying and failing to pull gum off her shoe on the moving platform, and I froze, overcome, almost eaten by the teeth at the end, where moving platform meets earth.

"Carrie."

"I'm trying to get this gum off. Wait. Crap, now it's on my hand."

"Can I ask you something for real?"

"Are you kidding? I can never tell."

"No, I need to ask you," I said.

"You sound serious when you're kidding and vice versa."

"Do you think you, would you have sex?"

"Would I? What makes you think I haven't?"

"No, I'm sorry, with me."

"What do you mean with you?"

"Do you think we might have sex?"

"I don't—Duke, why?" she grimaced and looked up from her shoe.

"No, it's sounds different asking out loud, but I think about it, me and you," I said.

"You selling that as news or what?"

"Exactly. I know you know. That's why I'm asking."

"Why would I do that?" she seemed to scoff, frowning inwardly. "I don't like that you asked me like that."

I looked up into the Geodesic dome—darkness—Spaceship Earth just kept rolling along. A few seconds later, after hopping off the moving platform and removing the gum fully, we began anew, as if nothing had happened. She talked cheerfully about genetic engineering, *when has it gone too far, what kinds of alterations should and shouldn't be allowed*, a favorite topic of hers. After graduating high school in Nebraska last year, she started Walt's gap-year internship program, where you live inside Walt, in the dorm (which is rigged up with virus-size video cameras, or so I'm told), and you work at one of the parks for a year before starting college. She's headed to Amherst to do pre-med, which sounds impressive to me. Her identical twin, free of acne, is in a coma in Omaha. Carrie stays optimistic, but it seems obvious to me that Walt is an escape for her, like almost everyone. I've never felt bad about my lust, coma twin or no, it had the power to heal, I believed that.

I guess I also thought, in one of my mind's black holes, that I'd be rewarded for being such a big person, elevating myself above caring about the pus minefield of her face. Actually, though, it was her unfortunate condition that made me think she'd even consider me viable; otherwise, I thought, she wouldn't have the time to address me. She always looked so driven and mental, which made me want to balance her with hot fingers, squeeze breath through her mind to make it bellow like a train whistle. I had no specific skills that made me think I could accomplish this. Just boundless self-doubt offset by desire.

No fool, Carrie, the red patches and whiteheads had a purpose for her, tiny badges of courage, scarlet letters she could defy, very high-school-English. Her face also gave her a degree of empathy that she instinctually lacked, and recognized she lacked. She was able to get something out of the embarrassment and shame, or at least note the deepening effect of the experience. She wore it well, with pride even.

Leaving work that day after Vand told me I was getting kicked off Spaceship Earth, I felt the panic set in, of losing Carrie, our bond as crewmates, our uniforms that seemed to suggest we were somehow the same.

When she grabbed me in the parking garage yesterday, Christmas Day, after being separated so long, months of working about as far away from each other as two people could at EPCOT, and tore my mouth open with her lips and tongue, impossibly quick and muscular, I was shocked to the point of inertia. She had no idea what was happening to me, the convergence of shit at home. That alone felt so good, being outside of it for a moment. She opened her eyes and said, "Come on, Duke," and it took another five seconds for me to realize time hadn't stopped for her, just me. I gave her a piece of my mind after that, though, which by her breath, halting and loud, I know she liked.

"Merry Christmas," she said.

Nothing more than mouth to mouth, but I felt it there, in her lungs, a depth. I've never seen Carrie act, not even once, without some kind of plan. It was my first kiss.

What happened to trigger Carrie's action was seeing me at lunch yesterday with Sigrid, a Swedish girl I met a few days ago. She just started working *The Maelstrom* ride and in the connecting store at the Norway entry in the World Showcase. Fresh-off-the-boat Sigrid.

The World Showcase, the second half of EPCOT, comprises a spectrum of nations, overblown travel bureaus with striking, genius reproductions of famous landmarks; rides and short films; good, expensive restaurants; and shopping, of course. The idea is a sort of permanent World's Fair with cast members from the host nations, or, in the case of Norway and Mexico especially, somewhere in the general vicinity.

Sigrid and I were in the Future World break room, my old hangout when I worked Spaceship Earth, away from the prying eyes of the World Showcase. A stream of characters in space gear—Goofy, Donald, Minnie, the originals—marched in, one by one removing their heads. They glistened, completely soaked through. Minnie bent over, spitting into the bushes.

"Goddamn it, it's hot today, heavy you know?"

Goofy concurred with a nod and a back adjustment. Sigrid and I sat down at a table, and I pulled out a four-inch notebook and pencil. I told her it'd take about three days to get to Los Angeles, and we could figure something out once we got there. But Carrie must have assumed that I was giving Sigrid my ear to later receive her other parts, her Nordic roundness, the succulent pear shape she commanded that gave a special dignity to the fruit. Nothing like that was happening, though, not in the slightest.

It was completely unintentional to force Carrie's hand, to cause her to unfold and concede that she wanted me after all, for her very own, wayward Duke, the dropout, the quiet flake, the good dog, the bag of nerves and ejaculate. It's strange to think of her in this moment, her mouth and hands, to think that I'm thinking of her hands, Iverbe gone two weeks now, no trace, Mom in shambles, the *Burgundy Five Star* notebook, me half out the door, just gathering a few more things before meeting sweet Sigrid at the Greyhound station tonight.

2

I've always loved the bus. School and public transit. Somehow, for my entire life, even as a pacifist, or maybe just a coward I guess, I managed to sidestep the role of the sacrificial lamb on the ride to school and back home. I had a friend or two over the years who'd sometimes come to the defense of whichever pitiful creature the bus thugs decided was the outlet for their shitty home lives. I had to shake my head. The feeble rescue would get shouted down, or worse, there'd be a slap or a threat of some makeshift pencil weapon. Sharpened and inevitable. The tormentors would never allow that space to go unfilled. They need to torment. Anyway I used the time to watch out the window, at the big nothing of Florida, and just think.

This city bus, at sundown, headed for the Greyhound station, is filled with a dozen people who want nothing to do with each other. I'm using this pack of rubberbanded 4 X 6 notecards and a Bic Stick as a shield and sword. I'm going to fill them with the words I find for my thoughts. I'll dedicate them to her—right now I can't bring myself to call her what she says she is—I'll drop them in a Ziploc bag as they occur, like a bag of questions. Then I can dump them out on her floor and let her put them all back together as one big answer.

On a pink notecard, I write:

We're almost there.
We're thinking about our almost journeys,
what comes just before.
We're either starving
or we're trying to digest something terrible.
We have the same glossy film on our faces.
We're farting and in denial about it.
We're palm trees.
We're strip malls.

We're trying not to ask
what the fuck we're actually doing,
on this bus, right now
But I got to thinking
about infinity,
how kissing Carrie … is,
how holding Sigrid … is,
how aiming myself at you … is
sewn onto the whole roll
of toilet paper
Hope, I guess, is infinity,
which seems to be what we're in.
I wish I wished for just that
instead of what I wish for—
or, even better,
that I'd just stop wishing
and use a different verb
as my go-to.

Front and back filled, I drop it in the big freezer Ziploc and feel a psychic burn on my shoulder. I instinctively turn around to see the source: a castaway's bearded face and body in far too many layers of clothes. Usually this would make me at least uneasy, being the object of a homeless stare, but tonight he seems like an audience, like rehearsal is over, the lights are up.

"Hello there," I say.

After a few seconds of no visible response, he looks down into his Arizona Iced Tea can.

"Good luck on your travels," I say, turning back around.

Sixteen days ago, my friend Melvin told me about *The Golden Ring,* which is roughly half my reason for being here on this surprisingly clean orange bus seat, instead of at home with Mom. It was the day before Iverbe left, a smoldering mid-December afternoon, the weatherman off by 15 degrees. Maybe the sudden burst of heat that day finally cooked the stew of shit that was on simmer inside of Iverbe. Inside me, too.

"That's what they call it? The Golden Ring?" I said.

"You got a better name or something?"

"I would think Swedes could be more creative."

"Fits, I think."

Melvin is, or now was I guess, my shift manager at the eatery adjacent to The American Adventure show, where I've been since getting the boot from Spaceship Earth. The show is sort of a remedial American History course performed by a cast of forty-three animatronic actors, and narrated to perfection by especially convincing versions of Mark Twain and Benjamin Franklin—Walt's ideal Americans. It's a ridiculous understatement to say it lacks the proper amount of horror and shame. All it has is a fairly hollow nod to the millions murdered and enslaved. There's a Chief Joseph scene. Frederick Douglass too. The show ends with a sweeping, musical number, a straight patriotic pander so well crafted (*America! Spread your golden wings! Sail on Freedom's wind across the sky!*) that I still shed a few tears when the song pauses and Kennedy flashes up there on the screen, asking us to *ask not*. There's a great Civil War number too, *Two Brothers*, minor key and catchy. The proper, mustachioed brother enlists in Lincoln's army, and the other, a shit-talking cracker, is decked out in slavery worshipping gray. They're assembled with Mom and Dad and little sissy, taking one of those new-fangled photographs on Mom's birthday. As the song goes on, Johnny Reb disappears from the photograph, his body strewn on the battle-field, full of holes. Great stuff. Sometimes being manipulated feels so good, I just can't resist. And I don't want to even try—that's the key. As if it's genuinely touching that someone cares enough to bother manipulating the likes of me. You could say I've developed whatever's at the poles of mixed feelings about The American Adventure.

"Anyway, all those blonde bitches over there are getting

turned the fuck out. Most of them won't come back from it, not really. Poor blonde bitches," Melvin said, filling the fry cooker with oil, swollen with genuine pity.

"Were they prostitutes in Sweden, before they got here?"

"Some of 'em, maybe. It's a gray area."

"Melvin, what's gray about it?"

"Shit. They's all kinds of currency, all kinds," he said.

I had no idea it had been happening for over a year, and I guarantee none of the attraction crews knew. The attraction crews in Future World couldn't leave each other alone for five seconds at work or in phone-brain. It was crushing, the endless, lonely chatter. There is no such thing as a kept secret among the Future World attraction crews—only false rumors—so if anyone, on any crew, knew about a prostitution ring being run out of the International Village, everyone would've known in seconds—less probably—whatever increment of time is just shy of immediate. There's a divide, it's true, between the immigrant workers of the International Village and us local yokes, but there are so many eyes in Walt's Kingdom, always watching, watching everything.

I met Melvin on my first day after getting transferred to the American kitchen. He just might have saved my life. He's a super-sized-super-human Black Sabbath half-Panamanian, into light bondage magazines, photography, heavy music. He'd been making hot dogs, chicken fingers and the other deep-fried baskets for six years and was finally promoted to shift manager. He ran the whole place with his mind. Melvin is a big man, width and breadth, and for some reason, my own ignorant preconceived notions I guess, I was surprised when after a morning shift, he asked me if I wanted to come by his place in Kissimmee. A couple of his friends were coming over to jam. From the first note, he played like a puppeteer and a wild boar. He seemed to be manipulating the tones from three feet above the neck, with bouts of heavy snarling. It was monstrous—full of sorrow and rage, with sections of raw freedom. I asked him to teach me a few things to get me started.

"Good," he'd said, "You should learn to play. You're a traveler."

"I am? What does that mean?"

"Nothing," he said.

In Melvin's reality construct, nothing has meaning, but everything is related and symbolic, a paradox he finds fitting and impossible to control to any degree whatsoever.

I bought a severely used white Dean for a hundred bucks, and after three sessions, I thought it was going pretty well—slow, but I was starting to feel something awake and moving in there, in the strum, in my thumb, loosening on its hinge. We began keeping our guitars and a couple microphones in the trunk, and after our shifts we'd drive in his Aerostar up to the top level of the parking garage and make recordings on his Fostex 4-track for an hour or so. If Walt had known, or better yet if He'd heard some of the music we made, doomsday carnival dirges and seal barking chants, He'd have fired us both on the spot, had us arrested for something. He could make anything stick. He had the law.

Even though I believed Melvin completely about the existence of *The Golden Ring,* I still had a difficult time fathoming all this was going on under Walt's nose. There was an ever-present smell of security in the air and a room underground where people were pummeled with bully sticks and chairs.

"Well, it's easy enough. The girls take turns playing the pimp and the pimped. You know how they got all those $300 sweaters in the Norway store?"

"Yeah," I said.

"And all that other shit, you know, sixty-year-old ladies stop and consider, hold up, put back, hold up again, try on, frown at, put back, all that?"

"Yeah."

"While that shit's going on, there's some half-bald fucker

holding bags looking dickless, thinking about all the pussy he wished he'd've got before it was too late. Or maybe he isn't thinking about it, but he's still thinking about it."

"Right."

"When the girls see some shit like that, a bell goes off."

"Like telepathy?"

"No, like an actual bell. See, you got two girls. One scouting and the other on what they call *the stage*. When the scout spots a mark, she rings the bell and the other girl hustles over to her spot. She walks over and asks him if he'd direct his attention to the girl currently on view by the window. Does he like the look of her? *Yes*. Isn't she a fine Nordic woman? *Yes*. Wouldn't he like to meet her at so-and-so place, at so-and-so time?"

"Holy shit."

"He either asks for the address or he gets so scared, he tears his wife away from the Teflon ski pants or whatever the fuck and gets the fuck out of there."

"Somebody would report it," I said.

"Pickpockets."

Some grease popped out of the deep fryer and caught my arm, which happened routinely throughout the day.

"What?"

"Oliver Twist shit. Little blond boys. They train 'em."

I remembered watching the musical version, *Oliver!*, with Mom—she knows every song by heart—when I was five and being charmed out of my head by Fagin, who sent the Godforsaken orphans out on the street to steal for him. The Artful Dodger, the greatest of the kid pickpockets, was my hero. Bill Sykes, just a dime-a-dozen thug really, was the big bad villain, and here was Fagin, the worst kind of parasite, living off the labor of homeless children, getting all the great musical numbers. It might have saved time if Mom had told me this is how it works in our fucked-up world instead of enchanting me with her spirited renditions of "Be Back Soon," and "You've Got to Pick a Pocket or Two," complete with Cockney and wild hand gestures.

"First he picks up the sign from the scout when the bell goes off. Then the blond boy does the job, and the scout walks over to the mark to sell the girl on the stage."

Melvin explained that if the prospective customer left after the approach, he'd eventually have to retrieve his property from the register, where the girls made sure *he knew* that *they knew* his name, address, all of it, and that they were fond of writing inventive letters to wives.

"How could they pull it off enough to support however many people are in on it?"

"Man, your head was so far down that chick's pants on Spaceship Earth, you didn't see a damn thing. How many sorry motherfuckers come through here? They get three time slots filled per girl per night—somebody getting rich."

It was true there was only The Carrie Situation in my thoughts most of the time. I'd barely even been seeing the guests waiting in line. They were props to me, except for splashes of horror and joy in kids' faces. It was the extremes that pulled me out of my head and made me grateful to work in such a place.

"Up in this bitch," Melvin said, waving an index finger in a spiraling motion, indicating the kitchen, "we don't see shit, but we hear shit."

"Well, I have to see this," I said.

"If you do, be discreet. And go in your civvies on a day off, not on your break. And don't say nothing to your white buddies."

"Melvin, obviously. And I don't have any, not really," I reminded him.

"It may take a while, but it'll happen. They turn that shit over, from what I'm told. Gold," he added.

"Yeah, I just can't believe it. I don't see how—"

"Man, do you really think Walt doesn't know?"

It was impossible to put *The Golden Ring* out of my mind the rest of that day, but I didn't have the guts right away to play the part of detective in the back of the store, maybe pretend to be enchanted by the sleek design of some Scandinavian toys, all the while noting each lump of middle-aged desperation and his proximity to the working girls. I'd actually stopped going to the parks on my days off after Walt demoted me. Something was missing. Plus, I spent all my time off playing guitar, badly, learning anyway. So instead I spent a few days sick with fantasy, in my bed, in my headphones and unzipped work khakis, envisioning a Swedish girl, about my age, a little older maybe. She'd tell me to drop by her dorm room, where she'd answer the door in a short silk robe, just finishing up painting her toenails powder blue. She'd give me a lesson, full of patience and sweetness and sweat, and tell me how I'd break hearts someday. I'd hand her the $200, but we'd exchange a look that clearly meant the money was just an absurd circumstance. Really, we'd just merged desires. I could sell that story to my own imagination.

In the middle of one particularly inventive session, though, I was ripped out by the sound of mumbled panic. I found Mom in her candy-striped Main Street USA uniform, now a full two hours late, frantically digging through a box of files.

"Iverbe left, Duke."

"Left where?"

Mom's face was a scrambled puzzle, her layers and years bubbling through her eyes and mouth.

"He's driving to Mexico," she said.

"What? How? Do we even have passports? Don't you need a passport?"

"Missouri. The town, Mexico, he grew up there."

"Oh, yeah. The LTD will never make it to any Missouri. Did someone die?"

"I don't know. He was packing a suitcase at four in the morning. He came over and gave me a kiss on the cheek, said he was going to Mexico, and was gone before I was even fully awake."

"Okay. Aren't you supposed to be at Walt right now?"

"Yeah. I can't. I'm scared, Duke."

"Why?"

"He didn't call in to work. They called and asked where he was."

"He didn't call in? Iverbe didn't call in? Shit."

Iverbe missed one day of work in four years of service to Walt, and that was because he was getting a cast put on his wrist due to a fall he took at the Ticketing and Transportation Center. He was trying to stop a runaway stroller with baby aboard, or so he thought. In his singular focus, he didn't hear the people shouting *It's just blankets*! Good thing, too, because he didn't quite get there in time, and the baby, safe on her dad's shoulder wearing Mickey ears, would've catapulted into the lake.

"He's been difficult to talk to lately, for a while now, I mean, you know. And I just thought—I don't know what I thought. I didn't think anything. I didn't care enough to think about it. I just ignored it," she said. "We never even went and put up the Christmas tree, Duke."

Mom cried, and I wanted to say, don't worry, it'll be fine, but the likelihood of that, considering Iverbe's failure to call Walt—and December 10th and no tree. It's true. I noticed changes in Iverbe when I quit school. His signature historical rants ceased immediately. No more talk about *the epic battle within Walt, greed vs. dream, the great society of tomorrow hinging upon such battles to save our culture*. And from the time he came into my life, I always caught Iverbe picking his nose, and he'd clumsily transition it into a sort of face scratch. He'd stopped any and all efforts to transition after I quit school. Even if I stared at him, he'd just go on digging.

"Maybe he just doesn't want to conduct the Monorail anymore."

"Maybe, I don't know," she said.

"What family does he have in Mexico besides Uncle Keith?"

"Uncle Keith died, Duke, you know that."

"Oh, right. Sorry."

"Oh, what does it matter? He doesn't talk about anyone. I know he has aunts, cousins, I don't know."

"Maybe he'll call," I said.

"His phone is on the dresser."

"Maybe he just needed to get out of Walt for a while. That's understandable."

"For someone else."

"I know," I said. "I know," meaning just the opposite.

Now I see plastic, day-after Christmas trees shining their light through the thick bus windows, sending dull knives into my eyes. About once every block or two, I see a row of the now-popular Christmas penguins holding red and green packages. It confounds and angers me, that we accept this, these penguins, it's just wrong, geographically. But deep down I know they have just as much right to be here as I do. I'm just like them, a mistake.

I finish another index card. Feeling that familiar burn on my shoulder, I turn around to meet the castaway's eyes. He's using, I think, a hot butter knife to slice me open.

"What do you keep writing down?"

"Nothing," I tell him.

The way his hair juts out of his red stocking cap, appearing both wet and hard, tells me I've just said the wrong thing.

"That ain't true. You writing something. Why?"

"Poems, like thoughts, for—they're for my sister," I call her for the first time out loud. "I don't know her, so ..."

"I read it?"

"Sure."

He takes the card from me and holds it between both sets of thumb and index fingers. I can see, now that he's leaning back, that he appears to be half-dressed as an attempt at Santa Claus, on the bottom, these sort of puffy red sweatpants tucked into black boots. Or the pants, I guess, could be warm-up pants from the early nineties, which you can get by the truckload at any Good Will in Florida, old people dying off and all. He steadies himself, preparing to read my poem aloud. The voice that comes out is reverent. He reads just like an eight-year-old.

"I keep thinking about you,
and this sort of plank
attached to nothing.
I inch my way out
and underneath me
is a wavy, moving platform
surrounded by a black ..."

He shows me the card and points to a word.

"Vacuum," I say.

"vacuum.
I can jump, or wait to be pushed
(by you maybe?)
but either way I land
on the platform,
explode in ink,
'The ink is how you lived!'
It's a stranger's voice
(as ink I can still hear)
and it scares me
to be this afraid forever."

He looks it over once more, hands me back the card, and looks out his window, as if we're now done.

"Thanks for reading it."

"That's no good," he says, without looking at me.

"Okay."

With just his eyes, he enters our shared space again.

"What do you have to be afraid of?"

"I'm not sure, I guess."

"I don't like your poem. You shouldn't give it to your sister."

He is right. It is different than afraid. I scratch out the last two lines and replace them with three:

And it makes me panic
to think of being
nothing forever.

I look over my shoulder to get his approval, but my neighbor's eyes are out the window, covered in a layer of the past.

The bus rolls to a stop, and the air inside rushes out, squeezing all the thoughts out of our minds. Now each of us has to direct ourselves toward an actual place and destination, toward other living people, toward their problems, toward a new toward. We're going there, to meet them and take on more troubles. Sweet Sigrid is inside this depot, actually waiting for me. We have plans. Together we'll be all right, I think, or at least we'll get somewhere. I catch the massive driver's face in the rearview and we lock eyes. *I didn't do it,* I tell him without speaking, and he rips the door open and barks.

3

Ten days ago Mom filed a missing persons report, but nothing turned up, or at least we couldn't get the police to call us back. I called the station every day to check, so Mom wouldn't have to, but I'd just sit on hold, listening to all the public service campaigns, warnings about abusing old people and watching for suspicious people—be especially watchful, it said, at the airport, theme parks, grocery stores, gas stations, hospitals, malls, schools, libraries, public pools, in, on, and around buses. Sitting there on hold every day in our beige kitchen, looking up at Mom's collection of Sergeant Pepper collector's plates, listening to the carefully chosen female police officer's stern voice, I just couldn't picture Iverbe, just doing Iverbe things, at any of these places. But I could feel a lack of Iverbe in each one.

And just six days ago, a Saturday, which is by law the most crowded day at all the parks, I woke up to angry rain. I knew it was time to see *The Golden Ring* for myself. If nothing else, I thought it'd be a distraction from watching Mom attempt to busy herself, trying to keep her mind off Iverbe and the liquor store across the street. She hadn't had a drink since before their wedding, seven years. I could feel that rock turning to mud.

The force of Florida rain is only duplicated, from what I've seen on TV, in the planet's rain forests. These are truly the best days to be at the parks, to experience the ugliness, the tiny generous gestures, the little truths that only show themselves in all out crisis mode. The leashed children, the cups of cocoa, the shrieks and the laughter. The rides are sweeter, more urgent, because they become necessary escapes from ferocious Mother Nature. The colors and details dreamt up by Walt's Imagineers leap out at you since the eye isn't in constant recovery from the searing Florida sun.

Of course, the stores are packed and the parks rake it in, in terms of merchandise and concessions. And while I believe Walt does truly love to see the kids bursting with delight, imploring their parents to brave the seventy-five-minute wait for the third pass on Space Mountain, he's sure as shit not oblivious to the beeps and swipes at the register. Basically, the downpour seemed like an ideal circumstance for hovering in the Norway store for a thirty-minute detective session, ride *The Maelstrom*, watch the pro-oil propaganda film (*The Spirit of Norway*), and head back to the store for another session. Repeat the process until I witnessed an actual transaction. I knew I'd have to keep moving so I didn't attract Park Security. You don't want to attract Park Security. These are serious fucking people. Melvin told me most of them were plucked from the FBI, CIA, NSA, or other intelligence. Melvin also told me about the bunkers where they administer the interrogations and occasional beatings, but I made him stop before he got to any particulars, otherwise I'd just picture it over and over, all day long, every day.

Last Saturday the sheer force of water was too much, the stores and rides were belching drenched guests of all ages and shapes back into the storm. Parents were being forced to choose between children, bringing one into their warm, safe arms, indoors, leaving the other to drown, screaming and pleading for her life.

I was knocked down near the entrance to the line for *The Maelstrom* by a group of sprinting, soaked German college students trying unsuccessfully to slow to a trot. Then, while on my side, I was kicked suspiciously hard about the kidneys and ribs by two boys who appeared to be Indian or Pakistani. It was an intercontinental beating. I knew from experience not to take it personally, but I did need a bandage for my elbow that wouldn't stop bleeding, and maybe some ice on my ribs. Repairs would have to wait, though. I scraped myself off the ground and hobbled to a corner of the store where they sold books of Norse mythology. Hardly anyone bought them or even understood what they were, and no one was considering them in the downpour.

During my fourth shift in the store, I was beginning to doubt if the girls would be able to do business at all. Even the horniest and most frustrated restored 1973 Mustang convertible owner wouldn't have the time to entertain the thought of a Scandinavian blowjob in the chaos. To my surprise, as I looked up from Thor's immense frame on the cover of six-hundred pages of myth, someone noticed me, my pattern. She was beautiful, round, and frightened—and she was walking directly at me with an intense focus. She pinched my wrist and I looked into glacial eyes, a slight tint of blue, but mostly clear. So icy, and yet they felt like a warm blanket over my face, like they were taking breath out of my lungs. I gasped to break the spell. She handed me a torn-off corner of yellow legal paper, nodded her head slightly, urgently. I became aware we had just agreed to something. Then she walked off, evaporating in the crowd. Before she did, though, I read her nametag. Sigrid. The sound of it echoed in my head, both burly and cozy.

I still have the piece of legal paper in my wallet that she gave me in the store on last Saturday. *Help*, it said. *1:30 a.m. Hess Gasoline Station, World Drive.* When I read those words for the first time, realized this girl was in some kind of danger, I felt a pang different from any before. I felt my ignorance, my distance from it all, everyone, I could see it in my face in the window's reflection, just another malignant mole on the earth's body, standard issue parasite. Train wreck. Must look.

It was as if *The Golden Ring* were just another attraction at EPCOT, something to watch, and yes, learn from, but learn what? In the moment that Sigrid handed me the note, among the drenched, stinking guests, she made that attraction interactive in a way Walt's Imagineers and marketing teams had failed miserably time and time again, since I visited for the first time, my child eyes full of stars. With each new attraction, or so-called update, I watched the decline of EPCOT, its arteries drained, a total collapse in understanding that its lifeblood was the infinite possibility it represented to people who dreamed of the future. Maybe that gradual breakdown made something like *The Golden Ring* possible.

Of course, I was at the Hess station at 1:30 a.m., like the note demanded of me. The monsoon had stopped around 11:00, so the streets were bare, and the air was a calm curtain of moisture. Sigrid was inside poking at a rotating hotdog, purple circles under her eyes, all the more visible and sad on her translucent white skin in the million-kilowatt fluorescence of the four thousand-square-foot "mini-mart."

"Sigrid? Hi. I'm Duke."

"You came. You know, I have seen you in America and between. You look nice. Are you nice?"

"Yeah, I'm mostly okay, I think."

"You have a car?"

"I have an Escort out there."

"There is person in the car?"

"No, sorry, it's a Ford. I share it with my mom."

"Oh. We can drive, yes?"

We drove off Walt's property, southeast on Highway 192 and took a turnoff near Lake Tohopekaliga. Her eyes kept shutting and flashing open, on the verge of sleep but choked back into consciousness by panic. I stopped the car in a spot Iverbe took me bass fishing once, overall one of the most relaxing days we ever spent together, listening to the Gators football game on the radio, even though I hate football. We caught nothing all day.

"I am not prostitute," she said.

"Yeah, I don't think you are."

"I am from a very small town in Sweden, live on a farm that fail."

"That sounds nice."

"We do not speak much English there."

"You speak it perfectly, or very well," I said. She left out an article or pronoun occasionally, but just her definite demeanor made her English seem stronger than my lapses into mush-mouth gibberish.

"I come here to learn better, to be not burden on my family. To see America also. You were looking for prostitute?"

"Yeah, my friend said—"

"Why you need prostitute? You have girlfriend? American girls—eh—not have sex with you?"

"No, well, no. But it wasn't for me. I was trying to find out if what I heard was true, about The Golden Ring."

"Is true. I am very tired. May please tell you the help I need?"

What she asked for was simple: money. If I just gave her $300, she could go back to the International Village and pay the head pimp, a six-foot ex-model named Marta. Her plan was to say she showed up and gave the hand job—"blowjobs cost $400, intercourse $500," simple enough. And if the John called the next day, furious about the hooker that never showed, she'd tell Marta he was lying—*there was the cash to prove it*! It could work once, she thought, and then she'd have to think of something else. I proposed that we keep passing notes. If she needed to tell me anything, she could leave them behind Charles Lindbergh's feet along the row of statues at the American Adventure. I'd check each day I worked, at noon if I worked the morning, six if I had a night shift.

"Who is Charles Lindbergh?" she asked.

"Oh, right, he's a famous pilot, a Nazi actually, although some people say that was blown out of proportion, so I don't know—does proportion really figure into something like being a Nazi?"

"Nazis, yes, we have them in Sweden. Okay," she said, and yawned.

She leaned her head against the stiff headrest at first, a few seconds of shifting left and right before drifting to my shoulder, and off to sleep. Her head was so light. We sat that way for a while, forming some front-seat union. I didn't know how long to let her sleep. I knew Mom would set her alarm for 2:30 and peek into my bedroom to make sure I was there. It was coming up on 2:20, and I'd "lost" the phone Mom had given me. Actually it lay in a drawer at home, intentionally dismantled during one of my *need to be disconnected* moments. I didn't want to scare Mom by staying out all night, but I was getting tired watching Sigrid breathe through her mouth, a tiny globule of drool slowly descending towards her circular chin. I looked down at her sturdy, translucent hands and thought of what they'd already been asked to do to strange, hairy old men. I couldn't stop myself from looking back at her mouth, trying to will old men's flappy genitals out of my mind's eye.

It struck me at about 3 a.m. that I was somewhere I'd never been before, that the focus had finally moved off Mom and Iverbe, how they affected me, the obtuse triangle we made. The shape of Sigrid and me, huddled together, was something like a still-forming potato, like I was waiting for angles and curves for my new shape.

There wasn't much of a decision really, I had to let Sigrid sleep and just tell Mom I'd gone on a sort of date, and oops, we'd fallen asleep looking at the stars by the lake. The thought of romance, young love, would soften her. Anyway, I dreaded going back to Mom's panicked, sleep-deprived eyes. I wanted to drive into the night, fused to Sigrid and the stars. Maybe I even anticipated right now, this moment, outside the Greyhound station, Sigrid and I bound together—but instead of the sky canopy of that night, we have the stink of human atmosphere at the station.

The buses line up, vibrating, waiting for duffel bags and their sacks of human cargo. Just maybe, though, the very fact that we're bothering to go somewhere at all speaks to some potential. On a blue index card I write:

Life in line

shuffling toward an attraction—
the glow of a giant
screen off in the distance
swallowing everything, maybe,
or just entertaining us.
No one is even trying to guess
what it's doing there,
they just shuffle like me.
Each time I consider
getting out of line,
other people's thoughts
form an amoeba
and absorb me
back in.
I call out, ahead in line,
some muffled response,
someone who seems to know my voice.
I call out to you
whether it really is you or not,
I don't care,
I'm running,
out of line
for the first time.

Inside, the station looks like someone brandishing a gun just cleared the place and casually walked out. The air conditioning dominates the lobby. I see a Cuban mother of three young girls whisper-shouting some witchy curse at them, her teeth gritted, the rings on her fingers shaking and spiraling. From the girls' non-reaction, it's easy to see her being tender again in a minute or two.

Sigrid appears to me like Waldo emerging from the page, hidden in plain sight on the other side of the ticket window, between a thick, cylindrical, concrete pole, a cello case, and a trash can. I see her clogs, standard issue from EPCOT Norway, sticking out lifelessly—dead-tired clogs. She is asleep.

I decide to leave her there for a minute, before entering her life in this way, as accomplices chained at the ankle. I drift to a metal bench, into my head, to Iverbe, and I miss him, not him, but something about him, that he exists, or, that he's there anyway. Only now do I consider a kind of *no-Iverbe scenario,* where he's been swept up into whatever. Nothing it is that comes for us. I hate my callousness, mainly because it doesn't come naturally. I have to will it, which makes it more fucked up. I decide I just don't know what I'm talking about, which is a calming thought.

Looking away, to the glowing vending machines, I see a hollowed-out-looking man in a tan leather jacket, a father. His phone envelops his attention, and he's allowing his four-year-old to kick at a jagged, broken corner of a tiled wall, over and over. The kid isn't even there.

A smutty-looking sideburned guy has appeared and is hovering over Sigrid's clogs.

"I got it."

"What?" he says.

"This is my friend. Get the picture?"

"You want me to fuck you up?" he says, and walks off, pretending to check something.

I note him, for the open-ended way he just left it between us. But this is not the man we're supposed to be frightened of. Sigrid's description is unmistakable: a shiny, golden-haired pair, a man and woman, same height, skin tanned by the Central Florida sun, *muscular like professional tennis players,* she said.

"Sigrid," I say, crouching down.

She remains unconscious, but her lips seem to form little words.

Again, "Sigrid."

"Djavlar! Shit."

"Sorry," I say.

"I'm okay, okay, I'm okay."

She has a few shirts and a few pair of underwear in a grocery bag, and a pack of peanut M&M's. I have some cinnamon bread, two bananas, four hardboiled eggs, six pens, eighty-something notecards, two changes of clothes, and my savings in my backpack—plus the $500 that was included with the notebook. We both jump at the sound of a man's shout—a pause—then the shriek of the kid who was kicking the broken wall. He looks down at his own little bloody ankle and turns up the volume another notch. The father, still inside his phone, throws the boy over his shoulder and hustles over toward the bathroom for triage.

"I have knife to my throat," Sigrid says.

"What? When?"

"In dream. Still there in my head. Like a cloud."

"You were sleeping?" I don't know why I say this.

"Yah. I have not slept more than few hours since your car."

"That was a week ago. Why haven't you slept?"

"I forget, forgetting English now. I cannot think."

She leans her head back against the thick pole, covers her eyes with two fingers on each eye.

"Do you mind if I write something down real fast?"

Sigrid answers by opening her eyes, lifting her neck off the pole, and studying the blank notecard and pen in my hand.

"Thoughts," I say, "it helps me calm down sort of."

"Diary is better. Thoughts should be together, to see more."

"But I have them separately, the thoughts. And I don't like the idea of all that empty white paper behind what I'm trying to write down."

Sigrid's head has returned to its original position against the pole. Her eyes are closed, and she gives no indication that she's heard me. I no longer have anything to write anyway, and instead I just feel lucky that Sigrid is making it so easy for me, resting with her eyes closed, ignoring me. A week we've known each other, and already being ignored feels like love.

"I look at schedule. Los Angeles delay," she says, eyes still closed.

"How long delay?" I say, a native speaker.

"One hour."

"Shit. In Walt, one hour is code for three hours. Do you think it's the same here?"

She shakes her head, brushing me away. I hand her a piece of cinnamon bread and a hardboiled egg from my bag.

"Duke, I am so scared. They said they cut my arm."

"Your arm?"

"Yah. At elbow all the way to wrist. This bread is very good, thank you."

"They're just trying to scare you. It's bad for business if you leave," I say, trying to appear as though I know anything at all.

"They break girl's leg. Kjella, very nice, good morals."

"Oh. Well, I don't know then."

"She has to penis suck with cast on her leg," she says, and coughs. "I am very dry, my throat. Thirsty."

"Is she still working EPCOT Norway?"

"No, she work the *real work* full time now. They take her out of *Maelstrom* rotation. Three times as much suck as other girls. I thank you for buying my ticket."

"Yeah, no problem. I should actually go buy them now. Sigrid, did you ever have to do it?" I don't mean to say this out loud.

"No," she says, and looks down. I can't tell if it's true, but I can't possibly press her more, nor should I have asked her that question in the first place. It makes all the difference, to not ask her that question, to be just slightly heroic. And what does it matter anyway, what she's done? It matters to her life, some future, but not here, with me, right now.

"We should hide, I think, after you buy tickets."

"I'm sorry, Sigrid."

"For what?"

"For all of it. America," I say.

"Why? The—eh—I don't know word, the *bad people* are Swedish."

"But they're here in America, doing the, you know, bad stuff. I'm just sorry."

"I'm not," she smiles. "There is you."

4

About 4:30 this morning (which already feels like a month ago now, sitting on the bathroom floor with Sigrid), I found myself driving Mom's car deep inside Walt, down Meadow Creek Drive toward The Commons, a labyrinth where they house all the international cast members and American college students. *The Golden Ring* was in there somewhere, sleeping off the night. So was Carrie, in her dorm. I could feel her vibrating with everything, loneliness, the oversized bucket of brains squeezed into her skull, her fleshy legs rubbing together, the constant worry over her comatose twin sister hanging there between planes of consciousness. After discovering her Dr. Pepper-flavored tongue yesterday, and before leaving with Sigrid tonight, I had to take an hour for myself, just to see—something.

But it took me an hour-and-a-half in the pitch-black moonless morning just to find her building. I kept repeating the same series of turns and ending up in this sort of nowhere zone between quadrants of dorms, with long rows of dumpsters and pigeons. All the dorms are three stories and a sort of nothing shade of yellowish wheat, very disorienting. And then there are signs and arrows pointing to more signs filled with combinations of numbers and letters, which bring more arrows, numbers, and letters. Finally I came upon the actual sign for building B08 A-C, Carrie's. The third floor.

Scaling the stairs two at a time, I felt a flutter of nervousness and excitement, which, I learned in biology before dropping out, register exactly the same way to a human body. It doesn't distinguish between the two. The crack of dawn hadn't quite shown itself, although looking toward what I guessed was east, the sun seemed to at least be thinking about emerging over the relentlessly flat Floridian horizon. I thought about waiting for it, that it might be some kind of wise and reverent action on my part, to watch the sun rise on the morning before a long journey. But the nervous flutter that'd begun in my chest moved down my shoulder, my elbow, finding my hand, which knocked, and knocked, and knocked on the door some more until Carrie appeared.

"Hey. It's like six or something," she said, rubbing her eyes, licking sleep from her lips.

"Yeah, I've been up for a while."

"So who's that girl you were with yesterday?" she asked me.

"Just a friend. Can I come in?"

"A friend."

"I don't want to talk about it," I whispered.

"You want some coffee? My roommate slept in her clothes again, so you can speak up. She's completely unconscious. You can smell her from the hallway."

Carrie sat down at the two-seater kitchen table against the wall, holding her knee against her chest—and it was true, I caught a whiff of stale fruit and vodka leaking into the kitchen.

"So," she said, "just what is happening here?"

"I have to go, Carrie."

"Well, this was a short visit."

"No, that's why I'm here. I'm leaving Walt. For good."

"I knew it," Carrie said, waking up officially, leaning back, smiling. "It's her. The Norwegian girl with the big ass, isn't it? What were you two talking about?"

"Swedish, and it doesn't matter right now. I'm leaving Florida. Today."

"What about your mom?"

"I don't—my mom doesn't know. That's not why I'm here. I don't want to get into my mom, or Sigrid or—"

"Sigrid?"

"Yes, Sigrid."

"Okay, okay. So what—you're not coming back?"

"I don't know. But I'm definitely leaving tonight."

"Well, I'm leaving too, in six weeks. So I guess you better sit down," she said.

"Yeah. I'll take that coffee you offered. Thanks."

"It's from yesterday. I just have to nuke it."

"I'd never know the difference."

I swill coffee, which I learned from watching Mom drink cup after cup as a substitute for cigarettes, which she started smoking to replace booze, which she drank in excess to kick cocaine. For the last couple years it's been tea, six to ten cups a day, which replaced coffee, until yesterday, when booze got the call again. Anyway, my cup was empty before Carrie could even sugar and milk her own.

"I'm finished," I said.

She smiled, told me to go sit on the bed, and disappeared down the short hallway. The door to her room was open. At first, I was surprised to see the walls covered in unpostmarked Walt postcards, taped up everywhere, alternating fronts and backs filled with Carrie's writing and drawings juxtaposed against The Mice, The Ducks, The Dogs, The Castles, and the rest. I reached out and touched the wall, trying to feel her thoughts in the ink. I ran my fingers over the graphite of her sketches of guests' faces—one face I recognized as mine, but better. She thought of me this way, nose pointed up at some light, squinting my eyes, the hint of a grin. Then I saw each postcard was addressed to her twin, and an electric current passed through my head.

"The wall is for when my sister wakes up. I'm going to make it into a book."

I whirled and saw Carrie's face, a smidgeon of toothpaste on the corner of her mouth.

"You're up there," she said.

"Yeah," I said, still touching the wall, "this is the intersection. With everything."

"Yeah, okay. How much time do you have?"

"Twenty minutes. I spent a really long time getting here."

She looked me right in the eyes as her T-shirt stretched over her head and dropped to the floor. Then her oversized pajama pants, summoning me in a perfect ninety-degree bend over her feet, one leg off, the other. It's hard to imagine ever knowing anything again, through the senses, like that first scent of Carrie's vagina, where my face instinctively traveled, tractor-beamed, pulled by a vinegar flower that mixed with my coffee-coated exhale. Coffee and Carrie, humid as Florida, the perfect smell, forever, I hope. God.

"Mm. Just stay there and take your time, just be yourself," she said.

This directive inspired me for the first time to consider the possibility that to be myself was a good thing, as if in my infinite inexperience, I might summon a flourish to take her to the place I'd imagined so many times while working Spaceship Earth. I was thrilled, after numerous, sort of generalized plunges and thrusts of my tongue, to find Carrie's clitoris. It was as if I'd been handed a violin and a bow, and just raked it across the strings only to produce a perfect note, which poured out of Carrie's mouth the instant the beautiful accident happened.

Through some kind of anti-language, we agreed I should remain there as long as possible. I could already tell, once invited inside, I'd go off like the fireworks finale of *Illuminations*—which is the brilliant old light show that closed every night at the EPCOT of my youth. Most of that holy time between her strong legs, I kept my eyes closed so I could concentrate on giving her what I imagined to be a variety of tempo and pressure—and so I could listen to Carrie's yips and breath. Each sound that escaped her mouth became my new favorite sound.

I looked up, once, over her forest of pubic hair to see her abdomen quivering, a series of three flexes with each exhale. Carrie's face, a pimpled constellation, appearing and disappearing behind her breasts, was everything I've ever loved about girls and women, that face just shy of tears, when you know they care.

She placed her hands on either side of my neck and guided my lips to hers. And my cock (which I now felt I had the actual right to call it), its lit fuse down to the end, exploded as her hand moved it inside her. One glide, one pull back, and I was sure some internal organ between my lungs and liver, my pancreas maybe, had melted. She gripped me everywhere, and held on, and on, and on. It was the most generous thing I've ever witnessed.

Lying there afterward, building a dam in my mind to keep out my life, I could feel it wasn't going to hold. Just as I'd felt Carrie's pull only twenty minutes before, now I felt an equally powerful pull from Walt, where Sigrid and I would rendezvous one last time to confirm and review our escape plans, where I'd bid Melvin, my compadre, goodbye, maybe forever. And Mom. Suddenly I felt scared and stood up, naked, and ran to the bathroom to submerge my eyes and forehead in cold water, over and over, until the fear passed.

Each splash of water brought a different face to the front of my mind: Mom-splash-Carrie-splash-Mom-splash-Carrie-splash-Mom-splash-Carrie. I had people now, finally. Still, it was clear, that as long as it took to gather a best friend and mentor, and to finally embrace Carrie how I'd always wanted, to discover her only wish was to allow me to explore her full depth—just as quickly I'd drop it all. Running from Mom, too, crumbling again, like she hoped she never would. All I could do in that moment, water falling off my face and splattering in the sink, was whisper something, which didn't seem to come from me (and I don't even know who I was referring to), I just heard my voice say, *don't die.*

"Stay safe," Carrie said, appearing behind me in a terrycloth robe, stolen by Carrie's drunken roommate from the Grand Floridian Beach Resort.

"You know," she said, "on the road."

She winked and tossed a heap of clothes at me—and with the smallest two-finger wave, she disappeared behind her bedroom door.

In that fragment of a moment, when the door blocked out the last inch of her long fingers, the light from the window, and then shut—that's what I sit with now, Carrie's fingers, a captive in the handicapped bathroom at the Greyhound station. A fully-clothed Sigrid on the toilet, head in her hands. I'm on the floor, which would be a disgusting thought if I hadn't scoured and dried it for a good five minutes. We're trapped here in silence. We should have already boarded the westbound bus, which leaves in exactly ten minutes. Instead we've been reduced to little children again, or worse, two little pigs with a couple of big, bad wolves outside, just waiting. And so I close my eyes and try to open Carrie's bedroom door again, live backwards in my head, but I can't get her face to appear as the door cracks. It's no use. I can't go further than those two fingers, the last moment. The rest has already turned to memory dust.

Less than an hour ago, the whole mood was bursting with optimism and excitement, standing in line for the tickets.

"I think I might be nurse for the old," Sigrid said.

"Would that be depressing? Maybe not, I don't know."

"Everything too much about depressing now. I don't like it. It is good to find a need and be the need, yes? You will be old and need care from someone. I think that person should be real person, alive person. Should look at old person like real person also, who is still alive."

"You're right. But all that death? Here one day, and gone. Nothing."

"No. It is not that way at all."

Sigrid's eyes suddenly retreated a mile into her head, and the color vanished from her faced in an instant. She looked down at the ground and dug her fingernails into my palm.

"She sees me!" she whispered.

"Marta? She's here?"

"And Jori also. Go, get out of line. Go to the place."

I pretended to search for my wallet, left the line, and headed for our emergency rendezvous point—here, of course, the handicapped bathroom. I glanced around for Sigrid, but she was already out of sight. On the way to the rendezvous point, my gait felt artificial, something in my neck, not exactly stiff, but locked in one direction. Looking over my shoulder, I met with Marta's eyes for a terrifying instant, long enough to catch the rest of her expression, not quite a grin, hollow and deadly. Next to her, Jori, just as Sigrid had described him, balding, blond and ripped, standing there blank-faced. There was no way to know for sure that she'd recognized me as Sigrid's accomplice, I told myself, mainly so I didn't have to invent a new plan. The bathroom equaled safety. I needed it to stay that way.

"If something goes wrong, you go in first," she'd said, finalizing contingency plans earlier today, "and I knock five times, five minutes after you go inside bathroom."

"Five minutes, five knocks. Got it."

I made it inside, locked the door, and found my reflection over the stained sink.

"Five minutes," I said to my reflection, and took out a notecard.

If this reaches you
and it's all bad news
about the brother you never met
know only one thing:
that you took the time to try
to do it the way you thought was right
and real to you
is the reason it matters,
what happens now.

I wanted Sigrid to knock and join me in the safe place that wasn't safe at all. Wrapped in that desperation, I again caught my reflection, and inside my face, I could still see it, twelve-year-old Duke, the first time I was truly scared right out of my mind, by adults and their broken heads. Maybe Sigrid shouldn't knock, I thought, maybe I shouldn't want that. Maybe she should just go. Maybe the plan was already fucked up beyond repair. Just then came five rapid-fire knocks.

As soon as I cracked the door open, a loud and short scream hit me between the ears. Sigrid slid inside, slammed the door and locked it, followed immediately by a fist pounding outside. A man's heavy hand. It pounded three times, then three more times, then stillness, then three more, and Sigrid burst into tears. I held her, my back to the door, trying to wedge myself between Sigrid and what was outside. We stayed that way for a while, until the last round of pounding.

The door has been silent, like the two of us, for the last half hour.

"I do not want to think about them coming here with knife. Tell me something, your life," she says, finally.

"Okay. I had sex this morning, you know, for the first time."

"Eckh. Something else."

"Okay. I just found out who my father is. I also just found out I have six brothers and two sisters. All from different mothers. But mainly there's this one."

"One what? Mother?"

"No. Sister. She's sort of in my head all the time now. She sent me this play about her life, to introduce herself, which is cool. But part of me thinks she might be insane, you know, like dangerously unstable. But maybe that doesn't matter."

"I have five sisters," she says, "they are always with me. Two of them are unstable—I think—fragile, yes? They will marry much older men."

"Are you the youngest? I'm the youngest, I'm told."

"No, oldest," she yawns. "I am so tired, Duke."

"What do you want to do? I mean we could—"

"Not yet. More distraction. Why your mother not tell you who real father is?"

"Okay," I say. "Well, I don't think she meant it to be a secret, but at that time there were a lot of—possibilities."

"Different men?"

"Yeah. She's an addict. She didn't really care for a while, about herself."

"Yes," she says.

Sigrid hugs me, and this is natural and easy. We aren't forgetting what's outside, distracting ourselves. This is preparation.

"Djavlar," she says, looking down, "this is a lot of shit we go through."

"Yeah."

We crouch together, foreheads touching, sucking air into our throats and expelling carbon dioxide in rushes. I touch my cheek to her ear, something Mom does that calms me. It's what I know to do. Sigrid rubs my back, wipes her nose on my shirt, her face is suddenly resolved.

"We get fuck out of here."

"Fuck them," I say.

"Yes, fuck them," her eyes narrow.

"Fuck pimps."

"Fuck," she says, chuckling with fear.

"Let's get on that bus," I say, then, it hits me. "No, no, no, wait. Think about this—just take the money. If we make it to the bus, they'll just follow us. And then kill us or something. Just take this money."

I give her the cash from my backpack, hopefully enough to take her somewhere, a motel room, and home eventually, back to her sisters and her failed farming town to fairy the elderly gently into eternity.

"Then you have nothing," she says.

"This is my country. I'm fine. Are you fast?"

"Yes, very fast. My family, we are foot orienteers."

"What?"

"Is popular sport in Sweden. Like a race across land you do not know, without compass."

"You're going to be okay, Sigrid."

"You also, Duke."

Sigrid removes her clogs and rubs her feet with her hands, waking them up.

"You're going to run. I'm going to block."

Sigrid palms my head like a basketball, grabs a little hair.

"You are *my* brother, also," she says.

I open the door and break into a sprint, aimed directly at Marta and Jori, sitting close together on metal bench. I'm visualizing my actions a split second before my body makes them happen, which I believe is called flow. I see myself diving headfirst, arms extended, hands extended, towards Jori's steel-toed right foot, Marta's high-heeled left. I will wrap them, become part of them, bind them together, drag them down.

In mid-air, I catch Sigrid peripherally. She is not a human. She is a lynx, her toes barely touching the linoleum, accelerating. I am on Marta and Jori, around their ankles. The inside of a thick elbow pins my trachea; I am choking and my eyes feel like they might pop from the pressure. I presume this is Jori's doing. I am holding—one second, five seconds, ten. Now a heel in my ear, jamming, searching for my brain. I hear barking and gasps—twenty seconds, thirty. Now fingernails, like fork prongs, scraping.

Through one half-open eye, I see a woman police officer galloping toward our impromptu brawl. Jori releases the death grip on my throat and takes Marta lightly by the arm. They stroll toward the front exit, ignoring the cop's commands to stop. She allows this escape and bends down, placing a soft brown hand on my shoulder. She looks into my eye, checking for consciousness, and brings her lips to a walkie-talkie, describing Marta and Jori as *six feet and blonde, possibly armed,* describes me as *an injured young boy*. I cannot disagree, although I want to correct her somehow. A wheelchaired man looks at me with suspicion, or maybe concern, and rolls into the handicapped unisex bathroom, from which I just emerged, now victorious. Sigrid is gone.

5

"How bad you hurt?" the officer asks me.

In her I see the actual purpose of police, the way she wears the uniform, with urgency and care. Her face is round, like a whole pie, her neck slightly spilling over her collar.

"Not bad at all," I say.

"You sure? Check that trachea. That motherfucker was leanin' awful hard on his elbow—on your throat."

"There's air coming through."

The officer demands my name and address, but I tell her I don't know any phone numbers, which is almost true. She writes it down in a notebook, something I didn't know officers did anymore, with technology.

"Where you supposed to be, Duke Brown? You got a basketball name. You don't look like a basketball player."

"I need to start my trip, to see some family."

"By yourself?"

"Yeah," I say. "I'm older than I look."

"What, thirteen?"

"Eighteen."

"Bullshit. Where you go to school?"

"I don't."

"Eighteen?"

"What does it matter?" I said.

"Mm-hm. You're bleeding, you just started bleeding. Here," she says, plucking five tissues from Kleenex travel pack in her back pocket, one after another like some industrial robot arm.

"I can feel it now. Is it gushing? "

"Dripping. You got yourself clawed, son."

I reach out, placing my hands on her arms, begging her with my eyes for an invitation to lay my head on her chest. The officer is a diamond, hard, warm, and clear. Her badge is a state of mind, a kind of deal she's made so that she can do good. Having spent all those days watching the millions of parents pass through Spaceship Earth and America—I've become a master at spotting them, the boundless ones.

"Who was that girl running, the one in costume?" she asks, gently pulling my cheek to her collarbone.

"Kjella. It's a uniform, not a costume," I say, almost a whisper.

"Shella what? What kind of uniform?"

"I don't know."

"That girl can *run*. How do you know her?"

"I tried to help her out of a tight spot, I guess."

Looking up, just a few inches over my eyes, I see her cheeks squeezing upward, irritated with me. All that caring makes it more dangerous for her, which is probably why they assigned her to the bus station. She draws me away from her body, keeping her hands on my shoulders, face to face.

"You going to be straight with me?"

"If I can be, I will," I say.

"Who were those people?"

"That was the first time I've seen them."

"That's not what I asked you. I asked you who they were."

"All I know is they were scaring the girl," I say, forgetting I've already used a fake name for Sigrid.

"You know more than that."

"They threatened her. They were going to hurt her. I can't say more, because, right now, that could—it's too soon."

"Come on. Let's call your parents."

"I'm on my own."

"Then your mother can tell me that."

"Please," I say, "I have somewhere else to be. It's family, I just have to, I don't know."

And her eyes expand in a way they can't, not really, in reality. "I know about family. You're in danger, son."

"Not if I don't put myself in any."

"Too late. Tell me what it is."

"I don't know exactly, a kind of confrontation. I don't want it, but I keep moving toward it anyway."

"You ever seen a lamb slaughtered? You won't ever eat no veal again."

"I need to talk someone out of doing something. Or maybe try to talk her into doing something else instead."

"You know when that will work?"

"When?"

"Never. Look what they did to Jesus."

"I don't see the connection."

"Huh. I know you don't," she says.

She shakes her head and looks over at a homeless man duct-taping his British Knight sneakers back together.

"Seventeen, huh?"

"That's right."

"You just said you were eighteen a minute ago. What you got in that sack?"

"A hundred bucks, and some stuff that doesn't matter to anyone else."

"You just watch out for the meth-heads in the small-town stations, you hear me? They're waiting for that sweet little face of yours. Take that shit and you lose your conscience. You know what you are without that?"

"Psychotic?"

"A devil," she says.

"I don't believe in that—in devils, The Devil."

"What do you think it was just scratched up your face and collapsed your throat?"

"I better get my ticket. Thank you, officer," I say—I want to tell her I love her, but I shouldn't.

"All right, go ahead" she says, looking down at her initial notes for the first time, "but you're not my friend, Duke Brown. You didn't give me a damn thing."

I want to please her, and I almost tell her to *follow the uniform*.

But if she did, and it led her to Walt, to *The Golden Ring*, the uncertainty of that, of Sigrid ending up maimed or dead—I decide to just nod, tell her I'm sorry with my eyes.

At the ticket booth, I discover that my money will get me to Houston, leave me with $11 and no way to get to Los Angeles or eat. I buy the ticket. The feel of it in my hand is like holding the sun, scorching and heavy enough to tear my shoulder out of the socket. Although an entire part of my brain knows it's just paper, I wrap my fingers around it, flex my arm, through the doors, straining, up the steps, past rows of seats, ending somewhere in the middle. My eyes feel strange, bulging and blurry. It's hard to keep the trash on the bus floor in focus. I swallow and swallow to keep from throwing up—breathe through the nose, out the mouth. Through the nose, out the mouth. The driver starts the bus, and a rush of air whips through. My entire head tingles like aggressive dandruff shampoo, and I feel myself tearing slowly, horizontal at my waist.

There are other people on the bus, how many I don't know, but I know they're sitting in seats somewhere, behind me, in front. I can feel them vibrating. Through a sleek sort of tunnel, I see the steering wheel and gear shift way out in front of me. I'm suddenly afraid to lose consciousness—if I faint, I'll die. I reach down blindly, into my backpack. I feel for notecards, pull two out, a pen—I can see them, I can see my hand, the pen in my fingers. If I can just write something down, I'll maintain consciousness. Everything is black, except now there's something outside the bus—somehow inside and outside. Or maybe neither. With my eyes on the object, on a notecard, I write to her:

I've gone through
some kind of portal.
And outside,
past the steering wheel,
in front of my eyes,

just hovering,
there's a kind of jellyfish,
all shot up with neon.
It looks real,
Like it's really there,
but I know it's not there,
in the same way
as the seats and windows
or me.
So many kinds of there.
I think I've been wearing
the same briefs since I was seven,
and now I've suddenly removed them,
climbed onto this bus
just me and jeans and a backpack,
and this neon jellyfish
and blackness
out the window,
there's a back and forth
between us
so specific but unspeakable.

The notecard is full—on another:

And what I say to it
doesn't come from my brain,
more from my intestines
so it's not words exactly.
And what it says back to me
goes to straight to my spinal cord
which knows just what it means.
I'm behind the curtain!

And just as I think that,

it closes, the jellyfish gone,
and I smell the other
passengers' breath and death
in tiny clouds above my head
and one by one
they appear again
in front and behind me.
Tonight I'll be sleeping
at a bus station,
in Alabama,
on the way through the mirror,
where I'd never wanted to go,
until you brought it all up
so *thanks for that.*

I paperclip the notecards together and breathe deeply, knowing she waits there, at the end, like the bust of her I've made in my mind, sitting there under a spotlight on a stage in a tiny theater. And then there is the other bust glowing in a dimly lit corner, one I can't yet look at for more than a millisecond, a sort of doughy-headed professional golfer with a finished wood-paneled basement, decorated with his collection of antique torture devices.

For hours, days really, with the engine around me, I'll chisel away little pieces of plastic until I arrive at His face, the two halves, the half that hates, and the half that believes he's right to hate—if what she says is true.

Tonight I'll be fine, though, I know it. The jellyfish told me so. It's tomorrow I can't picture.

6

Stop breaking down.

This stuff I got is gonna bust your brains out—hoo-hoo—it'll make you lose your mind.

I'm spinning in Texas, in a bar that still has a payphone, somewhere, fifty miles from Balmorhea, my last bus stop, as far as my ticket would take me—actually a little farther. I was able to ride a while past Houston before the driver checked my ticket. Balmorhea. The people must know, saying the name of their town, what it sounds like, like something that confines you to a filthy toilet, and they just don't give a shit.

This bar is some kind of local legend, hundreds of pictures of musicians who've played here, people I recognize but don't know. On stage, there's a harmonica being run through some kind of effects, and it's blowing me down. It's so fucking loud I can't even hear the heavyset girl screaming in my face. I don't know what she wants, but she's furious, jabbing her heavily manicured nail into my collarbone. What is that—the tiny likeness of a giant-titted Tinkerbell drawn onto her index nail—no, all of her nails. I can't even imagine that we've shared something, that some relationship exists, for her mouth to be so wide open, so close to mine, wailing at me. But then I look down, and I've spilled an entire plastic tumbler of beer on her red boots.

I nod, more out of need to remain standing than a desire to try to fix the damage I've caused, I hug her around her trunk. Immediately I feel my hair yanked, and I'm standing upright again, facing a different woman, but shockingly like the first, same ribbed T-shirt, but the same up-tilted nose and shoulder-length helmet of blonde hair, the same manicure. Just bigger all over. I look down, the same boots.

A black guy, sort of a kid, is suddenly between the three of us, and I remember that I'm not here alone. It's Willie. I know him. He's brought me here, this is his town, Alpine, and he's helping me now, talking down the nearly identical women with a series of hand gestures and nods. Black people are welcome here? Yes, I think so, and I feel my stomach relax just enough to hold the beer down. I just got off the payphone with Mom five minutes ago. I don't even know if she could understand me.

"Mom! I'm in Texas!" I shouted, "I'm all right! I'm really fucking drunk! I'm okay, though! Go back to bed!" and I hung up.

The kid I met on the bus, Willie, a freshman at Prairie View A&M, is a big talker. He got on in Houston at eight this morning, so we'd had all day, twelve hours of life story, probably at a ratio of about 6/1, Willie to me. Still, I felt like I gave him most of the picture in my allotted two hours.

I look up at the stage and there's a blues band, ancient-looking in their suits. This is Willie's grandfather, why we're here. I remember now—the harmonica, the loudest sound I've ever heard a man make. A high note rings out, and my eardrum is about to rip at the edges.

"Willie!"

"What?"

"You! I said your name!"

"Outside!" he says, pointing.

I look up at the stars, and it's just like they say they are. Billions, and they're all big. All bright. A rush of vomit shoots like a geyser, at just enough of a forward trajectory to not drop on my face on the way down. I feel better, good, like I'm nowhere at all. Willie hasn't noticed—I really didn't make any noise, just a sort of a gurgly cough.

"She's fuckin' here, man."

"Your girl?" I say.

He now sees some regurgitated hot wings in a puddle next to me. They glisten under the outside spotlight.

"What the hell, man?"

"I feel good," I tell him.

"Sit down."

"I'm good," but I'm not. I'm on the ground, on my back. Laughter that feels timed to my landing lashes me across the face. Willie helps me to stand, and props me against a pickup truck. He tells me to breathe.

Now I mean it. "I'm good, man."

"She's in there, man. With some corn-fed offensive lineman motherfucker. I don't even know what happened to Zambu or Zamhi or whatever the fuck. Maybe she's fuckin' 'em all, I guess."

On the bus, Willie told me just about everything a person could say about his girl, Janiece, a freshman at UT Austin. She was his everything, he said, but he was worried how much time she was spending with a graduate student from South Africa. Willie had written a concept hip hop/soul album about her body, titled, *Corpus Janiece,* and she didn't seem to care about all the effort he'd expended on it. A dozen songs, each dedicated to a different limb, digit, hair region, organ—he covered a lot of ground. Since I was captive audience for a live a cappella performance of the entire record, I felt like he might want my opinion after he finally finished.

"Willie, you're a great soul singer. You have some Marvin Gaye happening. And when you told me the concept, I was skeptical about the whole objectification thing. But you made it spiritual. But—you can't rap. You know that, right? Is somebody else going to do those parts?"

"Fuck you, man."

"Don't get me wrong. I loved the stuff in the armpit song, and the pussy song, as the centerpiece I guess."

"No man, see, that's it. Pussy's not the centerpiece. It's her ankles," he said, and then opted to quote from his own lyrics, *the foundation of your dance, upon which the rest of your life-force moves, smooth, summoning me to your womb.*

"Well, it's all really poetic. I guess I just had an experience with that recently, a girl, and her pussy, and you really got it, with the whole *pussy as universe* metaphor. But when you rap, it's like you're trying to sound so tough—"

"I am tough. I could knock your ass out right now."

"Which proves what?"

"Nothing."

"Exactly, man."

"You don't know hip hop."

"I know soul, though."

"Bullshit, man, you prolly like all that indie, masturbatory white-boy shit."

It was here I corrected Willie, and told him about the tiny, tingly inner celebration that would come when Mom would play her Smokey Robinson, Temptations, Four Tops, Otis Redding, and Sam Cooke records on the stereo. I saw Mom's glow when this music was on. Equal and opposite, I'd drop my head every time I heard the first few impossibly sticky, warm lines of *Sweet Baby James*. I wanted James Taylor to somehow un-exist, never have been. He was Mom's sadness, and I don't know how many times I saw her insides droop, letting her entire being get sucked into *J.T.* land.

Outside, Willie has his head in his hands. My head has stopped spinning. He keeps muttering things, *Janiece, you said, I was, Janiece, I fuckin' thought, like we were, Janiece, Janiece …*

"Willie, can we please go when your grandpa's done playing?"

"What?"

"I know you got this situation, but I have to get to L.A. tomorrow. I don't know how that's going to happen."

"I told you I'd get you the money, didn't I? Damn, man."

"I'm afraid you're going to ask me to help you do something violent. To that big guy."

"Fat fuck. No, man. Fuck that. She's not who she says she is. That's her problem."

"Now that's the spirit."

"You want to see a motherfucker throw some darts?"

After five games of Cut Throat Cricket, I've timed it, it takes Willie exactly five minutes to wipe his opponent's ass. I have to hand it to these people, they keep lining up to take him on. Five bucks to Willie if he wins, ten to his opponent if he even scores a point on Willie. They seem to think this is fair. It's not. It's not as if they can toss each dart exactly where they intend it to go. Willie can. He misses once each game, and he says the same thing each time, *awful*, which is supposed to be a self-critique, but I take it be more of a literal statement of fact. Full of awe. It's a spectacle. There's not even a need for some kind of hustle. They pay to see a show.

A semicircle has formed around us, a dozen or so cowboy hat Texans, half women, half men. I notice they don't cheer on Willie's greatness—they just stare blankly and shake their heads occasionally.

"You like him, huh," says a skinny woman, fifty or so. "I want to see the little son of a bitch miss."

"Does this happen often?" I say, pointing at the crowd.

"Yep. All these shit-kickers line up for the chance to say they beat Willie Cricket. He won't play unless the old man's up there with his harmonica, though. Been that way since he was a little shit."

"How little?" I ask, declining a cigarette offer.

"I don't know, six or seven. It's voodoo is what it is, and that's not even racist."

Willie decides he's given this giant belt-buckled guy enough chances to score, so he closes out all the numbers, then bullseyes. Once, twice, and … done. Untouched.

"Who else?" he says, whipping around like a boxer.

"All right, then, bring me that fat ass fuck," and with that he points at the hulking mass holding a whiskey and coke at the bar.

"No," I say, because Willie is wrong, this man is not fat. He is simply a giant.

I see who must be Janiece, standing with this man, her hands on her hips, squinting her eyes to form daggers. Incidentally, I heard songs about both her hips and eyes on the bus, and I note immediately how Willie rendered her perfectly. He is a genius.

"All right fat ass, hundred bucks I win, a thousand fucking dollars you hang one fucking point on me," he says, but the giant can't hear. He's across the bar.

"Tell him what I said, man," Willie says to me.

I walk over to the giant, who bends down in a surprisingly gentle posture.

"Willie Cricket would like to play you," I tell him.

"Is that right? Well, I guess that's something he needs to do, now isn't it?"

"He's actually trying to raise money for a worthy cause, for me to—"

"I don't give a shit. Tell him I'll play, boy."

"It's $100 if—"

"I told you. I don't give a shit. Whatever he wants."

The man's name, I learn from Janiece's disappointed call to him, is Kim.

"It's all right, Janiece," he assures her.

"Let's just leave," she says.

"That's not possible anymore." Kim walks over to the dartboard, past Willie, without looking, and drops a dollar into the machine.

"Go first," Kim says.

"I can't go first. It's not fair."

"Go first," he repeats.

The music stops with a big wallop and a *good night everybody*, and I watch Willie's grandfather wipe his face with a rag, soaking it all up. It's all hanging there in his gray beard. Willie turns to the stage, alarmed.

"Go on. Throw," Kim almost whispers.

A few people gathered nearby look interested, noticing Willie is about to throw without the music. He rocks forward and back, closes his eyes, opens them and fires three darts, all 20s. The number is closed. This is good, I've recently learned.

Kim steadies himself with a cigarette and closes 20 after three perfect throws. Willie looks confused. The object for Kim is to score at all, not to win. And yet, by closing out 20, he's trying to stop Willie from scoring—he's trying to win.

Willie's grandfather has disappeared, and now Willie looks unsteady, like he's wearing shoes that don't fit. A dart bounces off the 19, falls to the floor. Again. Again. The crowd swells around the game.

But Willie doesn't say, *awful*. He doesn't say anything. Kim merely steps up to the line, whips three darts into the 19, 18, and 17. I am about to vomit again, and I can no longer watch. I will know by the crowd. Groan, we win. Jubilant screams, Kim scores and we lose.

I head to the bar to get some water. Janiece is there, and her legs, too, as Willie described them. Normally I might just nod or wave, but I'm drunk. I take the stool next to hers and can't pry my eyes off of her ankles.

"You his new friend?"

"Yeah," I say.

"He only has one at a time, 'til they get tired of him."

"I like him."

"Yeah, well, it's all about Willie, isn't it?"

"I don't know. He's helping me."

"I used to think that, too," she says, sipping some kind of orange-pink cocktail. I tell her my name and she shrugs.

"What is that you're drinking?"

"Tequila Sunrise."

"You drink those at night?"

"Unless you're a drunk, you do."

"Oh, right," I say. Mom drank them in a more literal way on her days off sometimes, before I woke up, before Iverbe. I order some water from the bartender, who makes no return gesture that leads me to believe we've communicated.

"Why are you wearing a backpack in a bar? That's a real good way to get beat up."

"I'm on the road. And I'm pretty nonviolent, so it shouldn't really be a problem."

"I guess there aren't already enough stupid white people in West Texas."

"So how come you don't like Willie's concept album about you?"

"Because I don't," she says, emphatic. Other people might interpret her flared nostrils as desire to kill the topic.

"Is it the reason you broke up with him?" I ask and some tiny muscle softens at the corner of her eyes.

"It was all just too much."

"That's too bad."

"What?"

"Too bad. I like the armpit song. All of them, really."

"That's the problem! Like I want someone like you knowing all that, thinking about it."

"But, we all have armpits."

At this she gets up in my face, and I am suddenly Willie.

"We don't all have the *'juice of Venus' fruit trees* and the *'aroma of a peach in a salty sea of me, oh Janiece'* do we? And the shit's cliché anyway."

"You're just being mean. You know it's good." I say.

I hear the crowd hoot and shout, but it sounds more anticipatory than celebratory. I take three ice cubes from the plastic cup and hold them to my forehead. Janiece watches me administer the ice and sits, softening again. It's the little softening moments, I see it, this must be what kills Willie.

"Is it over?" I say.

"Kim is about to score. Willie hasn't closed 15 yet," she says, her allegiance vague.

I want to tell her I could make it without Willie's help, but that I'll take it. I want to tell her I only have one wisdom in the world, and that's letting people help me if I can see they know how.

"Shall we?" I ask, inviting her to the end of the game.

"Just tell him to move on," she says, applying lipstick, suddenly in a hurry.

I walk zig-zag over to the board, where the blood is boiling. It takes a few seconds to read the situation, where are we, what's closed, what's open, Kim hasn't scored, but he's closed everything. Willie has three numbers open. 15, 16, 17. He looks over his shoulder, searching the crowd. Janiece zips out the door, leaving a final flash of ankle in the air. Willie inhales deeply, finds my eyes for the tiniest fraction of a second, and whips around, rocks forward and back—17…16…15. GROAN. We embrace, Willie's fist in the air, my head in his armpit. The crowd recedes like a wave, filters back across the bar.

"When Gramps stopped playing, I got nervous, but then I just, like, remembered who I was. Motherfucker's at the ATM right now. I feel like I grew tonight."

"I talked to Janiece."

"Fuck all that."

"Yeah, I know. But I get it. She's something."

"She's fucked up."

"Thanks," I say, taking his hand.

"We gotta find Gramps before he leaves. If I'm not waiting when he's done, he just goes. That's it."

Out of nowhere Willie is on the ground, Kim standing over him. The giant tosses five folded twenty-dollar bills at Willie's face, hidden behind his hands, a trickle of blood leaking through his fingers. I take my backpack off, rise to my feet and look at this hulking man. His face is not unkind—it seems to be asking *What do have to say to me?* I give myself five seconds to think of an answer. One. Two. Three. Here's something—as hard as I can, I kick his Achilles tendon. It sends him leaning backward and, like blowing on a leaf, I push him over. Willie's bloody face meets mine with a cackle and we are outside. The F-150's tires crackle over the gravel, pulling out.

"Ho-ho-hold it! Grandpa!" He doesn't stop, Willie pulling at the door, knocking on the window. Somehow we are inside, cramming over. Our movements are deft. Gramps pulls out onto the highway and the cab of the truck sighs out the open windows. What we've done is not right exactly, but we know that. The giant is a principled man. It's in the service of the bigger piece. The work we're doing, Willie and I, pissing on things, owning them, inviting pain. I am living this way, Willie Cricket's way, and anything else is a lie, which is worse than wrong. We love the same way—we don't know how. I see it. I am the jellyfish. It is my job to swim and sting—and stop thinking.

Willie suggests we stop at a Denny's. The old man, drenched in guitar sweat, agrees without answering, or even acknowledging I'm there, on the other side of his grandson. Maybe I'm invisible to him. Or maybe I'm just somewhere else already.

7

Mom has this gaggle of figurines that the rare human who came into our home always mistook for the far more popular Hummels. They were very similar, which I found out from occasionally visiting homes of Hummel enthusiasts over the years. But her brand, Martigans, were a band of truly terrifying children. They were only made for a few years in the early 80s, and are pretty hard to get your hands on. I had mixed feelings when we'd head out to the swap meet, excited to be part of the crowd—you could actually touch all the crap, unlike the wretched department stores—but I'd implore whatever power was in control of such things to deny Mom new Martigans for her collection. There were subtle details in the faces that other people must have noticed too, which is why, I think, they became extinct—except for the few thousand floating around the swap meet world. They held a fright, as if the children had seen the horrors, or been brutally victimized, and were now attempting to do everyday tasks, tie their shoes, fill a bucket, fish at the old fishing hole. Their cheeks were strained and their eyes bulged, like they were moving slowly forward out of their skulls, looking at unspeakable things on their interior canvases.

"Mom, why do we need more Martigans? We have like thirty."

"I'd like to get the whole set if I can, the collection."

"But why?"

"Oh I don't know if I can say exactly. They're rare, and different."

"I don't like to be alone in the house with them."

"No? Well, they remind me of something, I guess."

She'd just shrug off my disgust in a way that made me feel like shit for saying anything.

"Your mother is so beautiful."

Iverbe would say this often when Mom walked into the room, which sounds very heart-warming, and I think it would have been, every once in a while, except that he didn't say it to me. He'd say it looking straight at Mom, but not to her exactly. It was hard to know who he thought was actually in the room. As a little kid I used to answer and say, "I know she is," but even that brief response felt wrong. Silence became my preferred answer, which he never implied that he noticed.

The closest thing we had to an actual communication—which I take to mean two beings giving each other their attention and saying something, as opposed to vaguely speaking to some unnamed, absent third party that he's chosen to substitute for me—was when Iverbe walked into my seventh-grade, third-period classroom, looking like he'd been struck by lightning. My algebra teacher, Mrs. Bicks, an obsessive creator of mnemonic devices, dropped her eraser on her chest, creating a puff of chalk that sent the class into five seconds of automatic derisive laughter.

"Hello, Mr. Iverbe. Are you all right?"

The movement Iverbe made about the head and neck wasn't a confirmation, and it wasn't a negative either, but out of fear of the unknown I guess, Mrs. Bicks interpreted it as a solid yes.

"Do you need to speak to your son?"

To this factually impossible question, Iverbe answered by reaching out his left hand. The extension of his arm brought into sharper focus that his standard vertical stripe short-sleeve dress shirt was completely untucked from his pants, something I saw only a few times a year when not at home or at a public swimming pool. My eyes traveled up the vertical lines to his hair, which was sticking in three distinct directions, but all jutting out from the right side of his head. To achieve this, I imagined he'd run his sweaty left hand through his hair, possibly unaware he was doing it, until there were three well-formed spikes of wavy, greasy, salt-and-pepper brown.

I was glad that algebra was a relatively lonely class for me, no friends. Only three other kids in my grade were even in there, and they were just hallway hello types. The rest were eighth graders. It made it easy enough to deceive them all into thinking that everything was fine, without being called on it later. Still, something told me not to go with him, to refuse his sweaty hand, to send him back into the hallway, to the negative space. Far, far away from me. Something inside pleaded to turn back time fifteen seconds, ask Mrs. Bicks for permission to piss before Iverbe thrust open the door. I thought of Mom, though, her deep understanding of him without any ability to explain it, her relentless protection of him from his attackers, the lesser teachers, she called them, who developed elaborate jokes about Iverbe receiving shock treatment, including brazen, rude imitations of his bizarre facial expressions that were equal parts extreme physical discomfort and breezy smile. I'd caught them doing it, too, in the hallways, whooping it up, but never knew how to confront them.

In the crosshairs of Mrs. Bicks' desperate stare, I put on a neutral face and walked briskly, but measured, out the door, gently pushing Iverbe into the hallway.

"No more no more no more," he repeated without punctuation.

At first the phrase, with a strange emphasis placed on the first syllable, was directed either internally, or to God, I guess. Or no one. A specter. Then Iverbe turned his face to mine, and again, for the smallest measurable increment of time, our eyes wrapped around each other's, and he sent the same words to me on a different plane. Attached to the phrase was an implied request, to simply understand. *No more.*

I had no idea how dangerous it would be driving to the high school to pick up Mom. I should've driven—twelve-year-olds can drive in an emergency. It's not that his hands were shaking, but they were experiencing jagged spasms sending us into oncoming traffic, until Iverbe either snapped back into the moment or I took the wheel. The first three times, I waited for him to correct our course, then I stopped waiting.

We glided, alive, into an open space and parked in front of the administration building. I still thought Mom could help, or just reset him. I nearly dropped the transmission when I put it in park with Iverbe's foot off the break. I ran into the office and explained to Mr. Heeves, the tenth-grade principal, that we needed Mom right away. He looked at his watch, disappeared behind a door, and just as fast Mom came flying back out.

"Ron, I have to go. I'll call you."

"Kaye, okay, Kaye, just call, okay Kaye," Mr. Heeves said, and seemed as though he may go on repeating this pattern indefinitely.

We jogged to the Civic and found him in the backseat, mostly catatonic, moving his lips just slightly, fishlike.

"Okay," Mom said, and I wondered what she meant exactly. Was this better or worse than she'd expected?

"Honey?"

He shook his head, just enough for me to notice it jiggling.

"Can you hear me?" Nothing. She leaned the driver's seat back and took Iverbe's pulse on his neck.

"Seems okay," she said, sort of to me. "Do you think we should go to the hospital?"

Then Mom simultaneously raised and slowed her voice, "I'm going to drive home now, let you sleep for a couple hours, okay?"

And sleep he did, for eighteen hours. Mom and I played Go Fish and War, and cycled through every James Taylor album Mom owned. We took turns holding Mom's makeup mirror under his nose and taking his pulse. I wanted to believe this was enough.

By one in the morning, we were both drained. I could feel Mom thinking, *if I just had a little ... to get me through the night*. Instead she said, in the guise of informing me of some kind of critical plan, "No, what I'll do is set the alarm every hour on the hour."

"I'm sure he'll be okay."

Mom snapped back in, gave me the assured face that we both knew was a fraud, but we agreed was part of the job of Mom and kid in that moment.

"We're going to be okay, Duke. Just help me, and I'll make sure of it."

The next morning, mercifully Saturday, when I woke up, Iverbe and Mom were at the kitchen table, drinking tea, a half-dozen donuts displayed on a big yellow plate. Iverbe was in his plaid pajamas with oversized buttons, grinning wider than I'd ever seen, his eyes like blue pinwheels lit by white and yellow spotlights.

"Look, Kaye, it's your son! He's awake!"

I almost turned around and walked straight back to my darkened cave of a bedroom, but the donuts lured me to the table. Before sitting down, I checked Mom's countenance. It registered somewhere inside the triangle of cautiously optimistic, relieved, and concerned. That was good enough for me, so I took a glazed chocolate and sat down. Iverbe poured me a V-8, which I don't drink.

"You know," he began, looking at the ceiling, "there have been important men and women in this century, excuse me, the last century, the twentieth century, men and women of authentic action. But only one truly carried the mantle of a Franklin, an Edison. And his legacy just so happens to be right here, not twenty miles away."

I'd heard the Walt speech before, obviously, and I'd seen the rare pictures of young Iverbe in Davy Crockett gear. There were only about a dozen pictures of him as a boy, and he's wearing the coon-skin cap in ten of them. While it wouldn't have been the first time we'd just acted like something difficult and painful hadn't just happened, this was different, a turn on the dial to a whole other station. I walked over to the sink, poured out the V-8, and sat back down at the table.

"Mom, could you pass me the orange juice, please?"

"There is absolutely no reason, I was telling your mother this," he said, keeping his eyes on Mom, "that we shouldn't take full advantage of our location and be pillars that sustain the crucial symbolic, and literal, really, structure of the American Dream. Hell, a world dream. All of us. And who doesn't love fun and ingenuity while you're at it?"

I looked over at Mom, and was surprised to find she was sold. I knew how it was with the office ladies at school, the shifty-eyed jealousy, the behind-the-back bullshit. Not that it has to mean anything necessarily, but the combined weight of office lady #1 and office lady #3 at the high school was between 430 to 450 pounds, give or take, while Mom still pulls off a bikini with ease. In some cases, I guess, people work for a common goal, but not at a high school.

"They love to hire teachers and other education professionals like your mother. Plus, she already has six years of service as a young woman."

"Three," Mom said.

"What about, you know," I said, "the test you didn't do so well on last time?"

"I never failed a drug test, Duke," Mom said. "I quit when I found out they were testing."

"We should have absolutely no problem whatsoever," Iverbe said, to no one I could discern.

Within two weeks, he and Mom were training, bringing home binders in the shape of Mickey's head. Hope was new again, revitalized, cooked in a scalding hot spoon over a burner and shot into our veins with a syringe full of gold dust. New jackets and shoes were purchased, stuff packed up, lifeless condo rented, stuff unpacked, haircuts all around. Walt even had the courtesy to ask Mom and Iverbe if they had a specific preference of cast member roles. Thusly, Iverbe donned the stripes of the monorail engineer, and mom returned to turn-of-the-century Main Street U.S.A. It was nowhere. It wasn't like anything, because it wasn't anything. It wasn't even a dream, until Iverbe whisked himself away.

Away…

Away…

Downtown Los Angeles looks like an island unto itself in the distance, through the rumble of the bus. I expected it to have more of an unreal quality, like Oz. Instead it just looks big and motionless, like it's waiting, and not with interest, but just with knowledge of what's coming.

On a notecard I write to her one last time:

I read what you sent me,
the play,
your life,
by the pool
where I used to live.
Before this bus
which is where I live now.
It is, by all accounts,
a very shitty pool,
chairs with plastic flaps
lying on the ground,
an inch-thick surface
of mosquitoes and bees
blanketing the water.
People still swim in it though,
and retain all their limbs
as far as I know.
Sitting there,
Reading and reading,
years ago in my mind
but only a few days, really,

I thought I might grow
an extra finger
or some body part
not so easily attachable,
like an elbow
or a pancreas,
after finishing the story
that is now my life, too.
Cue the unanswerable questions—
or not,
maybe not unanswerable,
maybe the answers
are shockingly simple
and just too horrible
to integrate into life
on Main Street
or Future World—
You sank it all
into the deep end
of the mosquito pool—
which might as well
be 20,000 leagues
under the sea,
because I wasn't going to
dive in and save it.

We sit on the freeway now under downtown, sort of carved into the ground. Every other place I've been, I've always gotten the feeling of being welcome or unwelcome immediately, and I don't remember ever being wrong. This is the only place I've felt pure neutrality. It doesn't give a shit that I'm here. Why would it really, but every other place has, in some way, either disapproved (more often) or given me a little smile. But this place, nothing. I don't know what to do with this. I want to laugh at the weightlessness, but it's real now, and more chaotic the stiller it is.

I have five miles to walk tonight, once we reach the station. Pointed west on Sunset Boulevard, to her boyfriend's house. I'm afraid to beg for the money to catch a bus or train, not afraid, but sort of ashamed, or maybe just starving. And I want to be alone. It seems like it might be easier to exert whatever I have left through my legs and feet, one in front of the other, two hours—it seems reasonable after so much sitting, listening to my stomach on the Greyhound, still feeling grateful for the old toothless guy in Kingman, Arizona, who gave me a banana.

Sunday night at 10:00 and the city surprises me with how little life moves around. Rows of tents with sneakered feet hanging out the ends next to sushi restaurants and sleeping hotels. On every corner, steam rises from somewhere, though I can't locate the source. I didn't account for the giant hill I'd have to scale to get to the north end of downtown, where I'd hit Sunset Blvd., and hang a left to her. My head swirls and my stomach might be outside of my skin. I reach for it with one hand and search my body with the other to find the hole to stuff it back in. Steam everywhere, engulfed. I sit down and lean back on a chain-link fence, under a "for sale" sign, contact Roger Holmes, 323 667 6129. More steam. A face emerges, attached to nothing, and the almost wise little kid I used to be, and still rely upon, tells me it's not really there. But it's there enough to see. It's the bust I've been working on, chiseling away at, doughy and sure of itself. It's impossible that anything exists in my stomach, and yet …

What comes out of me, up through my esophagus, is liquid, but it's raw acid really. As I grasp at the air, the face fades. If I don't stay awake, who will find me in the morning? In the night? My task is to find thoughts in my mind that energize my head enough to keep it from tipping over.

Carrie. Lift me to my feet, the lightning in your tongue, the bite in your voice. I love you, how inaccessible and judged you are. I love the subtle distrust it creates in the cast members, that you let me in. What is it about me that opened you? *Fuck that guy,* they might think, grinning, an eyebrow cocked. Will you be waiting for me in Massachusetts, for some surprise weekend, to see if we really can wear each other out, and then decide what to do next? I want that visit, and my legs and feet want it, it almost seems possible because I am stomping down Sunset Boulevard on a hot winter night, out of downtown, fifty-foot strides.

Gentle Sigrid. Propel me past Dodger Stadium, past these vintage clothes and auto-repair shops. The pace is measured and constant, like your heart, and to rush isn't as important as to save myself for the final stretch. Sigrid, name your first child Duke. Don't listen to your brawny bearded husband, Hampus, or something, always carrying tools, wanting to name the boy after his grandfather. Toss little Duke into the air and catch him with one arm. Put some kind of cold herring dish out on the table, maybe a specialty of your stout white-haired mother-in-law, Helenka, while you put the final touches on the venison. Everyone in crocheted sweaters, even little Duke, eight pounds new, floating up and down in the air, a tiny trapeze artist.

"Sigrid," Hampus might shout into the kitchen, "you know your Papa likes his buck rare. You've been in there a long time is all."

"I know, Hampus, I know how Papa likes it. Things take time."

"I think little Duke is hungry again."

"Then bring him over here and get back to building the sled."

Sigrid is big and real. I can't hate Hampus, possessor of all things I lack. We would get along probably. Yes. Hampus would understand. Sigrid knows Hampus understands just about anything that's important to her. If he doesn't, he just forces himself to, out of real devotion. And so that's what we share, Hampus and I, devotion, one of the few sentiments that at least has the possibility of lasting.

The homeless are everywhere here, even though they don't

exactly crowd the streets. I walk from one homeless man to the next, then to a woman, bent over, hands folded on her back, than another man, grumbling—they're markers, bus stops for human traffic—I feel whichever person I walk past until I get to the next. They cast a big mental net, and I wonder if I should guard my thoughts, so I can stay focused. Something is telling me to think of nothing except walking, the rhythm on the pavement. I even start humming *there she was just a walkin' down the street singing do wah diddy* ... At Tang's donuts, there's a crowd of five men smoking and talking quietly, they are going to call out to me, I think, but they only stare when my steady gait crumbles and I stagger towards the street, another dizzy spell, a slow-motion strobe, which I refuse to accept, one two one two, I see a hazy red light hanging in the air and use it as a guide, where to stop until the haze turns green.

Sirens put me on my knees, sound is everywhere and there really isn't anyone around. There's always been someone, which I never took the time to notice until now. My hand is stuck to something, that much I can feel, and my eyes register a free weekly paper, some burlesque girl on the front, tassels spiraling. It's enough to put me down—I ask myself, is it worth it, to sleep now, a sleep which may not end in sleep? I dry heave again, just a little escapes into my mouth, which somehow seems to unstick my hand from the pavement. It's like fuel. I am on my feet, only a mile to go, I tell myself, even though it's two.

At the corner of Sunset and Vermont, it's Mom's face planted firmly between my ears. The one bad thing about the post-cocaine-post-booze Mom was she stopped singing all the time. I knew her as a singer, and then suddenly she just wasn't, except for the odd special occasion, birthdays, maybe a Christmas carol or two, when it was obligatory, which ruined it. She sings tonight in my head, Stevie Nicks, *I have always been a storm,* which she used as a lullaby, which worked without fail, which gave me love of lightning and thunder, which always sounded and looked like

Mom and vice versa. The very same song I belittled her for singing to me when I turned thirteen, after she mentioned it at some breakfast, hearing it on the radio, *Duke, remember I'd sing this to you*? But thirteen, a good excuse as excuses go, my party line was that I hated Fleetwood Mac. *It makes me want leave the room, the way she sings,* I said. I see Mom, though, behind my forehead. I listen to her low voice again, always more of a rasp than a belt, and I see it, see why she chose the song, how it admitted everything to me, the confession of it. I am a monster. We are monsters, never listening, pretending not to understand when we do.

I see Western Avenue ahead of me. I've passed it. *If you hit Western going west, you've gone too far west, and must turn back to the east, not far east, just a tiny bit east,* she wrote, on the printout folded into the back pocket of the notebook. 1566 Harvard Blvd., how could I overlook Harvard, such an obnoxious street to live on. On the corner is a Thai spa and herb shop, and for just a second I imagine my body loose under the touch of some beautiful masseuse, my face clean, puke out of my mouth, some kind of Krachappi plucked song in the background. I learned about the Krachappi instrument from the Thai folk group they hired at EPCOT to wander around between Japan and China, serenading the guests, Duan Sib they called themselves, nice people, voracious, silent eaters. I am that spare instrument now, or the vibration of the strings.

I am here, 1566 Harvard, the left side of a square Craftsman duplex, and spiraling toward the door, before I can knock, she is there. She is the bust of herself, except I expected hair. Her face is my face, the part that's always looked like a stranger to me. Her eyes hold me up, her arms around me. Her legs are strong and her fingertips on the back of my head are good. I know her now.

Part IV
Whirlybird

Preface to Scene 5 of *Burgundy Five Star*

Everyone on the plane from Orlando to L.A. could've spontaneously combusted as long as Kaye continued to sleep with her face wedged between my chin and collarbone. Before she dozed off, over Arizona, she began doing something with her voice, contorting it, opening it, as if it had been knotted up before. Now it came out raspy and soft, and we were suddenly on the inside of her walls. It was goddamn wonderful to be out of mine, enclosed in hers, where she turned it all over, and over again. I closed my eyes and tumbled with it, like being thrown around a dryer, rhythmic warm blows to the head. Just listening.

"The last six months I was on coke I started setting up a lawn chair in the parking lot while Duke was asleep inside. There was this guy, a vet, used to set up his tent almost every night on the patch of dirt, which was usually mud, in front of his parking space, about ten spaces down from mine. I didn't have a car, but I got a space anyway. He had one of those tiger-striped dogs out there with him, and he'd lie still, outside the tent, but if I got within ten feet, the tiger dog would leap up and just woof and woof, really low, until I'd point myself in another direction.

"I'd get out there about three in the morning in my leather jacket and sweat pants, start in on a pack of Camels and giant mug of English Breakfast Tea and wait for the sun to come up. I know I thought and thought and thought, nonstop, but if you asked me I couldn't tell you one thing that went through my mind. But I was always aware of the guy in his tent, The Camper. And if he ever actually slept in his apartment, or somewhere else I guess, if I went out there and didn't see his tent, I'd go back inside and watch infomercials with the sound turned down until I fell into a sort of burned-out resting state. He always knew when I was out there, too. We couldn't bring ourselves to look at each other on the stairs, but in the parking lot he made me feel good, like I was safe, with his dog, and his lantern. Whatever was racing through my head, if I had a question, I'd ask him what he thought, you know, and he'd give one word answers (I gave him a sort of Jeff Bridges voice), and his answers seemed unrelated on the surface, so I'd have to slow down and try to figure out what he meant when he said, 'equilibrium' or 'blender' or something. Duke was six, at the same time hyperaware and in his own world, you know. One morning, I was in pretty bad shape, teeth chattering in 85 degrees, my nails were stubs, and the sun comes over the horizon and just splits in two. And I see Duke's face behind my eyes, on both suns. One is looking down at me, that expressionless expression he still has, a million little sparks coming out of his head, with his face perfectly still. The other face, on the other sun, is looking off into the distance, and I keep trying to get his attention, get him to look at me so I can ask him what he's thinking about. But I can tell he doesn't know I'm there, like I don't exist. And the first face is still staring at me, and all I can think to do is try to get the other one's attention and I can't. Suddenly I'm hyperventilating, and crying. So I asked The Camper, with my mind, if I was going to lose my son. He said, 'alarm.'"

The last hour, with Kaye asleep, was bumpy, and I was treated to her partly bare breasts shimmying in the choppy air, which really just reminded me that I'd already fallen. Each time she exhaled, it was like she poked miniscule holes in my bile reservoirs. I could feel them draining, and wondered how I would feel when they were empty. How long would it take? To think I almost missed it.

How to help this boy. What would help entail? How in Hell's name can a person even be remotely confident his action would cause a chain of events that would actually benefit someone else? And the old wheels turned: *Does the boy need help? Why does he leave home at such a crucial juncture for his mother? What difference does he hope to make by leaving? What are the opposing forces inside/outside of Duke Brown? Answer these questions and any others you find to be essential to Duke's struggle. Provide* *evidence*. *Five paragraphs, at least two textual quotes per paragraph. And remember, your contrary idea that precedes your thesis statement is key. The better your opposing argument in the first body paragraph, the stronger the heart of your thesis and its supporting paragraphs will ultimately be.*

I knew nothing of help. All I had was zeal of the ignorant converted. That would have to do.

Kaye opened her eyes and looked over at me during our descent, like our heads were on pillows in an expensive hotel bed we'd saved up for, our empty suitcases resting on top of each other in the corner of the room—maybe even our toiletries share a nylon travel bag. The flight attendant gestured with her neck and hands, and I said no thank you with my eyes. We'd call room service if we needed anything.

"You know, if I hadn't gotten pregnant with Duke, I was going to take a job with Delta," Kaye said.

"If I hadn't been beaten with a trumpet, I was going to kill myself, so I guess we're even."

"I hope that's true, because otherwise you shouldn't joke about it," she said.

"What would you say if I told you I loved you?"

Kaye shut her eyes.

"Hmm?" I asked.

"I'd say I'm feeling far too upset to even respond to something like that, especially when you mangle it by making it into a question. Teachers."

"Mmm. Yes."

The woman in the window seat, reading *The Celestine Prophecy,* perhaps rereading it for the tenth time, made no effort to hide her disapproval of the content of our conversation, shifting her flanks and passing a gassy admonition out of some hole in her face. I took a pocket comb someone had left from the pouch in the seat in front of me, and I leaned slightly toward the woman.

"Would you like to watch me comb this woman's hair?"

"Stop it, Craft," Kaye said.

"Say my name again."

"Craft."

"Again."

"No."

"All right."

"I like you, okay? My kid's down there."

"I know. We're landing soon," I said.

It spoils nothing to say that Lila Bell chooses to end the final scene of her play with the entrance of two new characters: Kaye and Craft. These two bring a desperate headwind into the scene and connect the scene's two principles, Duke and Lila, beyond their own imaginations. This particular choice runs the risk of striking the reader, at first glance anyway, as amateur-hour Deus Ex Machina. *Along come mommy and the fallen ex-mentor/lover to save the children from themselves.* But with this writer's blunt tool, like every tool ever invented by Human Kind, it's all in how you use it. I submit Exhibit A, with certain knowledge of its influence upon the author.

Exhibit A: *Lord of the Flies*

Lila once threatened to cut class when I told her that in our next unit we were indeed going to the island with the boys and the beast.

"I read the goddamn thing last summer, Craft. I want to keep reading plays. I'll come back when you're finished. Just hurry up and get it over with, all right?"

"Oh, this is just like a play, very dramatic. You really should come."

"No, I don't think so. Just write me a hall pass and I'll wander around or something."

"There's something I want you to see, and you won't see it unless you participate."

"Oh yeah? What."

"Well, I was very critical of your last play, as you know, and I just think you have the wrong idea about *Deus Ex Machina.* You have Jesus hopping down off the cross at the end to negotiate the resolution between the goat man and the lizard woman—the author's hand is too visible."

"I think clumsy was the word you used."

"Yes. Well, I want you to see what Golding does, because rather than simplify and resolve, his God pops through the trap door, rips back the curtain and complicates everything for each character, for the rest of their lives. It's quite wonderful."

"They're saved. He picked the happy ending."

"Oh no, Lila. They're not saved. They're most definitely not saved."

"Yeah? All right, Craft, you convinced me, I guess. But I'm skipping the fucking day when they kill Simon. It made me want to throw up last summer, and I hate it."

"I wouldn't ask you to go through that twice," I said. Though now I'm sure that was a lie.

SCENE FIVE

Hot Lights on the same Japanese platform bed from Scene 3, Morely's bed, but where we viewed Lila and Morely from foot to head, center stage, now the bed is down left and facing backwards, so that we see DUKE and LILA's faces, resting on their forearms, hanging over the headboard of the bed, not unlike Linus and Charlie Brown at the conversation wall. They have talked all night, eyes bloodshot, hair sticky sweat. LILA wears a long T-shirt and white socks. DUKE in jeans, no shirt. Sweat, or a tear, runs down his neck.

We hold there, still, and let their faces emerge from what they've just finished. DUKE's mouth is a heavy arch, like the slightest wind from the open window could send it into quivering tears.

LILA's face is half undecided, half resolute. It tilts one way or the other like the flag in a game of summer camp tug of war.

The Hot Lights fade slowly, very, very slowly.

We sit in silent darkness for ninety seconds, or until every person in the theater, perhaps even the actors begin to doubt that the lights will return. Technical difficulties? Finally, softer lights arise center stage, morning, BIRDS are singing wildly through a window over a pink two seat café table in Morely's kitchen. DUKE enters in his jeans, and has found a spare T-shirt of Morely's. It is far too big. He notices the horrible sound of a bird outside—it's as though it were having its eyes pecked out. He opens the window behind the table. A large animatronic SPARROW, five times scale, is perched on a limb right outside. DUKE thinks to shoo it, but the moment he moves his hands to swish the air, the Sparrow shrieks at him and DUKE recoils. After a moment of trying to orient himself, DUKE puts up a hand of truce to the Sparrow, who immediately begins to whistle beautifully, but more human-imitating-sparrow than actual sparrow.

DUKE: *[to the Sparrow]* I'm just getting some orange juice.

[He enters the darkness stage left, then comes back with a glass of juice and sits at the table, wary, but intently studying the giant creature. LILA enters with an omelet, toast, and a cup of coffee. She plops the plate down in front of DUKE and drinks the coffee herself. He starts to indicate the Sparrow to LILA, stops, doubting his own eyes.]

DUKE: Wow, this looks great. Again. You have any more of that coffee?

LILA: I've never seen anyone eat like this. Three omelets.

DUKE: This is nothing. You should go to Hometown Buffet any night of the week.

LILA: You're right. I should. I should sit down at a table and strike up a conversation. A hundred conversations. I forgot how important they are, the buffets, in the scheme of things.

DUKE: I don't see why.

LILA: Yes you do.

DUKE: You're right. The old and the obese. We need them to be human.

LILA: See, you tell little lies, too, pretend not to understand when you understand perfectly. *[She gives him a shoulder squeeze. He doesn't react.]* Are you ready to make a real film?

DUKE: *[rote]* I'm here right now, aren't I?

LILA: Look—I know I said it was all true. I know that, but truth, and family are much more than facts. You need to get past it. I need you to—

DUKE: I'm going to get some coffee and change the subject. Are you ready? *[DUKE stands and walks off stage right. The giant Sparrow powers down and lowers slowly out of sight.]*

LILA: Ready for what?

DUKE: *[off stage]* To change the subject?

LILA: For now.

DUKE: Now don't whip around, move very slowly, and look over your shoulder.

LILA: What? *[DUKE enters with a cup of coffee.]*

DUKE: Over your shoulder.

LILA: Okay, I'm over my shoulder. What?

DUKE: The giant sparrow.

LILA: What sparrow?

DUKE: Are you kidding me?

LILA: Where is it?

DUKE: Behind you!

LILA: Stop it, Duke. Listen, Peru was a setting I chose to make it feel like it really felt—like a jungle. It was just I went through it in a hotel room in downtown St. Louis, by myself, a zip-lock sandwich bag full of cowshit-mushrooms instead of a jungle. It was terrifying and I had to do it. I had to die a little. And I had to tell everyone I was in Peru, Duke. Even you. Because I was next to the river, and I saw my illness, I was shown.

DUKE: You did say all this last night. You know that right? I listened to this already—with a pretty open mind I think.

LILA: But I need to say it again, because you're not with me. Like *with me* with me.

DUKE: So you didn't really go to Peru, *but you really went to Peru*. You said there were nine of us, not three. You made up six people. How do I know he is what you say he is?

LILA: He is a killer. It was his job.

DUKE: In, like, objective reality.

[The Sparrow rises onto its perch behind them, lifeless, turned off. It suddenly clicks on, mechanically flaps its wings.]

LILA: You want facts? Little scraps of inert, surface information units?

DUKE: I'm not like a big fact guy or anything, but yes.

LILA: He was the handler. He took orders from the top of the ladder down to the bottom, to the mercenaries. He managed mercenaries. Don't you think there's a special place in Hell for mercenary managers?

DUKE: It makes a very good story. To tell me. To get me to go with you. It's believable.

LILA: *[tender]* Please, Duke. Don't do that.

DUKE: Tell me again that this is real. Real real.

LILA: It's as real for me as it is for you. That's the truth. *[They embrace, DUKE burying his face in LILA's collarbone. She holds the back of his head. He sobs lightly, more wet breathing than crying. The Sparrow suddenly expels five long shrieks. LILA whips around, shooing it away from the window. It breaks into beautiful song again, then clicks off, lowering down, out of sight.]*

DUKE: But that's it right?

LILA: What do you mean?

DUKE: There's nothing else I should know, right?

LILA: Nothing. Except this. *[LILA places a gun on the table.]* It's the only way to make him talk to us—to make the film work. *[Duke jumps up, at first recoiling, then leaning into Lila's space.]*

DUKE: You said we were just going to expose him.

LILA: We are. It won't be loaded, so that's all we'll be doing.

DUKE: *[nodding at the gun]* That's conspiracy to commit assault with a deadly weapon—or whatever. It's really bad. And it's wrong.

LILA: No, it's just a tool in a circumstance. Just like the cameras. Why do you think it's wrong?

DUKE: You're becoming him, just using it.

LILA: No, I'm showing him what he needs to see so that he becomes visible to the world.

DUKE: What if he figures out that he's on camera?

LILA: Morely's good. He's subtle—he won't know.

DUKE: I don't want you to do it. It's fucked-up karma.

LILA: The world would be better if he were dead. I believe that. He's got to believe that *we* believe that. Even if he thinks we wouldn't actually do it.

DUKE: I don't like that concept. All that black and white, should, shouldn't be alive. I'm no judge.

LILA: Does the world need more or less evil in it?

DUKE: It's not like that. I think a person picks things to care about, and some people get so angry, about, just, what it is, how hard it is, just being alive, so they fuck everything up for everyone else and they do terrible things.

LILA: That's too easy, you're letting him off the hook.

DUKE: There's no hook! You just look around, you're told things, and you start deciding. And the stuff that's easy to grab is pure shit.

LILA: It's not random like that. It's inside of us—there's a higher language emanating from space. It's attracting us. You either listen and try to become fluent, and follow it toward something real, or you ignore it and let yourself get sucked into the black hole of destruction.

DUKE: Destruction, okay, yeah, I see destruction, but either way, good things get fucked up. I just don't think it matters like you do, righting wrongs. There are too many other people I want to get to know now, other people who get it, whatever it is, you know, that something, and it changes, but it's the same too, getting it, like giving, giving yourself. People who do that. I feel like I almost get it, so I'd rather just focus on that, on those people.

LILA: And what if a killer took away one of your 'giving people'? Every day, one more black hole and one less giver.

DUKE: I don't know okay!

LILA: You're out there trying to learn how to live, and the giving people give you things, but the black hole just keeps getting bigger! And bigger! And now it's not just sucking in the killers and the manipulators and the abusers, now it's sucking in the weak and the destitute, and the harmlessly stupid, and regular sort of nondescript people—

DUKE: All I know is—

LILA: What if you could stop it from happening? What if it really is a war, all of it? What if the burden of understanding is the obligation to strike?

DUKE: Strike?

LILA: With force. Nullify one killer. There's your karma.

DUKE: That is not karma.

LILA: Exposure. Expose him like a gaping, diseased asshole. Stamp it on his face. Let the people watch it unfold, all over the world. Let them judge.

DUKE: Yeah, okay, but I don't think anyone really cares who our government used to kill a long time ago—how much do they care about the people they're killing now?

LILA: It's a story. It has life already—It's already viral. I'm a missing person.

DUKE: No one will care. He's a retired killer, so what?

LILA: Is that what you really think?

DUKE: No.

LILA: They'll care.

DUKE: They actually don't.

LILA: No, they actually already do.

DUKE: Is that what *you* really think?

LILA: We're going to be something, you and me. Big and good. What does he have in his life? Let's make a list. Come on. Get a pen and paper. Let's make a list. *[DUKE takes out a pen and paper from his backpack.]*

DUKE: A job.

LILA: Burn it.

DUKE: Connections.

LILA: Burn.

DUKE: History.

LILA: Expose.

DUKE: A daughter.

LILA: Douse with his shit.

DUKE: His country.

LILA: Strike.

DUKE: His whole, you know, construction of reality.

LILA: Boil it for ten minutes and make him grab it with his bare hands.

DUKE: I don't know, probably a Lexus or something.

LILA: A Range Rover actually. Leave it untouched. The film is going to be good, Duke. It's going to *do* good.

DUKE: Okay. *[She swells with happiness and takes both of his hands in hers.]* Where's the camera going to be?

LILA: I don't want you to know. That way you're more natural. Let's chant.

DUKE: What?

LILA: Chant with me.

DUKE: Do you have something worked out?

LILA: How about Strike Force?

DUKE: Okay.

LILA: Go.

DUKE: Okay.

[The Sparrow rises and turns on to join their chant.]

DUKE & LILA: Strike Force Strike Force Strike Force!

[A door slams shut. CRAFT, 47, and KAYE, late 30s, enter from stage right. The four people, related in a cat's cradle of string, regard each other, trying to connect each string, almost accomplishing that, then faltering in confusion at just who is there, together, now, and why. CRAFT regards The Sparrow in awe. It clicks off and sinks out of sight.]

KAYE: Duke, are you all right? Who is this?

CRAFT: My student, former.

LILA: Hi Kaye. I'm Duke's sister. Lila. It's good to meet you.

KAYE: *[just noticing]* She has a gun!

LILA: Oh, it's not loaded, unless Morely loaded it.

CRAFT: Lila, put that down. What in God's Hell are you doing with this boy?

LILA: Craft, this is my brother! Amazing huh?

DUKE: *[to KAYE]* Who's this guy?

CRAFT: Hello, Duke. I'm Craft. Pleasure to meet you.

KAYE: He's a friend.

LILA: *[to DUKE]* He's my old English teacher. *[to KAYE]* And former lover. Briefly. You should know. You two seem like you're here together.

CRAFT: It was after—she was grown, like she is now. And it wasn't—

LILA: It was one night a month ago. *[KAYE looks slightly repulsed, but not surprised.]*

CRAFT: Thank you, Lila.

LILA: We have nothing to be ashamed of, Craft. You should tell Kaye what you did. It was gallant, I thought.

DUKE: What the fuck is going on here?

LILA: *[She puts a free hand on DUKE's shoulder, making a circular, circle-of-life gesture with the hand holding the gun]* It's a good sign.

CRAFT: Listen, now. We're here to help you … both of you, whatever you're into.

KAYE: Duke, we have to go home. Right now.

DUKE: Mom, I have to do something first. I have to be there. For support. *[LILA walks over, holding the gun, and gently takes hold of KAYE's forearm.]*

LILA: Kaye, I'd like to sit down over tea and talk to you for hours. And we will, I know that, but Duke and I have to leave in five minutes. We're confronting our father. It's important to us.

CRAFT: Give me the gun, Lila.

LILA: I can't, Craft. You know that.

KAYE: Duke, you're not going anywhere with this girl. She's clearly ill. I should know.

DUKE: Not the way you think, Mom. I think it'll be okay.

CRAFT: *[leaning in close to LILA]* Wherever it is you think you're going, I'm coming with you. I promised someone.

KAYE: No. Duke and I are leaving now. Together. *[KAYE crosses to DUKE and places her hand on his shoulder. He takes a step back.]*

DUKE: Mom, I'm going with her.

KAYE: *[reaching]* Duke … Iverbe's dead.

LILA: Oh, Duke. I'm sorry. *[Duke drops to his knees.]*

DUKE: No more. *[LILA bends down, takes DUKE gently by the shoulders.]*

LILA: One more. Just one more thing. *[KAYE crosses to DUKE and swipes LILA's hands off his shoulders.]*

KAYE: You leave my son alone!

LILA: I'm sorry, Kaye, but Duke knew. He's known. Last night he told me, he felt it, when he died, about a week ago, he felt him pass.

DUKE: No more.

CRAFT: Listen to your brother, Lila. He doesn't want to go with you. You're going to stop this. *[CRAFT takes a step toward LILA. She points the gun at him calmly, resolute.]*

LILA: Craft, do you even know what you're trying to stop?

CRAFT: That's not loaded. Now stop.

LILA: It isn't? How do you know? Craft, we need this.

CRAFT: You've found each other. That's all you needed.

LILA: No! He's there, whistling his way into eternity. No fucking way I let that slide.

KAYE: Listen to me, honey. You're all juiced up—I get it, okay? But this is going nowhere. My son is going nowhere with you.

LILA: Kaye, we'll be back in two hours, three tops. I'm sorry about your husband. I want to bond with you someday. I know we will.

KAYE: *[to CRAFT]* Tell me what's wrong with her!

CRAFT: She leans toward the abyss.

KAYE: *[re: gun]* I'm going to take that from you right now. *[LILA aims it at KAYE.]*

LILA: This is my life. And this is Duke's life. Please understand that. Please. Duke, it's time to go. Are you with me? Are we together?

[DUKE looks up from his stupor, around at the room, at everyone, separately, together, gives the slightest, faintest nod in LILA's

direction.]

The lights fade very, very slowly.

8

(from *The Kingdom*)

Morely's silver VW Golf whizzes over the hill like Spaceship Earth on fire. What he has under the hood I don't know, but in the cab great volcanoes rage, waiting to spew. Mom vibrating next to me in the passenger seat. Her hand flexed so hard, she's about to break her left middle and index finger. I knew Iverbe was dead but my mind hadn't formed the sentence. It's probably better that Mom said it, so that's what I'll remember, instead of my own voice, in my head, on repeat: *Iverbe's dead. Iverbe's dead. Iverbe's dead.*

This guy, Craft, is next to Lila in back. I want to hate him, or think I should, but there's something about his face, a rodent quality that I like. For his part, he sits there with his hands on his knees, seems to be trying to project calm, even if it's fake. Nobody's said anything since Lila's last direction. What's there to say? She's holding a gun. Craft and Mom have almost accepted it in a way. We'll be there in ten minutes.

"101 North," Lila says, her voice sliding straight into my skull, the headrest being the only thing separating her lips from my ear.

I catch her eyes in the mirror. Pure whirlpools. Mom looks over at me and buries her face in her hands.

"Don't do that, Mom."

"I'm terrible. I'm a terrible mother," she says.

"No, you're not. We're just in this. I'm not going to get hurt. Nobody is. It's just a stunt."

Up and over the hill, into the valley. The descent isn't too steep, but I feel my organs sink and tingle anyway. I let the Golf coast, down, down until we hit bottom, and I take a turn off, a series of lefts, Lila's *go through that light, one more, that light, you missed it, turn around,* and I am in some canyon, spiraling. There it is, The Pinnacles, the entrance emblazoned with blue on a silver crest, a picture of a mountain top with sunbeams radiating off of it—this is it, the end. I blow past the entrance.

"That was it!"

"I know," I say, "I just couldn't turn in—my hands. I'll turn around."

"All right, everyone," Lila says. "Ready?"

"I don't have a choice," Mom says, much calmer than I thought she'd sound right now.

"Kaye, I appreciate you coming," Lila answers.

"Stop it."

"I really think this will help reduce risk. If Craft asks at the gate instead of us, the pig will come unsuspecting."

"You said that already, about fifteen minutes ago," Mom says through gritted teeth.

In the great negotiation that played out in Morely's driveway before we left, Lila's offer to let Craft and Kaye come along if they'd be part of the plan was the final straw from Mom. She just threw up, right there, into Morely's neighbor's yard. I noted how gently Crafted touched Mom, her hunched over, his arm around her waist, the other hand holding back her hair.

Anyway, Mom knew she had to let it go. Just abandon everything that felt right. I forced her hand. It was a shitty thing to do, but I did it.

"Do you have anything in particular you want me to say to the security guard? I'm guessing you have it written somewhere, how you imagine it playing out," Craft says.

"Yeah, pretty much," Lila says. "Tell the guy at the kiosk, in your own Craft way of course, that you found some kids on your front porch brazenly smoking dope. You asked them to leave, but they said they were too tired to move. Then you asked them where they went to school, and they said, *leave us, plebian*. That's how you knew they must be Pinnacles kids."

I pull into the entrance. The school's buildings seem to grow out of the canyon walls, walkways connected by steep staircases. People my age go to something they call school here. The same word I used a few months ago, but this is something else, an ideal. The field to the right, the only flat surface of land—our rendezvous point.

"There's visitor parking. Take that spot by the dumpster," Lila says. "Craft, do you want to run your lines?"

"I'm through with that sort of thing, Lila," he says.

"What's that mean?"

"It means I'm going to say what I'm going to say."

"Say what I said to say."

"I'm getting out of the car now," he says. "Kaye, darling, would you mind?"

"Darling?" I say out loud, not exactly on purpose. Mom's eyes drop to the floor. She gets out, allowing Craft to crawl out of the back of the Golf. Still projecting calm, he straightens and tucks his yellow oxford into his brown pants. He runs his hand over his stubbled rat face and leans into the passenger window, looks me dead in the eye.

"Duke, I know this moment isn't typically when a person might say something like this, but I don't think it matters anymore, the set and setting. I love your mother. I'm in love with her."

"Craft!" Mom shouts.

"Kaye, let me finish."

"You should let him finish," Lila says to Mom. I see Mom's hand start toward Lila in a slap, but she pulls back, just before it becomes obvious, what she was about to do.

"Duke, I'm here because I met Iverbe in the hospital. He asked me—well, that's not exactly right—he contacted me on another plane of existence and commanded me to find you and protect you. He didn't say *protect*, he said *comfort*, but comfort has turned into protect. That's why I'm here. When your mother opened the door and I saw her face, it confirmed everything. Do you understand?"

"Yes," I say, because I do, and there's no point pretending that I don't.

"That was very beautiful, Craft," Lila says. "That's why I always loved you."

"I'm a little angry at you right now, so fuck you if I don't kiss your cheek."

"Oh all right, Craft, all right, like you didn't poke me with your hot poker every day in class and pour gasoline on me. It was a years-long fomenting process, but I got the message. You're half the inspiration for all this."

"I'm sorry to you, Lila."

"For what?"

"Lust."

"You waited, Craft. Not everyone would've."

"I didn't wait. I was obvious with you. I wanted you to know. I'm sorry for that."

"It was just my brain you wanted, the rest was secondary. I knew that."

"Damn it, now. Let me apologize."

"I won't let you. You almost saved me—and now Morely has. I mean, what we've been able to do, you wouldn't believe—"

"I'd like to get this over with," I say.

Any more of this line of thought from the two of them and I'm going to vomit again. I almost did when Mom spilled her innards back at Morely's, but I was able to pull it back, remain calm, which I felt was significant at the time.

"You don't have to do this," Mom says. "They're not your family. Any of them. I am."

"Mom, we could've helped each other, brother-sister, that's the point, right? To help with all the crazy? Now we have this," I say, pointing sort of everywhere. "But it's ours," I tell her.

"Duke, I knew my father, your grandfather. He was around. Believe me, you don't have to know your father."

"I agree, Duke," says Craft, "I never met my father, but I can't imagine it would've done me a shred of good."

"Craft," Lila says, "we're not going to get to know him, we're going to destroy him."

"You can't!" Mom says, wheeling out the Quaking Voice. I've only heard it a dozen times in my life, when the top of her head pops open like a cuckoo clock, and out shoots a kind of horrified, bald animal.

"He's … I didn't want you to ever see him!"

"So he's a psychotic asshole. I get it. I'm not afraid," I say.

"No! He's not an asshole—he has strange powers. Sickening powers, Duke," she says, now whispering, and on the dilapidated movie screen in my head is Mom in some terrible room, on her knees, makeup running down her face. I squint and pull my cheeks as tight as they'll go.

Mom breaks down, silently, in her hands, her face vibrates. Craft and I both place a hand on her back. Lila, too. She allows this.

I look out the windshield, a security guard is jogging, sunglasses, hand on his radio. Three people comforting a weeping woman in visitor parking. He has to call it in.

"Security, on the way," I say.

"Shit," says Lila, "ten minutes, Craft."

Craft turns around to meet the security guard's girth.

"You folks okay?"

"We've just had a death in the family," Craft snaps at him.

"Oh. I'm sorry to hear that."

"Could I speak to the head of security, please?"

"Certainly, sir. Can I ask you why?"

"It's a matter for him, I afraid."

"All right, I'll get him. Follow me, please."

Craft looks over his shoulder at Mom, and I see it flash—I've seen it, in the mirror, reflected in Carrie's eyes, Sigrid's, Melvin's, Willie's, the officer's, and Lila's when she opened the door to me.

Mom reaches out the window, her arm outstretched, but Craft has already turned to follow the security guard.

"Eight minutes," Lila says.

"What's happening in eight minutes?" Mom asks, not mocking her exactly, just furious.

"My boyfriend's meeting us. I mean, I've only known him a couple weeks, but we've been doing intensive work—"

"Can I please just have a neutral image in my head? Something else, anything," I say.

"You said you liked Morely."

"I like him, he's great, just don't explain what you two do. Please."

"It's natural, Duke," she says.

"Just, can we just concentrate on what you want to say?"

"You're right. Okay, you start."

Before Lila finally told me that she'd taken egregious liberties with the concept of fact when writing the play she billed as one hundred percent true in her letter that was taped to the cover, we'd gotten pretty excited out in the living room, smoking an eighth, I was told, of Morely's dope, swilling two pots of coffee, writing this whole good cop bad cop of justice confrontation scene. She liked my straight man, said it was understated and powerful. Then we got to talking about the play, and she clarified her version of reality, Peru, yes, Peru, but more so our nonexistent siblings, and I tore up our pages of notes, our speeches, all of it. So we have no script anymore, but I know we both remember it all. The whole night is still imprinted on the back of my head, reverberating, like a foggy crystal.

"I don't need to practice it," I say, "I mean, we should just, like, visualize it."

"Okay. There will be four headsets. I didn't figure on Craft, which is a shame, because—there he is!"

At the bottom of an impossibly steep staircase, Craft stands with an old man, not a with a pig face, just a regular-looking, droopy-eyed old man, arms folded, cul de sac, sunglasses, shined black shoes, mustache-goatee, suntan, meat gut, walkie-talkie in hand.

"What the hell is Craft saying to him? He's talking and talking," Lila shouts in my ear.

"I can't look," Mom says. "Duke, just drive away."

I can't answer her. I'm extending out the window, to hear any sound, any indication of humanity in the way the man, my father, listens and moves.

"Look at him! God, he's just putrid," Lila says.

"You have no idea," Mom answers.

"Oh, don't worry, I know exactly—"

"No! You do not *know exactly* one fucking thing."

Mom sticks her index a hair away from Lila's face, which I understand.

"Mom, I'm going make sure nothing bad happens."

"He knows how to control your mind, Duke, he can move you around like you're in a game."

"No one can control my mind—not even me," I say.

"He has a very strong head, Kaye. You did a great job," Lila says.

Mom buries her face, melting, again.

"I'm changing my name, Mom," I tell her.

"What? Duke, this has gone far—"

"To Iverbe. When we get back."

Mom leans and reaches around to kiss my forehead. Out the window, a woman has joined Craft and the old man, my father. She's blonde-coifed in a navy blue suit and sensible shoes, big shoulders and head. Definitely looks related.

"Is that her?" I ask Lila.

"Yes. Shit. No. Good. I'm glad she's there. I'm fucking glad, you hear me!"

"Mom, that's my other sister over there with Craft and my father. I don't mean to call him *my father*, I mean, to upset you, but I just don't know what else to call him."

"She's older than me," Mom says.

"Hell yes. She could be your mother, Kaye. That's a horrible thought, but you know, she's old enough."

This woman, our sister, Diane, points a finger in Craft's face. As soon as I see him move to swipe the finger away with his hand, I get a sharp pain to my stomach. Suddenly Craft is on the ground, my father standing over him, Craft's hands outstretched and pleading.

From behind us, a bright yellow helicopter rumbles overhead and plants itself in the air over the field.

"Go!"

I open the door. I am out, Lila out, running, half hunched, toward the violence.

"Show me your hands! Now now now now now now now now!" Lila is stuck in a loop, screaming at our father and sister, their hands up, but not convincingly.

"We're getting in the helicopter!" I yell, but she keeps going.

"Now now now now now now now," her eyes locked on our father's sunglasses.

I clap my hands and Lila stops.

"Move!" she shouts.

We are hustling down bleachers, across the track and onto the field, approaching a helicopter the way we've seen it done a thousand times in movies and old reruns of M*A*S*H, crouching and alert. It hovers, hovers, feet off the ground, and down. Morely kicks open the door, waving us in. Deafening, compressing my head, I cover my ears and find my place in the single file line. Craft, my father, me, Diane, and Lila. I count four actual seats—we smash together and the door closes like an oven. The proximity is scalding.

Craft's nose drips blood, and I notice for the first time he has freshly healed scars on his head, neck, and arms. Out the window Mom sprints toward the chopper, but we're off the ground. Her face bounces off mine and sticks to Craft for a moment before we lose sight of her. Lila, gun drawn, hands me a headset. Our father, robotic, and our sister, appalled, sit on either side of me—so the gun is more or less pointed at my chest.

"Testing, C.I.A. C.I.A. C.I.A., testing," I hear in the headphones. I give Lila a thumbs up and hand them to my father to put on. He doesn't acknowledge me or the headphones.

"Put them on!" Lila shouts.

"Don't shout so loud," Morely says from the pilot seat. "You just about blew out my ears."

Lila points the gun at our father's chest. He mocks the act, but puts on the headset. Morely weaves the controls of the chopper, and I notice we're making enormous figure eights over the field.

Something buzzes by my window.

"Well, shit, that was fast," Morely says.

Police helicopters, two, three, four, five of them, circling the perimeter of our figure eight.

"We know," Lila says, looking him dead in the eyes. I'm surprised she can do it. But she's doing it. I feel it, the power of her gaze. I can do it, too, if he looks at me.

"We know you sent decent people to their deaths. We know what kind of people would do something like that, over and over again for years."

He faintly grins and I look to Lila, her eyes tightening.

"And you raped my mother. She told me."

"We have no relationship."

"Here I am," she points to herself. "Rape's flower."

"He's done no such thing!" Diane screams, reading Lila's lips, I guess.

When Lila explained the scene to me last night, as told by her mother, how she'd flirted at some fancy dinner for some corrupt senator, how exciting it was at first, a real spy, she'd thought, how she got drunker and drunker, how she told him to stop, because she couldn't see, how he ignored her until the end, until he finally answered her: *that's what you wanted.* That was pretty much what sold me on needing to be here, this moment, to hear her say it all to his face, to see his reaction. And it's like no other feeling in the world, feeling him receive it with nothing, total emptiness.

Diane grabs the headset from our father, spitting into the little microphone.

"My father's indiscretion that unfortunately resulted in you was during a time in our lives that you wouldn't understand. My mother was ill and incapable of ever improving. You and your mother mean nothing to us."

"Admit it," Lila says.

"Give me the headset," he says to Diane.

"You don't have to acknowledge any—" and she stops, handing it to him.

"I'll tell you the truth," he says, turning to Lila. "Your mother was a boring drunk. It was a boring night. I hated those official kiss-ass dinners. So I waited around until I was done waiting. There she was, obliging and desperate. What, too simple for you? You're exactly what I'd expect from the hour of her blubbering I had in my ear that night. Exactly. It was a horrible mistake made by a grieving man. My wife was a saint before she fell ill, and my daughter is a great success. I am both a fortunate and deserving man, despite my faults, to have lived the life I've lived. You ought to be thanking me."

I see it first, Lila's hand shaking, her cheeks quivering, her eyelids acting as a dam. Before I can even make a plan of what to do, it rings out. One shot into the floor of the chopper. My father and Craft are on top of Lila. She is overwhelmed, on her back.

"Hey, hey!" Morely shouts from the pilot seat.

I flash to the bottom of the pile and see it, Lila's hand, his hand around her wrist, squeezing, the gun about to drop out of her hand, Craft's face, driven into the floor by my father's knee. I see a knuckled hand driving into Lila's sternum. Morely has all but evacuated the pilot seat, leaving only his left hand to keep us in the air.

"Hey! She's pregnant!"

"Morely shut up!" Lila screams.

I grab it—I am holding a gun for the first time, pointing it at my father, but picturing a tiny Lila inside Lila.

Craft and Lila scrunch into the seat next to our father, Diane next to me on the opposite side now. We've all shifted, but I don't know what's changed exactly. Somehow I felt safer with Lila holding the gun, although that makes no kind of discernible sense.

"Of course she's pregnant," Diane says, near my ear. "She thinks it gives her some kind of power." Why is she speaking to me? How did she get a headset again?

"Duke," Craft shouts. "You can end this now. Tell Lila's boyfriend you want to land."

"A baby?"

"Tell him, Duke, tell him to land," he says.

"I found out an hour before you showed up," she says. I expect this to change something, about the situation, end it. Resolve. But it doesn't. It goes on.

I look out the window, counting, one-two-three-ten police copters in a perfect circle around our flight pattern now. In the bleachers below, students fill the rows, like it's some halftime show extravaganza. Finally I turn to meet his eyes.

"You have the microphone now," he says. "Damn, you don't even look a thing like me. *She* does, I'll give her that. Well, go on."

"How did you meet—"

But I stop, because I've already put it together, something central anyway, from his rationalization, what he said about Lila's mother, how Lila came to be. It is hideous how I came into this world—worse, it is common. What he is. What he's done. What we are. We are common. I see that now. I want to burn it out of me. I can't.

"You come all this way to see me? See where you came from? Trying to figure out what you are? I have a unique point of view—though limited, I'll grant you that."

"Duke, whatever he says is a lie," Lila says.

"Who's lying to you, boy? Look at me! Now do you want to know what you are or not?"

"Do you wish we didn't exist?" I ask him.

"I don't wish anything," he says.

I wish that I'd just stop wishing.

I wrote that myself to Lila just a few days ago—something like that. I already want to peel those words off the index card and send them to Hell.

I think of Iverbe, his whole life a wish for a gentler world, a sort of padded room earth, without a need for revenge, punk rock, guillotines, oil wars, assassinations. Finally he just stopped, when even Walt's vision couldn't keep them all outside the gates. I hold the gun in my surprisingly steady hands, the gun itself a wish, a wish for change, to make things feel different inside, something other than *shouldn't even be here*. It's the wrong tool, I know, but can there be a wrong when there is no right? What could I hold in my hands that would answer the question?

"Yes," I say. "Tell me what you think I am."

"Take off your headsets," he says, pointing to Lila and Morely.

"No!" Lila shouts.

"Both of you, this doesn't concern you," he whispers, the sound of his breath in my ear searing my brain.

Morely turns around, nods his head to me in some kind of show of support. I turn to my sister, meeting the half of her face that doesn't look like mine.

"You don't have to," she says.

"I do now," I tell her. She drops the headset.

"All right now," he says. "After I retired, I had the pick of jobs, across the world. More money than I ever thought I'd make. All the highjackings, and the Russians gone, it was a crazy world—of course I knew it was going to get worse. So I took the job in Disney World—worst decision of my life. That place was a goddamn mess. Anyone, anytime could walk in there, open fire, kill five thousand, ten thousand people before any kind of response. Shit. So I cleaned all that up.

"Internally, now that was the real problem. But I cleaned that up, too. After six months, I'd tripled the security budget, hired my people. But one day, we come to realize, there's a thief. Plundering the break areas, taking cash out of wallets, jewelry, anything worth anything. Now we'd also been finding little baggies in the trash, remnants of powder. One day, one of the ex-cops I hired says to me, 'What we have here is a coke whore, plain and simple.' Do you know what a coke whore is, boy? Do you know what happens when you put those two words together? Well I'll tell you. You figure it out real fast, the possibilities in a place like Disney World. So I ask my friend, how do you catch a coke whore? He says, 'You take away the fat girls and the blacks. And you look for the white girls who act like they know how to fuck.' And so I brought them in, one at a time, and sat them down, and I stood over them, make them look up at me. And I told them I knew about the cocaine. And then I asked them if there's anything else they wanted to tell me, and they said no. And I told them I knew there was *something else*, there's proof, and I could send them to jail. See now, they don't like that. It gets in the way. Now they're scared, because it sounds like there's no cocaine in their future. And I asked them how they planned on getting out of a jam like this. This is a big jam for someone of their stature. And they might hem and haw a little—but sometimes not at all. Not your mother, anyway. She knew exactly what to do. I didn't even have proof. In fact, I didn't really think it was her. Are we done?"

I consider his question, because at this point, it's the only question that matters. Not only do I have no answer, I've also lost the meaning for the word, *done*. What have we done? When are we done? What were we doing? I spin with the phenomenon of how something can seem clear in a certain point in time—confront evil with knowledge and a threat to expose that evil—until we find ourselves in a whole other field, where everything is doubt, or no longer exists as it did. All the conviction, which was the fuel, turns to sand. In the new field, it simply is—the doings of life, done.

But below us the bleachers are filled with students now, and more crowd the walkway behind the bleachers, looking up to the sky at something they've never seen on their secluded campus before. They see something distinctly *not done*, something still happening, in motion. News trucks, tiny cameras, tiny men, zeroing in on us.

I look across at Lila, feel her head spinning in the same field of doubt. I implore her eyes to meet mine, to scrape themselves off the floor of the helicopter. In the moment they do, I bring their force of vision to meet mine, and I drop the gun.

At first I can only look at our hands, together, and I feel we are back in our field of conviction and purpose. When I look up to check on the effect of this action, I see genuine surprise on our father's face, mouth open, tongue emerging from a dark hole as his hands reach down for the gun. Craft pulls my shoulders, Diane's head wedges between Lila and me, close to our father's face, and then she disappears. A gunshot. Who has it? Faces search for the hand that fired it. No one took the bullet. Limbs are indistinguishable now, except for my hands, Lila's hands. He has the gun. Who? Craft's hands wrapped around his wrist. A work boot shoots out from the pile as if spring-loaded.

And then it is over, done, like he said, *done*—the door is open, Craft, purpose, wishes, why, behind us, below us, wind rushes in, the door, the door.

13

(from *Craft*)

By the time Kaye and I finally reached the Los Angeles airspace last night, made our descent, landed, shuffled off the plane with our shared bag and rented a car, it was about 1:30 a.m.—too late to call upon Duke with the news of Iverbe's death, for the love of God. We reasoned we'd get as close as possible to the address he left behind on the envelope in his room, which put us at a shockingly expensive Best Western just north of Hollywood Blvd., not that it mattered. The precious, retro diner downstairs was open, so we piled late-night eggs and sausage into our silent mouths, drained refills of coffee just because it was there, and hurried up to our room.

I clicked on the TV to get the weather. I wanted any possible advantage, any leg up on what was waiting for us, come morning. It took me by surprise when Kaye began undressing in the chair by the window, standing and reaching behind her neck the way women do, that singular gesture of taking off a necklace before bed. When she pulled her T-shirt over her head, I made a move toward the bathroom.

"It's all right, Craft. I'm exhausted, but I want to."

She undid her bra, and the rest, let it all drop to the floor, not in a heap, but separately. For the first and only time in my life, my own disrobing caused not a single self-conscious thought rooted in shame, though my beaten body looked worse than it ever had. The lights were low, and there were framed pictures of Marilyn Monroe on each wall, looking rehearsed and vulnerable.

Kaye entered the space between the top and bottom sheets, holding the blanket and sheet across the tops of her breasts. Her invitation lacked humor because there was none. And I was glad. She didn't want me to smile. She didn't want me to wait. She wanted me to kiss her, to give her my life for the night, for all of it. She didn't want it to last long, and she didn't want to let go. She didn't want music on, and the plumbing rushing in the rooms above and below us just reminded us of ourselves.

I woke up at 6:01, like always, no matter the time zone, the locus in the universe. There, for just one instant, was Kaye's face, hovering, studying, absorbing, caressing mine. I caught her there, in my net of filth, my life, my love, obscured in my near-sighted gaze, and I didn't care about the harm, the death I'd already suffered and died on the way to her, and to her son.

"I should—well, I don't know if I should, but I'm going to," she said.

She told me everything, how Duke had come to be, from start to finish in six breaths. I imagined it had been something like that, but less overt, maybe. And on the last exhale, she looked away, placing her face in the middle of a Bermuda triangle formed with her elbows and neck, perhaps suggesting our conversation had never actually happened.

"Do you think we can talk him out of whatever he plans on doing?" I asked her, her face in the middle of the triangle her elbows formed with her neck.

"I've never talked him out of a single thing."

"Yes. I had a couple students who were that way. My favorites, actually."

"You're that way."

"No. I can be talked out of anything."

"Only if you're lying."

"Where the hell were you all this time?" I said.

"Don't do that."

"All these years, goddamn it!"

"There's no point in that!" she said. "I was fucked up. You would have hated me. Everyone ended up hating me."

"Not me, goddamn it."

"No, you too."

"Listen to me, now!"

"You would have."

"You can't tell me that! I don't understand one piece of this life! I don't understand the need for the hell we have on our hands, the greed and hunger, the need for it, the need for you or Joyce or Gandhi or German Expressionism or Lily Tomlin. What's the goddamn use, except it's there? So bless it! It makes no sense that I understand love right now, because I don't love anyone! Except you."

"All right, Craft, not you."

And she got up from the bed, but turned around to place a hand on my shoulder before washing up and preparing for the day.

Watching Kaye blow-dry her hair under the row of spherical hotel bathroom lights while I pretended to look through the travel bag—I was able to take that room, that construction of that room with Kaye blowing dry inside, and I was able lodge it into the sacred few scrolls of forever. I felt the moment it took hold, so I could let go. Just let go of her there. In the Volkswagen. Parked at a high school.

Some kindred quality of Lila's boyfriend's car, like my defunct Subaru and Tim's Tercel, the age of it, ten years, maybe just that it was a Volkswagen, assured me that as I left Kaye I was still jogging in the same direction from which I left St. Louis—toward life. I was the messenger again, a sort of de-winged Hermes, a punishment, perhaps rendered because I could never get it right—the message—until now. And so I knew I couldn't very well recite Lila's script. I knew that Iverbe sent me to explode in the right place at the right time.

When their father walked up, I couldn't help but notice how extremely high he considered his waist to be, and how he buttoned the top button of his polo shirt, and how his sunglasses suggested that he had no eyes. He and I were different kinds of animals.

"Who are you, sir, and what are you doing on this campus?"

"My name is Craft. I'm a teacher. Who are you exactly?"

"Plowman. Head of Security. Is there a problem with someone in your party?"

"Yes. There is, Mr. Plowman. Although, it isn't the type you're going to be able to easily solve—not in any mutually satisfying way."

"Don't fucking play with me you weak little piece of shit. Who are you in all this?"

"Oh, you have nothing to be afraid of," I said.

"I know who's in that car. All I have to do is make a phone call, and I know whatever I want to know. Do you understand that?"

"That's all fine," I said.

"Do they think I'm going to allow them come here and ruin what I've built, what my daughter's built?"

He gestured to his left and there she was, on cue, the administrator of this facility. After quickly appraising and dismissing my worth, she seemed to be attempting to remove the Volkswagen full of problems with her mind. Her forehead scrunched up slightly and I could see her eyes beaming out irritation and disdain.

"I said you have nothing to be afraid of."

"Is that a threat?" he asked.

"It's a reassurance, which is the opposite of a threat."

"I want all of you gone. Now. That's the last civil statement I'm going to make."

"I'm afraid this is not about what either of us wants, Mr. Plowman."

"Who is this man?" the daughter asked the father.

Plowman put up a hand, indicating some degree of control he was confident that he could maintain. Then he grinned suddenly, took two steps toward me, and turned away from his daughter so that she'd have to strain to hear his near-whisper.

"I know who you are."

"Oh?" I said.

"You married her, didn't you? Reform that little piece of trash? Clean her up? You a big hero?"

"I'm on a whole other plane, Mr. Plowman. That sort of baiting won't serve you the way I'm sure it has in other situations. Anyway, you're making it far too complicated."

"How's that?"

"They're very good kids, your offspring. You could just pretend to be happy for them, for their lives, move them along, and still go on being the same diseased beast on the inside. It can be done. I did it for years."

The punch originated from his right shoulder, so powerful from such an old fist, so completely flattening my body and consciousness all at once. On the ground, in a heap, the only posture from which I've been able to truly see the world, I caught a perfectly clear image of Lila and Duke running, matching each other stride for stride, moving from their points of origin in the Volkswagen toward Plowman and me, the two of us locked in predictably one-sided brutality, our essences played out in miniature. I felt Lila and Duke with me in that moment, and it crystallized—how this moment would galvanize them. They might spend hours in drifting thought, trying to apply logic to it, or metaphysics, or Time. Separating us, Craft and Plowman, holding us up, disassembling us and putting us back together. He and I belonged there, entangled, at war, fighting like a cobra and a rat. And Lila and Duke belonged in motion, running toward us, forever, running to prevent, to rectify, to overcome, and, in the utter futility of future daydreams, to change the outcome.

But on the helicopter, it was the principal who opened the door behind me. Lila's boyfriend tried to grab her, but the woman's flanks were considerable. He had a terrible angle anyway. Once I saw the old man's gritted teeth, the force of the kick to my chest didn't surprise me as he extended his work boot. I'd just felt his hammer of a fist moments before, so I knew what lay beneath the surface. No, it was their coordinated effort, the father and daughter, that took me off guard, their immediate telepathy, like one body, as if they'd been ready to execute the plan the moment they boarded the chopper. The open door, the death-blow, and the great digital infamy that awaited Lila and Duke upon their return to their lives on the ground.

Though it may seem odd, on the way out the door the feeling that overtook me was far from the self-pity of the victim, some casualty of a curse. Yes, the kids invited death to our little party, the way they dug up the past and shook it wildly. But the real cost would fall to Lila and Duke, not me.

"I'm sorry, Craft," Lila would whisper into her pillow, both in prison and after, growing a new life inside.

"I'm sorry, Mom," Duke would tell Kaye every day with his eyes, meaning Iverbe, but also me, a little anyway.

In forging themselves together, both the onus and the ecstasy of thousands of new, heavy dawns became theirs. Any regret would have to evolve into something more useful, for the beasts live. The days that await them require more than a cocktail of compassion, doubt, and longing for *what if*. I know of what I speak when I say that medicine leads to quick, certain, and fruitless death.

Anyway, for my part, I'd already become some mangled Orpheus, returned to the underworld, carrying my own restored heart aloft like a trophy, an enchanted bird singing a triumphant song of—yes, even fleeting—love. And so the sensation of actually falling through the air, face up to the sky as if I were floating on the surface of the ocean, was familiar, how natural, how almost routine and expected—yet how vital it felt, that I remember, keep the feeling forever, or give it away entirely in that instant. Despair wasn't in or on my mind, tumbling with such speed as to almost seem still, but rather a curiosity as to what the Astroturf felt like, my old friend the ground whom I'd fall upon for the last time. Five feet to go, I felt my face with my hands, the shapes it had been and become, how it finally loved another without restraint, how it had burned itself onto the trunk of this family.

It was not just Lila who was pregnant.

Acknowledgements

I thank these humans, whose support and wisdom made this book possible: John Maurer, Dennis Cruz, Holly & Steve Wilson, Lab Twenty6, The Writing Club, H-W, Michael Paul Gonzalez, Ariana Kelly, Tom Smallwood, Meghan Ward, Seamus Young, Tuva June, Chance Louise, and, yes, Sarah.

About the Author

Ryan Elliot Wilson's writing has appeared in *The Painted Bride Quarterly*, *Thunderdome*, *Drift*, and the anthology *IN SEARCH OF A CITY: Los Angeles in 1000 Words*.
He lives with his family on the East Side of Los Angeles.
SPIRAL BOUND BROTHER is his first novel.

We live in uncertainty. New ways of committing crimes are discovered every day. Hackers and hit men are idolized. Writers have responded to this either by ignoring the harsher realities or by glorifying mindless violence for the sake of it. Atrocities (from the Holocaust to 9/11) are exploited in cheaply sentimental films and novels.

Perfect Edge Books proposes to find a balanced position. We publish fiction that doesn't revel in nihilism, doesn't go for gore at the cost of substance — yet we want to confront the world with its beauty as well as its ugliness. That means we want books about difficult topics, books with something to say.

We're open to dark comedies, "transgressive" novels, potboilers and tales of revenge. All we ask is that you don't try to shock for the sake of shocking — there is too much of that around. We are looking for intelligent young authors able to use the written word for changing how we read and write in dark times.